TriQuarterly 106

Fall 1999

Editor
Susan Firestone Hahn

Publisher
Kimberly M-- ''i

Editor of T'-

Associate Editor
Ian Morris

Production Manager
Bruce Frausto

Gini Kondziolka

Production Editor
Josh Hooten

TriQuarterly Fellow
Brian Artese

Assistant Editor
Francine Arenson

Editorial Assistants
Gina Carafa, Russell Geary,
Cristina Henriquez

Contributing Editors
John Barth, Rita Dove, Stuart Dybek, Richard Ford, Sandra M. Gilbert,
Robert Hass, Edward Hirsch, Li-Young Lee, Lorrie Moore, Alicia Ostriker,
Carl Phillips, Robert Pinsky, Susan Stewart, Mark Strand, Alan Williamson

TRIQUARTERLY IS AN INTERNATIONAL JOURNAL OF WRITING, ART AND CULTURAL INQUIRY PUBLISHED AT **NORTHWESTERN UNIVERSITY.**

Subscription rates (three issues a year) — Individuals: one year $24; two years $44; life $600. Institutions: one year $36; two years $68. Foreign subscriptions $5 per year additional. Price of back issues varies. Sample copies $5. Correspondence and subscriptions should be addressed to *TriQuarterly*, **Northwestern University**, 2020 Ridge Avenue, Evanston, IL 60208-4302. Phone: (847) 491-7614.

The editors invite submissions of fiction, poetry and literary essays, which must be postmarked between October 1 and March 31; manuscripts postmarked between April 1 and September 30 will not be read. No manuscripts will be returned unless accompanied by a stamped, self-addressed envelope. All manuscripts accepted for publication become the property of *TriQuarterly*, unless otherwise indicated.

National distributors to retail trade: Ingram Periodicals (La Vergne, TN); B. DeBoer (Nutley, NJ); Ubiquity (Brooklyn, NY); Armadillo (Los Angeles, CA).

Reprints of issues #1–15 of *TriQuarterly* are available in full format from Kraus Reprint Company, Route 100, Millwood, NY 10546, and all issues in microfilm from University Microfilms International, 300 North Zeeb Road, Ann Arbor, MI 48106. *TriQuarterly* is indexed in the *Humanities Index* (H.W. Wilson Co.), the *American Humanities Index* (Whitson Publishing Co.), Historical Abstracts, MLA, EBSCO Publishing (Peabody, MA) and Information Access Co. (Foster City, CA).

the best fiction, poetry, and

North America and

THE END IS ~~near~~ NEAR!

2K

TRIQUARTERLY'S DOUBLE MILLENNIAL ISSUE

POETRY BY

Stuart Dybek
Edward Hirsch
Paul Hoover
Mark Irwin
Sandra M. Gilbert
Cleopatra Mathis
Campbell McGrath

Alicia Ostriker
Carl Phillips
Peter Dale Scott
Tom Sleigh
Gerald Stern
Susan Stewart
Pimone Triplett
Alan Williamson

NEW WRITING FOR A NEW ERA

Preface

Classics and Contemporaries. I woke one August morning and walked out on the porch with a cup of coffee in my hand and the phrase on my lips. But it was too good, too perfect for my uses. No wonder: Edmund Wilson's "Classics and Contemporaries" is one of my most thumbed books. The Northshire Bookstore in Manchester didn't have a copy in stock. Looking over the clerk's shoulder as he studied the list of books under Edmund Wilson's name in *Books in Print*, I rediscovered that he called his collection of essays and reviews *Classics and Commercials*. But I will take this coincidence as a chance to pay homage to that curious man, Edmund Wilson, whose *Axel's Castle* was the most influential book about modernism by an American.

One central tenet of modernism is that the classic is contemporary. And that artists can communicate across time and space. What does Ulysses demonstrate if not the unity of all times and all places?

Classics and Contemporaries ranges freely across time and space, from little known gems in the Greek Anthology to some of the most original writing being done on the planet today. Some of the writers represented here, though well known abroad, are just beginning to be published and recognized in the United States. I picked up Alan Warner's *Morvern Callar* in a bookstore and was blown away. I feel lucky to have obtained a chapter from his wild new novel, *The Sopranos*.

Literary translation has become a defining point on our compass. Charles Martin's *Metamorphoses* and W. S. Merwin's *Purgatorio* are likely to become known as the best modern American translations of those works. David Slavitt's versions of de Sponde's sonnets are dark, honest, and terrifyingly immediate.

I am drawn to work that pushes at the border of genre: lyric and narrative, poetry and prose, translation and "version," the letter. Having become identified with the long poem of late, I looked for short poems that make up in intensity what they lack in length.

Then there's luck: it was my good fortune to happen upon amazing and unusual things: pivotal unpublished letters by James Schuyler, an essay revealing Louis Zukovsky's affinity with Apollinaire, a section of P. N. Furbank's work in progress on the novel, a dark and moving essay by

Howard Norman, a radio play by John Berger and strong poems with an innovative use of form by James Lasdun, Claudia Rankine and Barbara Guest, among others.

I have tried to create an anthology in which the various genres will interact to form a living organism—to dissolve any contradiction between looking backwards and forwards at once.

Mark Rudman, Bondville, Vermont, August 26, 1999

Mark Rudman wishes to thank Catharine Savini and Mike Wexler, the English Department of New York University, and Susan Hahn for their assistance in compiling this issue.

Contents

Editor of this Issue: Mark Rudman

Cover painting: "The Clearing" by Jake Berthot

Six Letters from James Schuyler

edited by William Corbett

James Schuyler, who died in 1991 at the age of sixty-seven, has been grouped with John Ashbery, Barbara Guest, Kenneth Koch, and Frank O'Hara in the first generation of the New York School of poets. Schuyler's letters resemble those of Elizabeth Bishop in that they are all of a piece. They cannot easily be divided under subject headings like travel, literature, art or politics. Like Bishop, Schuyler wrote not to think out loud or as a warm-up for writing poems or to pontificate but for the most civilized of motives, to entertain. That said, these letters have in common attention to literary matters. The letters to Donald M. Allen and Miss Batie are unique among the nearly two thousand Schuyler letters I have gathered. Although he was a novelist, poet, and art critic Schuyler wore his profession lightly. He did not feel compelled to remind friends that they were hearing from a writer. He wrote letters less to express himself than to engage his friends and so get letters in return.

Schuyler's punctuation, spelling, and grammar have not been corrected. His eccentricities in all three departments mark the letters with a trace at least of his unique voice.

—William Corbett

*

[Fairfield Porter (1907-1975), painter and art critic, became Schuyler's best friend. They met in 1952 but at first Schuyler was put off by Porter. At the time of this letter they had begun to form the friendship that would lead, in 1961, to Schuyler living with the Porter family for twelve years in their Southampton, Long Island home and on Great Spruce Head Island, Maine, where they spent their summers.]

To Fairfield Porter

Bastille Day eve 1954

Dear Fairfield,

Your letter delighted me. I think it's the wittiest one I've ever gotten.

We were in town yesterday afternoon and evening, and, after seeing a movie at the Art, I ran into Larry[1] in the Cedar, and we were all sorry to hear that your back is bothering you. I hope the shots help.

New York seemed rather frantic and tense yesterday; I'm so glad I'm not spending the summer there. I suppose one has to be out of it a while to feel its size and self-absorption, it's peculiar toughness. And then Larry was hung-over and silly, and there was a scene with the waiter, brought on by Gandy Brodie's[2] rudeness (whatever his problems and qualities, I think it's all right to say that as Gandy stands, and sits, he's a horrid young man).

I am so interested in what you say about "willed" and "organic;" it's a problem I find myself stuck with every day with my novel.[3] Parts of it seem to me to go along very well; unfortunately, from the beginning certain dramatic events are implied, and each time I try to go into the implied story (as opposed to the story that gets invented page by page) I seem to lose my tone. The tone seems to me anti-melodramatic, but I have willed the characters into a melodramatic situation, so that while they can talk about what has happened or will happen, it seems almost impossible for a strongly active situation to occur. I don't know if this tells why I think organic has anything to do with it; I suppose I mean partly a quality in a work of art of completeness in itself, as delightful in art as it is in a melon, and also, a way of making art. That if, at the beginning, I had not implied events outside the story more dramatic than those I describe, I could more easily bring natural and spontaneous drama out of the story itself. So this melon of mine, I am afraid, will never thoroughly ripen. (I take consolation in the maxim of learning through doing).

Arthur Weinstein bought a Hartl oil. It looks lovely in his apartment, and I gather from John Hohnsbeen[4] that Hartl badly needs the money. It's nice to know of an exchange that gives satisfaction in several quarters.

I can't work up any strong feeling about Connecticut[5]; it's very busy. On the other hand, it has pleasant semi-rural moments, and I love paddling in the unnaturally blue waters of the pool.

I don't know yet when we leave for Austria; probably the first week in August. I keep forgetting I'm going, and then when I remember, I feel thrilled. I'm afraid for me Europe will always be followed by an exclamation point. It's such a treat to go there.

Your touch typing improves by leaps and bounds. I hope this finds you feeling better. Take care of yourself, and let me hear from you soon. Arthur sends affectionate greetings.

As ever, Jimmy

[Kenneth Koch (b. 1925), poet and teacher. Like John Ashbery and Frank O'Hara, Koch went to Harvard. Following graduation all three came to New York. Ashbery and O'Hara introduced Koch to Schuyler in 1952.]

To Kenneth Koch

Summer, 1956

Dear Boy,

I've been thinking—no, that's not the way to put it: I've an idea—no, that's not the way either; I've been lying on the bed and it seems to me that
we should
all do
a lot
more
of it
(so that's how W.C. Williams gets that look)—anyway there is the question of these painters who insist we make public spectacles of ourselves. According to Button & Blaine[6], we're limited to 170 (one seventy) words per poet per painter (I mean the poet *including* the painter, not 170 words each); well, I started mine about John and found that after a page and a half I had hit the 600 point and hadn't even gotten to him yet. So I planned a plan with my room-mate[7], once again a minion of the M.O.M.A. has given his seal to it. He says he doesn't care what happens and it might as well be this way as any other.

All it is that we each write a sentence. Isn't that simple? (Climb back out of the bay, dear, it's cold and you'll get the plate in your head all rusty). I mean like, Sentences about Howard Kanovitz, Sentences about Marry Abbot Clyde, Sentences about John Button, Curses about Herbert Machiz[8]. . .You know sort of like The Cheerful Cherub: "You keep out of my way and I'll keep out of yours;" "Don't tell me how to wear hats and I won't tell you where to part your hair;" and so on. Just a lot of nice home-made sentences. Anyway, you must do it right away because while no one cares whether it ever happens it has to happen now if it's going to happen at all. That you aren't better acquainted with your chosen artist's work doesn't much matter, as it turns out that if you try to describe a teaspoon in 170 words it may turn out sounding quite a bit like Gitou Knoop. So let'er rip, Big Red (and remember it's not 170 sentences they want from us, but words).

Isn't Great Spruce Head beautiful? I could go on quite a while telling you about it, but then, you are there.

J & J[9] came back from Mexico, very tan and smelling of coconut oil and a little weary. This time I think they were a little less staggered by its beauty (our Jane isn't taking any sass from anybody) and more at home. It's always hard to say whether they had a *good* time anywhere, but they did visit the gladiola center of Mexico and the cucumber center and saw a lot of movies with Spanish subtitles.

The frothy New York social season keeps on draining away; tomorrow night we're going to dinner at David Noakes's[10] and Stuart Preston[11] will be there. No wonder all the ovens in New York are being converted to non-toxic natural gas.

(Larry called up just now and managed to make so many innuendoes in one and a half minutes my head feels like the merry-go round at the end of *Strangers on a Train*[12]).

Oh I also saw Larry briefly yestereve (ah, bit sticky and muggy it was, the Chihuahua for all its hairlessness was asweat) and he said he'd read your "G.W. Crossing the D." aloud to some Southampton Big-Wigs and they loved it, they broke up, they thought it was terribly funny. Isn't that cute? Anyway Larry seemed to think it was a step toward the Southampton auditorium, Broadway and too many pickles too late at night at Sardi's[13] (John Button knows a marvelous pill for indigestion that cures acidity without setting up an alkali whateveryoucallit). Anyway, it occurred to me I've never heard Larry read from any work other than his own, and I wish I had tuned him in on this little device I have that picks up what anyone is saying anywhere in the world at any time. (I had it trained on Harry's Bar in Venice at the time; pigs all of them).

We love Janice's[14] postcard. We love Janice, and we thought and talked about her a lot of her birthday, and fulminated against a social order that prevents us from expressing our sentiment in a tangible form. I would call a diamond tangible, wouldn't you? But then, alas, so are pralines.

I had lunch with my editor from Harcourt, Brace, and it's a shame that an unusually kind heart, gentle tongue and faulty memory prevent me from reporting the conversation to you. Anyway, they seem to like it enormously, and have plans for publishing it during my life time—and I don't mean I'm taking the short view of my span, either. Though when illustrations were suggested, on the grounds that it would make it more "of a package", I did almost bring up my Chef Salad Marmiton. Then I thought, oh well, at least it doesn't have to be pressed into clay like the works of those poor Babylonian novelists. Think how the author of Gilgamesh must have felt—he didn't even have reprint rights. The people at Harcourt are extremely proud of the way their books look. Since I think only books printed in France and a few subsidiary states can be looked at without experiencing one of the major disgusts, I don't care what they do to it. After all, the origin of our art is the spoken word, isn't it, Kenneth? Ho ho ho.

We misses thou and thou moglie and thou bambinakins. I hope baby K[15] soon gets over her xenophobia so I can rush in and smother her with kisses without getting socked in the eye. Hurry back; the telephone is a dead thing without you.

Love,

P.S. and do your sentences tout-de-suite and send me them; John Myers[16] wrote from Venice that he doesn't want this show to lay an egg Isn't he cute?

[Donald M. Allen (b. 1914), editor Grove Press. Allen had begun work on the anthology that became The New American Poetry 1945-1960.*]*

To Donald M. Allen

Sunday, Sept. 20, 1959

Dear Don,

Here, from the welter of papers I've been carrying about, are a few poems; and a copy of the play that amused Frank, and (of "historical" interest), an imaginary conversation, written after seeing Frank's first book and walking up Park Avenue with him one May evening. I may send you a few more, but there aren't any I like better that "February", "The Elizabetheans Called it Dying", and "Freeley Espousing."[17]

I was so interested in what Frank told me about his talk with you last Sunday. Olson may well be right, and there is a real point in putting in "background" or older poets.[18] But if you want to represent the influence of readers as systematically omnivorous as Frank, John A., Prof. Koch and, me too, well: wow. Frank sometimes seems to cast the splendid shadow of his own sensibility over the past, as well as his friends, and while a brush of his wings is delightful, it is also somewhat heady. I thought you might be interested in what I remember people as actually reading.

John Wheelwright: particularly the poems in Rock and Shell.

Auden: like the common cold. Frank and Kenneth still profess; I grudgingly assent (though if Auden doesn't drop that word numinous pretty soon, I shall squawk).

For the greats: Williams, Moore, Stevens, Pound, Eliot. I doubt if any very direct connection can be found between Moore and anyone. I wanted to write like her, but her form is too evolved, personal and limiting. After a bout of syllable counting, to pick up D.H. Lawrence is delightful.

Eliot made the rules everybody wants to break.

Stevens and Williams both inspire greater freedom than the others. Stevens of the imagination, Williams of subject and style.

Pound I wonder about. Like Gertrude Stein, he is an inspiring idea. But a somewhat remote one. A poem like Frank's Second Avenue might seem influenced by the Cantos, but Breton is much closer to the mark.

Continental European literature is, really, the big influence: the Greats, plus Auden, seemed to fill the scene too completely—so one had to react against them, casting off obvious influences as best one can. In the context of American writing, poets like Jacob and Breton spelled freedom rather than surreal introversion. What people translate for their own pleasure is a clue: Frank, Holderlin and Reverdy; John A. (before he'd been to France), Jacob's prose poems; Kenneth and I have had a go at Dante's untranslatable sonnet to Cavalcanti; I've translated Dante, Leopardi and, fruitlessly, Apollinaire and Supervielle. (I like the latter's stories better than his poems). But Pasternak has meant more to us than any American poet. Even in monstrous translations his lyrics make the hair on the back of one's neck curl.

But back to Americans. The horrid appearance of the sestina in our midst (K. and Fairfield Porter used to correspond in sestinas) can be traced directly, by way of John Ashbery's passion for it, to one by Elizabeth Bishop. It's title eludes me: one of the end words is coffee, and it is in her first book.

Hart Crane: very much, and perhaps for extra-poetical reasons that aren't so extra. But he has exactly what's missing in "the poetry should be written as carefully as prose" poets: sensibility and heart. Not "The Bridge", of course (not yet anyway)—I think it's impossible for anyone not to premise so overtly an "American" idea. I don't mean that I don't enjoy the poem; but there is, at bottom, the rather hick idea of America challenging Europe, when Whitman had already conquered with a kiss.

But do look at "Havana Rose" in the uncollected poems, or "Moment Fugue" (I'd give the tooth of an owl to have written that or a song like "Pastorale":

> No more violets
> And the year
> Broken into smoky panels.

What a beginning.

John and Frank not now, and Kenneth perhaps, admire or admired Laura Riding; but she wouldn't let her poems be reprinted. I have always found them rather arid going, myself.

On reflection: I don't think I'm right about Gertrude Stein. Certainly the Beck's[19] production of *Ladie's Voices* (on the same bill as Picasso's *Desire Caught by the Tail*, in which Frank and John A. appeared as a couple of dogs, night after night) in 1952 influence me immediately and directly. To represent her by a work like *Ladies Voices* would be truer than to include almost anything of Eliot's. I like Eliot but what Parson Weems was to other generations, *The Wasteland*, was to us; Pablum.

Also, in tracing influences—the important ones—there is this: that while John Wieners by chance first got the word from Olson at a Boston reading (then later went to Black Mountain College) and put it to good use, it is an experience unlike that of any other talented poet I know. Frank studied with Ciardi[20]; but if another writer had been giving the course, Frank would have taken it. (Olson's own allegiance to Pound-Fenellosa can't be generalized for others—unless you have room for all of Proust, *The Golden Bowl*, *Don Juan* (very operative on Frank and Kenneth) and Lady Murasaki. All through high school one of my sacred books was Mark Van Doren's *Anthology of World Poetry*. (In which I first read poems by Thoreau; I'm not all *that* international).

I was so delighted to hear that you asked Frank about Edwin Denby's poems; I hope you have seen *Mediterranean Cities* as well as his earlier book. His harsh prosody I find a relief.

There is a poet who died whose name escapes me[21]: Frank and John admire his work very much, and I think Frank has copies of *QRL* with poems of his. Perhaps Frank has already mentioned him to you.

I trust we'll talk soon. I didn't mean to go on at this length, but if you can find anything for your anthology in these maunderings, so much the better.

> Yours,
>
> Jimmy

To John Ashbery

[John Ashbery (b. 1927) was, in company with the artist and writer Joe Brainard, Schuyler's favorite correspondent. In this instance Schuyler is sending Ashbery a letter Schuyler had written to Chester Kallmann. Poet, librettist and W.H. Auden's companion from 1939 until Auden's death in 1973, Kallmann (1921-1975) was probably Schuyler's closest friend from the mid-1940s to 1950. Kallman's book of poems Storm at Castelfranco *(1956) was dedicated to Schuyler. In his poem "A Few Days" Schuyler wrote, "Chester Kallmann was a martyr/to the dry martini."]*

September 3, 1960
49 South Main Street, Southampton, New York (c/o Porter)

Dear John, I thought it's be well advised to let you know about this—no I have not turned my back on modern art.   XxxThe Rat

Dear Chester,
    "N'est-ce plus ma main. . .?"
    I hope you're having a marvelous lederhosened summer, full of (I wanted to list a lot of double entendre Austrian tasties but my German spelling, you will be surprised to learn is inferior to my English).
    Business first: I "and others" (it is a deep secret; the other is John Ashbery) are invisibly editing an anthology-magazine.[22] It will go to press on Majorca in October—part of its unstated objective is a riposte at THE NEW AMERICAN POETRY, which has so thoroughly misrepresented so many of us—not completely, but the implications of context are rather overwhelming. Anyway, for issue one we want a cheerful, serious, international, kind of Paris-New York edited contents, and that of course means you. Have you any new poems? If not, I'd like very much to represent you by the scena from the *Rake's Progress*, "Has love no voice", to finish of act.[23] Two other contributions are previously published (Edwin Denby's "Mediterranean Cities"—entire: "we" may all know that book, but I know how little known his poetry is; and Anne Channing (Porter's)[24] poems; which came out in that well known magazine *The Bonaker* (—I will tell you what a Bonaker is in this fall). Is there any copyright complication? Is there a detachable piece from the Berlioz story? What are you working on now? Well, you know best what's on hand. Please send what you like, up to fifteen pages—preferably less: I'm plopping in a quite short story sort of in the *Alfred & G* style; one of Frank O'H's poems is a 1952 effort called "Party Full of Friends"; George Montgomery makes a few terse utterances—and so on. I think, in general, you will approve.

Why, Saint Restituta, do you send your winds over Lake Agawam each time I decide to typewrite out-doors? *"Ma ai, stupidone, chettle le serre mi da'vent alle piacevole prate di patete . . . Patete!!!"*

When are you coming back? Who will call who first? My tattered bull-headedness (oops—that was supposed to be tattered bullhead-dress, like those Mexican hot-chas, but let it pass)—can't wait to tell the Plaza typewriter folks what I think of this re-conditioned so called Royal portable de luxe—

I think I will contribute that paragraph to the Larry Rivers Get Well fund.

Look, when you hit the States, why don't you telephone the Museum and, in a disguised voice, say you are Kurt Brown, Mr Kallman's secretary and that Mr Kallman is back? Then my so-called secretary, Mrs Berit Potoker, will leave me a note that someone whose name is either Hurt Krassner, Rock Hudson or Ashley T. Jeffington called; and I will KNOW. Oh well, really, I do look forward to seeing you, and I hope the coming season (of which I shudder I had a glimpse last night: you should meet Bob Rauschenberg's pet Australian marsupial, Sweetie) won't be full of mutual acquaintances—dare I call some of them friends?—such as Merton Glasscock, Tits Galore and Merkin O'Toole looking at me askance and saying, while I am secretly trying to get the pickled onions out of my sherry toddy, "I saw Chester last night." Followed by a fraught pause.

The wind has dropped. I suppose that means the fog is ready to do its stuff. Considering its lethargic look, it can move with surprising speed. And it is only the fact that it is Saturday evening that prevents me from going into the house and calling the Plaza Typewriter folks this minute. That, and the fact that a check I gave them recently may have bounced. Thank goodness there's no mail delivery tomorrow or Monday which, ugh, is Labor Day.

I hope in all this camp you can discern that the "Occasional Anthology" is a serious opus. Please send what you like prontissimo, to: John Ashbery, 35 rue de Varrene, Paris VIII, France. Or to Mr Harry Mathews[25], (just a sec. While I step into the barn & find Harry's address). It is: Mr Harry Mathews, La Haut de Peuil

Lans-en-Vercors (Isere)
France

which I believe is near Grenoble. Have you met him? He is a young writer, an ardent *Rake's Progress* fan, he and his wife live either at Lans-en-Vercors, on their farm, or in Paris; although they spent this summer at Wainscot (near here) visiting family.

I set my face against non-paying publications, and the profits realized from this pub. will be on a divide the profits, per page, basis. Mother will count pages but she draws the line at lines; and will only count pica if the designer appears to be fibbing—no problem here, since I am not about to visit Majorca.

If Wystan is with you, please tell him he's of course invited to contribute, too: I only hesitate because I feel that at this point there are so many demands for his work. But if he would like to jump into the pool, the other otters would love to have him. Since I am (but don't tell John Ashbery) more or less no.1 editor of issue 1, a page of his pothooks would thrill all of us.

Oh. (The sun is now straight in my eyes—I suppose I could move my chair, but the last time I did, a batch of paper clips vanished into the lawn. Criminetties;;;all the Diffenbach boys just plunged through the hedge. They are playing a game, I guess. Go away little boys or I will change you into swans—and remember, you do not have a little sister. A nephew of Anne Porter's, whom I like very much, or did when we spent a month or so together in Maine a few years ago, is convinced that Wystan once translated *The Calk Circle in C's*.[26] (sic. For calk: the ribbon is functioning so that I see each line only when I reach the next): I am uncertain whether Laurence M. (Bunny) Channing, Jr. hopes to produce it at Cambridge (he has a healthy contempt for—is it Bentley's very own? Hashing), or is writing a thesis or what; anyway, I have no recollection of same: has either of you? If it exists, is it available? From what I know about Bunny, if he wished to produce it, it would be for either the Poets' Theater, or some follow up to the Brattle. (This is based on a conversation Anne had at another nephew's wedding last Sunday). Anyway, Anne owns all of Auden in American editions, except the plays, and so far I haven't traced it; but I have a recollection of some translations in that magazine called _____, where I first read your work in print. All that comes creeping back in the disheveled twilight (the temp. just dropped thirty degrees) is an image of a more-or-less pocket sized magazine, and some German Englished by Wystan.

I am going back to work next Tuesday, but please write me here. (And please do write, dear boy!) I intend to keep coming out here for long weekends—quite possibly until well in the summer.

There are a million things I meant to tell or ask you. Like: At Julia Gruen's[27] birthday party yesterday (her second) Larry R. said, "Hey I heard from John Myers it was so stormy flying he says he said Hail Marys for an hour and a half! He relapsed!" For once I think I had the taste not to say anything witty, I just stared past Morton (call me Slim) Feldman[28] at the Henry Ford's distant manse and wondered.

What would cause Bunny a thrill I can dimly recall the great age of . . . would be if Wystan wrote a yes or no on a postcard and sent it to him. (About Brecht, I mean).

Laurence M. Channing, Jr.
Wareham, Indian Neck
Massachusetts

Did you know that Fairfield Porter is a sort of cousin, quite close, of T.S. Eliot's? I guess that's why his older brother is named Eliot—though scarcely for T.S., who may be younger than Eliot, who is an attractive grandfather; for family reasons I mean.

Supper time. The youngest Diffenbach just pointed out that in the house I could type with the light on. How true. WRITE! Love,

P.S. Dear John: I'm not cross with you anymore. xxxxx Pip.

(In his letters to John Ashbery, Schuyler habitually addressed him by a name other than his own, that of a movie star or famous, and now forgotten writer, such as the once best-selling novelist Joseph Hergesheimer. Schuyler usually signed himself with a similar borrowed name. For the most part Ashbery addressed Schuyler in the same joking way.)

To John Ashbery

July 13, 1968

Dear Joseph Hergeshimer,

First things first: I'm afraid I can't help with your Sherwood Anderson query, since I spend a good deal of time sedulously avoiding his works. This is not because I dislike them, but because I don't know much about them and prefer to keep it that way. When I was a child, back in the days of flagpole sitters, Billie Dove, the Golddust Twins and Knee-Hi Grape, a baby sitter once treated me to a read from what I've always fondly imagined was a novel of his, which concerned the thoughts of a man while hopping the midnight freight to get away from his wife. So I've always imagined that true maturity would be to read, enjoy and understand a Sherwood Anderson novel. A day I hope to postpone as long as possible.

(Liz says I promised to go swimming *right now*. Well, I wouldn't want to keep Rose Anne Shepherd waiting. . .)[29]

July 14th. Good grief, it's almost time to go swimming again. Though I may just skip it. Even if it is mighty warm for Maine, it's still damn cold.

Well, since breaking off yesterday, life has been more that usually exciting. First there was a dip in the cove, with the exciting Haskell children from Stonington. Then Bruno and I took a long walk. True to his character, the great gun-shy duck retriever refuses to learn to swim. I spent quite a long time at Fisherman's Beach throwing sticks just out of his depth, and a couple of times actually got him to be briefly water-born. But he eluded my attempts to grab him in (these trys can be made when Liz is not around). Then I found a thrilling new (to me) sort of cranesbill growing on the Double Beaches, and gooseberries. So home to supper, a few games of solitaire while Fairfield read some more of *Middlemarch* aloud (a marvelous book—how odious that Leavis[30] should be right about anything) and so to bed and up before the larks (5:30) and to Stonington, where I visited Bartlett's Market in search of local newspapers (rather dull today) and yearned through the closed antique shop window while Anne and Liz were at mass. And so the days wear away.

Apropos George Eliot: I don't remember *Silas Marner* as very funny-on-purpose, do you? *Middlemarch* is—it's sort of a highbrow *Barchester Towers*, or so I conclude at this point. We've only decimated its thousand pages. Do you, by the way, have any inside info on how to pronounce Mr Casaubon? I suppose it's anglicized . . .

I'm sorry you missed the visit to the island of Mike Strauss's Parisian cousin, minus any English at all. Well, the couple didn't have any, but their post-college son, who works for a farm-machinery branch of Sperry-Rand in Lancaster, Pa., had a little, so I cottoned on to him—though without ulterior motive, since the person he most resembled is David Sachs. He seemed quite startled when I suggested that Lancaster is a rather pretty city. It would have pleasured your ears to hear him pronounce Ottawa. I had my usual *fleuve-riviere-ruisseau* French conversation, and learned to distinguish a *crique* from a—I forget what—an *ance* perhaps? I'm sorry I've forgotten their last name, which was nice and plain, but Mama's first name was Monique. I wish they had stayed longer. It's nice that the French have such an instructive bent. I'm sure one could sustain a lengthy cocktail party simply by asking the names of the Departments of France. (Hmmm—it just occurred to me that may be my own one Gallic quality).

I loved your ad. In the *New York Review of Books*, and have been dining at home for a week on the story that you are on tour with Bobby and Arthur in the two piano reduction of *Façade* . . .

Tee-hee.

The Portland paper of a few days back got used to start a fire before I could cut out a recipe for you, Golfball Dessert. However I doubt that you would have wished to make it: chocolate sludge containing angel food cake torn into pieces the size of golfballs. Mold and chill.

If you've a mind to try Irma's fool-proof popovers, you may do so with this caution: if you use individual custard cups do not, as she suggests, try to line them up on a whippy cookie sheet. When you pick up the sheet, you will see why. The survivors were delicious. As was my Swedish tea ring, for which I invented a memorable currant-cardoman filling (and how). It brought gasps from the Laurence Porters and friends, so I don't risk any squeals until they had left. The meat pie, which I preferred, (or CHICKEN POT PIE TOPPING (pg 421) however . . . Irma says it will soak up a lot of gravy. But only, I find, if contact is intimately established between gravy and topping. Otherwise all you get is Beef Stew Under a Cloud, and a cloud which is rather like biting into a motel pillow.

There is a phonograph here, but it is not of an epoch you could do much for. The records that go with it have grooves on only one side. In fact I played one for you (the trio from Lombardi, I believe) but it seemed to suggest to you that your presence was required at the crowning of the Miss Maine Broiler Queen in Bangor, so I turned it off.

Now I can't find your letter before last, 'case it contained any queries. Shucks. But the "tawney hockey pucks" are unforgettable.

Guess I will pull on my impeccably tailored Lastex trunks that have lost their stretch and my dyed-to-match pearlized Keds and go for a dip. Marian Christy to the contrary, I wouldn't mind a bit having a gray mink boa over my shoulders on this heavily air-conditioned island.

Keep me posted as plans mature for your projected swing through the New England States. And don't forget to leave time for a bite at Wildwood Park.

Love,

Starling F. Scruggs

("Dear Miss Batie" turned up among Schuyler's letters to John Ashbery. I have not been able to identify Miss Battie. Nor do I know if Schuyler ever finished the letter. If he did, did he send it to her? Again, I have no idea. As far as I have been able to determine Schuyler wrote no other letters in which he goes in detail about a poem of his. He is discussing "February" which appeared in his book *Freely Espousing*.)

March 25, 1969

Dear Miss Batie,

Thank you for your letter. It is always pleasant to learn that someone takes an interest in work which one enjoyed writing. In the past I have declined to comment on my own work: because, it seems to me, a poem is what it is; because a poem is itself a definition, and to try to redefine it is to be apt to falsify it; and because the author is the person least able to consider his own work objectivly. Though as for the last, one certainly has to try. However, I liked your letter, and I have a great curiosity about Vancouver, so I'll see if I can think of anything that may be of use to you.

Of the ideas you suggest, the one that seems closest to what I might think is that of "an art where everything is ambiguous until superimposed into an entity." To change your phrase somewhat, I know that I like an art where disparate elements form an entity. De Kooning's work, which I greatly admire, has less to do with it than that of Kurt Schwitter's, whose collages are made of commercial bits and "found" pieces but which always compose a whole striking for its completeness.

I had no religious intention, though I can see why a poem whose "idea", if we may call it such, is that of an essential harmony, or perhaps congruity is a better word, might suggest one. However, intention needn't enter in, and if a reader sees things in a religious way, and the work is dogmatically acceptable, then I don't see why it should not be interpreted in that way, as well as in others. In this case, though, I really can't see that purification comes into it at all. Part of the point would seem to be that junk, like the trucks and the lions, and things that matter, like flowers, the sea, a mother and her baby (in an ascending scale of value) have each its place, and that it is the world in its impurity which is so very beautiful and acceptable, if only because one has so little choice.

As for evocation/communication, I don't find the first separate from the second, though subsidiary to it. The aim of any poet, or other artist, is first to make something; and it's impossible to make something out of words and not communicate. However, if a poem can be reduced to a prose sentence, there can't be much to it. (Someone, I believe, has said that, "What a poem communicates is itself." This seems to me true.)

I am not quite sure what you mean by the "development" of the poem. If you mean it in the sense used is music, I hope it's there in the poem; anyway I have nothing to add to it. If you mean how I came to write it, well, let's see.

It was late February and I had very recently returned from Europe, where for the first time I had visited Palermo, and made an excursion to see the temples at Agrigento (where there were also wild snap-dragons in bloom among the lion colored drums of fallen columns), a rather dusty and disappointing affair at the time, but which was a pleasure to recollect. The day on which I wrote the poem I had been trying to write a poem in a regular form about (I think) Palermo, the Palazzo Abatelli, which has splendid carved stone ropes around its doors and windows, and the chapels decorated by Serpotta with clouds of plaster cherubs; the poem turned out laborious and flat, and looking out the window I saw that something marvelous was happening to the light, transforming everything. It then occurred to me that this happened more often than not (a beautiful sunset, I mean) and that it was "a day like any other," which I put down as a title. The rest of the poem popped out of its own accord. Or so it seems now.

I do not usually revise much, though I often cut, particularly the end or toward the end of a poem. One tends to write beyond what's needed.

It seems to me that readers sometimes make the genesis of a poem more mysterious than it is (by that perhaps I mean, think of it as something outside their own experience). Often a poem "happens" to the writer in exactly the same way that it "happens" to someone who reads it.

As for stimuli, I hope you won't "perceive a similar response" in this instance, since what stimulated me to write was the apathy following on the disappointment of a wasted day. However, what seemed like waste may have been a warming up. Who knows? Not me.

Notes

1. Larry Rivers (b.1923), painter. Fairfield Porter painted his portrait in 1951.
2. Gandy Brodie, painter.
3. *Alfred and Guinevere*, Schuyler's first novel, was published by Harcourt, Brace in 1958.
4. John Hohnsbeen, friend of Schuyler's. He worked as an art dealer. Leon Hartl was a painter whose work Porter admired. Arthur Weinstein was friendly with Schuyler in the 1950s.
5. Schuyler spent part of the summer in Alice Esty's in New Canaan, Connecticut. It had been rented by the pianists Arthur Gold and Robert Fizdale. At the time Gold and Schuyler were lovers.
6. John Button and Nell Blaine.
7. Frank O'Hara. Schuyler, O'Hara and Joe LeSueur were sharing an apartment at 326 East 49th Street.
8. Herbert Machiz, founder and director of the Artists' Theater.

9. Joe Hazan and Jane Freilicher, painters and husband and wife.

10. David Noakes, a Schuyler friend to whom he dedicated the poem "Greetings from the Chateau."

11. Stuart Preston, man about Gay Manhattan in the 1940's and 1950's. He appears in the memoirs of James Lord and others.

12. A film directed by Alfred Hitchcock.

13. Broadway restaurant popular with the theater crowd.

14. Janice Koch (1931-1981) first wife of Kenneth and a close friend of Schuyler's. He dedicated the poem "Money Musk" to her.

15. The Koch's daughter, and first child, Katherine.

16. John Bernard Myers, director of the Tibor de Nagy Gallery and impresario of the arts. His Tibor de Nagy Gallery Editions published Schuyler's second book of poems, May 24th or So.

17. All three poems and the poem "Salute" appeared in *The New American Poetry*.

18. Charles Olson had advised Allen to include in the anthology poets who had influenced the poets of 1945-1960. Allen came to reject the idea as too cumbersome.

19. Julian Beck and Judith Malina, actors and founders of the Living Theater.

20. O'Hara took the poet John Ciardi's creative writing class at Harvard.

21. David Schubert (1913-46) whose only book, *Initial A*, was published by MacMillian in 1960.

22. This evolved into the magazine, *Locus Solus*, which ran for five issues and was edited by Harry Mathews, Kenneth Koch and Frank O'Hara in addition to Schuyler and Ashbery.

23. Kallmann collaborated on this libretto with W.H. Auden. Igor Stravinsky composed the music.

24. Wife of Fairfield Porter.

25. Harry Mathews (b. 1930) novelist, poet and resident in France for many years.

26. Bertholt Brecht's play, "The Caucasian Chalk Circle."

27. Daughter of composer and writer John Gruen and the painter Jane Wilson.

28. Morton Feldman (1926-1987) composer and essayist.

29. Liz Porter, daughter of Fairfield and Anne. Schuyler writes this letter from Great Spruce Head Island in Maine's Penobscot Bay.

30. F.R. Leavis, English literary critic.

from Purgatory

A Translation of the Purgatorio of Dante

W.S. Merwin

Canto XXIII

While I had my eyes focused among the leafy
   green branches, as they are used to doing
   who pursue birds and lose their lives that way,

"Son," my more than father said to me,
   "come along now, for the time that is allowed us
   will have to be put to better use."

I turned my face, and my steps as promptly
   following after the sages, and such was their talk
   that the going was at no cost to me.

And then we could hear, "My lips, Lord," being sung
   with weeping in such a way that it brought
   to birth joy, and at the same time grieving.

"Oh, sweet father, what is it that I hear?"
   I began. And he, "Shades, perhaps, on their
   way to untie the knot of what they owe."

As pilgrims do when, deep in their thoughts, they
   approach those they do not know, on the way,
   and they turn toward them and do not stay

so from behind us, moving more swiftly,
   a crowd of souls, silent and devout,
   came and stared at us in wonder as they passed by.

Each was dark and hollow about the eyes,
   their faces were pallid, and they were shrunken
   so that the bones were showing through the skin.

I do not believe that Erysicthon
   was ever so withered to a crust
   by hunger when that was what he dreaded most.

In my own mind I said to myself, "These are
   the people who lost Jerusalem, then
   when Mary drove the beak into her son!"

The eye sockets looked like rings that had no stone.
   Whoever reads OMO in the human
   face would have recognized the M clearly there.

Who would believe that the smell of an apple
   and the smell of water could make that happen
   by begetting longing, if they did not know the reason?

I was wondering then what it is that starves them,
   not having seen yet what had made them
   so thin, with that miserable crust on them,

and there, from deep in the hollow of his head
   a shade turned his eyes on me and kept them on me,
   then shouted in a loud voice, "What grace has come to me?"

I would never have known him from his face
   but I was certain, when I heard his voice,
   of what his countenance had erased of itself.

That spark lighted again all that I
  had known once of those features that had changed,
  and I recognized the face of Forese.

"Ah, do not stay in dispute with the withered
  scab," he begged, "that discolors my skin,
  nor with the absence of the flesh I had,

but tell me the truth about yourself, and who
  are these two souls who are escorting you?
  Do not wait longer before you tell me."

"Your face that I wept for once when it was dead
  gives me no less cause now for weeping," I answered,
  "When I come to see it so distorted.

Therefore, in God's name tell me, what strips your leaves so;
  do not ask me to speak while I wonder still,
  for someone whose will is elsewhere cannot speak well."

And he to me, "From the eternal guidance
  virtue drops through the water and through the tree
  now left behind, and that is what so thins me.

All of these people weeping as they sing,
  for having followed their appetites to excess,
  in hunger and thirst here remake their holiness.

The fragrance of the apple and of the spray
  over the tops of the green leaves spreading
  inflames a longing for drinking and eating,

and not once only is our pain freshened
  on this level as we come around;
  pain, I say, and I should say comfort,

for the will that leads us to the tree
  is the same that made Christ say, 'My God' gladly
  when out of his own vein he set us free."

And I to him, "Forese, from that day
    when you exchanged the world for a better life,
    until this, five years have not come around all the way.

If you no longer had the power to sin
    before the hour when that good suffering
    overtook you that weds us to God again,

how is it that you have come up here so soon?
    I had thought I would find you lower down
    there where time is repaired again with time."

Then he to me, "It is my Nella who
    with the pouring of her tears has brought me to
    drink so soon the sweet wormwood of the torments.

With her devout prayers with sighs she has brought me
    from the hillside where they are waiting, and
    from the other circles has set me free.

That much dearer and more to be cherished by
    God is my dear widow whom I loved greatly
    as in her good works she is solitary,

for the women of the Barbagia
    of Sardinia are more modest by far
    than those of the Barbagia where I left her.

Oh, sweet brother, what would you have me say?
    A future time appears to me already
    from which this hour will not seem very old

when from the pulpit the impudent women
    of Florence will be forbidden
    to go showing the nipples of their breasts.

What barbarian women, what Saracens
    ever needed spiritual disciplines
    or any other, to make them keep covered?

But, shameless as they are, if they really
  knew what swift heaven is preparing for them
  their mouths would be open to howl already

for if our foresight here does not deceive me
  they will come to sorrow before he has
  hair on his cheeks who is lulled now by lullabies.

Oh, brother, do not hide your story from me
  any longer. See, it is not only I,
  but all these people are staring at where you veil the sun."

So I said to him, "If you bring back to mind
  what you were with me, and what I was with you
  the present memory will still be a sorrow.

That one before me turned me from that life only
  a few days ago when," and I pointed to
  the sun, "his sister appeared round to you.

He is the one who has conducted
  me through the deep night of the truly dead,
  with this true flesh following behind him.

With his heartening he has brought me here
  climbing and turning around the mountain
  that makes you, whom the world twisted, straight again.

He will be a companion to me, he says,
  until I come to where Beatrice is,
  where I will have to be left without him.

It is Virgil who speaks so to me,"
  and I pointed to him, "and that other is
  the shade for whom all the hillsides, just now,

of your kingdom shook, as they let him go."

Notes

line 11 Psalm 50, "O Lord, open my lips and my mouth shall proclaim your praise."

line 26 Erysichthon, son of King Triopas of Thessaly. He cut down trees in a grove sacred to Ceres and was punished with hunger so fierce that he ate his own flesh.

lines 28-30 From Flavius Josephus, The Jewish War VI. When Titus laid siege to Jerusalem a Jewish woman named Mary was driven by hunger to kill and eat her infant son.

lines 32-33 According to a belief current in Dante's time, the Italian word for "man," "omo," was visible in the human face: the eyes as o's and the brows and nose forming an m, at least in the uncial script.

line 48 Forese Donati, friend of Dante's and fellow poet. They wrote sonnets sparring with each other, in the convention of the tenzone but not with unfailing good humor. In two of the sonnets Dante speaks of Forese's gluttony, as other commentators did.

line 74 Matt. 27:46 ". . . Jesus cried out with a loud voice, saying, 'Eli, Eli, lema sabacthani?'" that is "My God, my God, why hast thou forsaken me?"

line 87 Apparently an abbreviation of Giovanella; Forese's wife was named Anella.

line 94 La Barbagia. A mountainous region in central Sardinia, where the inhabitants were said to be descendants of prisoners left there by the Vandals. In the Middle Ages they were notorious for their lax mores. It was said that the women exposed their breasts.

line 96 The Barbagia Dante is alluding to here is Florence.

from Rocks on a Platter

Barbara Guest

The empirical sun

        on the disturbed border
in the animal-clad wood   gone down,
magick within   begs extension
disappointed   at eye level;
grey-streaked sky, sea.

          less
     less mourning less
       sandy mourning!

Frail sentence moved by

the seismic sway of existence,

under a shaken tree

is cultivated outside us.

Words, inflammable,

                    lie   in bricks

                        this changes.

                    White
perpendicular lights   attached to the shoulder
I touched the wrist with my writing finger   and from the center
the orb of the eye was enough fire   to light the writing lamp and
afterwards   the blade   withdrew from the writing shoulder and
that writ
blew away   flame lit with nothing   and nothingness stayed.

    Skin of the lost paper
        Knuckle smooth   (touched the writing).
            Nietzschean   thumb on
                    the trout
                and they disappear.

Elegy (A Little)

Donald Revell

Linoleum and half a dozen eggs
In 1960
           Many towered Ilium
A brand name and a shopping list too

Memory distinguishes all things from
Only nothing
              I was born and grew
Rooms stacked up into houses
A few trees (maples) weltered in their seasons
Wildly like sea birds in crude oil
                       What amazes
Me now amazed me always but never
Often eyesight is prophetic instantly

Seeing broken eggs on the linoleum
In the kitchen 1960
I saw a broken lifetime further
On as now I see my happy sister

Skywatch

Jan Heller Levi

> Between Aries and Andromeda lies the small constella-
> tion Triangulum, the triangle. The most important object
> here is the 33rd object in Messier's catalogue, described as
> a hazy white glow of almost uniform brightness.
> —from the *New York Times*: Week of November 3

Who is this Messier and how do I get
his catalogue? This week my
stars swerved like New
York cabbies. You tell
them where to go
and they take you.
Sometimes. Where
can I find Monsieur
Messier, with his
dossier of objets d'sky?
I've had too much
coffee this week, too
much frothy cappuccino
which is a vile
drink, not to mention
institution.
I thought I saw my major
ex- across a room
at a poetry reading
but it was only

a hazy white glow of almost uniform
brightness.
Who is this Messier,
physicists must know him,
or meteorologists.
I'm probably only 3 degrees
of separation from someone
who slept with him,
or his wife,
now there would be a messy love
triangulum.
Here are, I think,
the first 14 of the 33 objects
in Messier's catalogue:

1. the rubber-stamped constellation that sings:
   "You are not an idiot"
2. young hair
3. the H's behind our knees
4. the astronaut pen that writes upside down
5. house with its face split open, cut lip of bedroom,
   bleeding parlor
6-14. the Scottsboro Boys, all nine of them—pinwheeled
   in the heavens, arms and legs reeling. Especially
   Clarence Norris, 18, who *Life* Magazine, 1937,
   called *the dandy of the outfit, . . . plasters his hair*
   with strong-perfumed grease, keeps his shirt and
   overalls neat and clean.

Unlucky stars, are those lights in the trees,
or rain?
Are those stars in the heavens,
or the buttons of overalls,
polished neat and clean?
Professor Messier, I assume,
would know.
Last summer
the palm reader
took my hand
in his,

traced out a comet's tail.
My skin flamed
with an almost-uniform
heat.
This is your life
line, he said, it breaks
off here, but then
begins again.
Here. He looked at me
with some concern.
Expect some great
change
in the middle
of your life, he said.
I'm older than you think,
I said,
it's already happened.
I already died.
He consulted no book,
no manual,
but touched his fingers
to my brow,
I swear I saw 7 objects
of Messier's catalogue
swirling celestially
behind my eyes:

15. Madame Messier's suitcase. Packed. She's leaving.
He spends too much time with his head in the clouds.
16. A copy of Leaves of Grass from the Texas Book
Depository.
17. The little engine that tried but just couldn't.
18. My mother's underwear, a hazy white glow of almost
uniform brightness.
19. The idealist who writes his love in the dust.
20. A window in Robert McNamara's Pentagon office, 1965.
He turns to see my distant Quaker cousin, Norman
Morrison, douse himself with gasoline on the Plaza
below, and set himself afire.
21. The pick-ax still quivering in Trotsky's brain.

What is the difference between desire and ambition?
Desire, I think, is a river,
ambition a boat,
but in a hazy glow, the river mist takes
the form of a boat,
and sails you
away from
ambition.
In fact, it was my major
-ex I saw,
from the window of a cab.
Uptown, downtown,
from the perspective
of the Great Galaxy
in Andromeda, known
as sector M31,
whose separation
from earth is a mere
750,000 light-years.
I hopped out at the nearest
park bench,
sector M33,
from which Earth would be
a faint curiosity.
Indeed it was.
And odd it was
that she was
carrying a papoose.
And I-Ruined-Your-Life
came and sat down
beside me. And
I-Plucked-You-From-
Safety-and-Threw-
You-to-the-Wolves
said, hey, how have you
been. And I answered
cordially. Cordially
mind you.
Then she drew
from her papoose

a woolen blanket,
more than all the colors
of Joseph's coat.
We lay down in the great
sheep meadow,
our ankles, hips,
and shoulders touching.
The sky came close,
like a doctor with a thermometer.
Messier's milky waters
and boats swam into our eyes.
  Look, she said, there it is:
        22. Your heterosexuality, a little tattered, but still usable.
And I said what?
And she said,
look, there it is:
        23. Your own divided heart, its chambers of desire and chambers
        of dread overlapping.
And I said what?
And she said,
look, there it is:
        24. The amethyst bauble at the throat of Countess Gemini in
        Portrait of a Lady. "She lived," Henry James wrote, "it might be
        said, at the window of her spirit, but now she was leaning far out."
Oh, I said,
I thought it might
be something like that,
and she said,
look, I've got to be going.
I said what,
again?
And she said
yeah and left.

Lucky stars,
you've been dead so long and still
you shine,
apples in the night
from the tree of regret.
Madame Messier has packed her bags,

and is moving on.
When I left my husband,
a friend said
don't do it,
before you know it,
you'll be one of those
dames in their 40s,
alone and bitter,
taking taxicabs,
knowing exactly what to tip.
Last night,
reading about Messier's catalogue,
I thought about the story
of our lives,
the ones we tell ourselves
about ourselves,
how they're packed with themes,
but so few symbols.
I thought I'd make a list
of things, of objects,
the ones we carry with us,
the ones we leave behind.
But the columns wouldn't
split properly,
I wanted two boxes,
I kept getting a triangle.

from Mozart's Third Brain

Göran Sonnevi

Translated from the Swedish by Rika Lesser

[Translator's note: *Mozart's Third Brain*, Göran Sonnevi's thirteenth book of poems, is divided into two parts. The first part, "Disparates," contains shorter poems written between 1958-1996. The second part is the title poem, which is divided into 144 sections. Section 48 follows.]

XLVIII

We are here with all the dead, their
shadow that always grows   We look in
toward the light that is casting the shadow
Look into the transparent forms of the light

European music is playing
I hear its worlds of sound
cut into one another, as in a counter-
point of worlds   Ricercare   That
conceptual universe   Old
knowledge; old suffering; old phobias
How are we to understand the suffering that exists
when we are not prepared to do anything about it?
The treachery of this   Old treachery
as if it were completely new; risen again

The whirlwind of ash at my feet, invisible

Where shall I set them down?
The firing goes on   We are vessels of clay in the fire

The orders of crime increase in enormity
When did Antigone become genocidal?   Creon always was

The rage and the blinding that appear
in large groups of people   The orders of murder
The orders of pain   As if they were logical hierarchies
A Gödel-ladder, where the rungs are knives, razors
or some even thinner blades   Cutting through everything
Through all dimensions   Blood everywhere

In mosques, churches, synagogues, temples, all the thousands of homes
Also in the royal caesura, the whitest center
Not a word, no counter-movement is excluded   Not a single child

And if contemporaneity does not exist   And we are
isolated beings, inside the whirling storm
of confused signs   When we touch one another
we are wholly alien   Then we can breathe   Light   Darkness

The invention of dodecaphony involved
a whole new way of structuring relations
among tones, I said to J   In the architecture
of sound   Which cannot be taken away   Even if
Schoenberg was wrong about the method's
general efficacy   Saw before me the tower of nothing
Then I   thought: dodecaphony is also *prayer*, to the one,
                              the only one, the unimaginable
That which has no image   But it is
only one way to pray   There are infinitely many
Trotzdem bete ich   When song comes, in the face of annihilation
there is only one   One single people   My kin
The universal language tells us this   From all directions

from Disparates

Here waiting exists, and small, small
wings of death
Like blade wheels
in an invisible turbine
Where water, or the invisible streams
thundering, dark, transparent
Visionary images are released, projected
on the inner skin
A landscape
that cannot be controlled
The ecstasies are performed there,
they whirl, with empty
centers of oblivion—Also
centers of zero
From aborted vortices lifeless faces sink
The body's system of vortices
balancing in their inner relations
All of these points
of zero
of birth and
death   The tree in its growth
through the brow of space,
its roots boring through
the cloud of earth

So many people

The silences, the ecstasies
reach out for
them like plants
toward the light
Only there can one live
Where will you be born? Where will I?
How do I break through the walls of muteness,
your wall, my wall
Yes, the chink
that sparks as it opens

That is where you are, where I can
enter, where you can
receive me
How do I open to let in all the flowers
growing from the soil of your inner gray skin?

All the small, invisible vortices inside there

from The Book of Sounds

Beggars can be seen now in the cities of Europe   As parts of
the new economy   Large groups of people
enter into hopelessness   Aimlessness, which
also erupts in the absence of all society

New cities rise up out of their ruins   Metallic
glass, umbrella-shapes, towers   In the distance
a Tower of Babel, in the architecture of the previous century
heavy, still bound to the earth   Now the stones will

float   Light, gray   Or sparkling with darkness
like the beggar woman's face   In exhibition halls you can hear
the hum, language without language, for whom are all

these words   No one knows   Maybe someone hears someone
Whom did I hear, in the room of sounds?   An organ was playing
In front of Bach's grave I bowed down   Once

from The Sopranos

Alan Warner

Our Lady of Perpetual Succour School for Girls

No sweat, we'll never win; other choirs sing about Love, all our songs are about cattle or death!

Fionnula (the Cooler) spoke that way, last words pitched a little bit lower with a sexyish sideways look at none of the others. The fifth-year choir all laughed.

Orla, still so thin she had her legs crossed to cover up her skinniness, keeked along the line and says, When they from the Fort, Hoors of the Sacred Heart, won the competition last year, they got kept down the whole night and put up in a big posh hotel and . . . everything, no that I want that! Sooner be snogged in the Mantrap.

Know what the Hoor's school motto is? Fionnula spoke again, from the longest-legs-position on the wall. She spoke louder this time, in that blurred, smoked voice, It's "Noses up . . . knickers DOWN"!

The Sopranos all chorted and hootsied; the Seconds and Thirds mostly smiled in per-usual admiration. Quietly, so's only the Sopranos-half of the wall could hear, Fionnula goes, Look girls, the Hoors're no even IN it this year. Shows how chronic the standard is; we stick thegether on this and there's no ways we'll win, won't even get in the second round! We'll be plonked on the bus an back here in plenty time for the Mantrap slow dances and all manner of sailors' jigs.

That's IF submarin-ers are in the Mantrap. And that's IF we get past that new bouncer, he hasn't got off wi a single one of us! (Ra)Chell was calling out, just from along, where some taller Seconds and Thirds separated her.

(A)Manda Tassy recrossed her legs, looking a little uncomfortable, cleared her throat and announced, I've got in the Mantrap three Saturdays running! Manda who could never afford cigarettes an was aye bumming them, placed one of her big sister's duty free Camels into her lips without even offering round, an from a pack of twenty!

Kylah squinted severely, though Manda was next her, Kylah went, That's cause you're the dying image of your big sister.

Are you JOKING Kylah? Manda blew smoke, Have you SEEN Catriona's suntan!

I'll no see a thing the day, Kylah muttered.

Orla giggled and smiled, her braces showed, Yon medallion man, the bouncer, he's only there cause he couldn't get a chef's job anywhere. He's from the Island. He'd get on well with Chell cause he has a love of animals; he can only tell the ages of sheep!

Aye, goes Chell, From behind.

Those within earshot laughed. Manda coughed.

Kylah, chortled, frowning up and down the line as if watching a fast tennis rally and says, The Island, where no horse is safe as long as there's a table or chair left!

Fionnula shrugged shoulders laughing, lit another cigarette an goes, As long as we ALL stick thegether. It was spoken as what it was: a warning to any Seconds or Thirds who might be taking the competition too seriously and who didn't have the priority of a night on the town later; it was a threat to anyone with delusions of grandeur.

The Sopranos leaned forward an looked at Kay Clarke from Seconds who, virtue of her limb-length, sat trapped, sombre and silent amongst them, then they glared down the length-of-legs school wall towards the short-arse end and Ana-Bessie.

Snobby Kay Clarke and Ana-Bessie Baberton fee-paying (their Old Men, one Port Solicitor, one Consultant up the Chest Infirmary) stared stubborn cross-square to the statue of JL McAdam, surveyor, advocate of tarmacadam and national hero. Kay and Ana-Bessie were aye willing to admit bursary girls like Fionnula had "colourful character". Inwardly, the two middleclass girls consoled themselves: Fionnula's legs were "actually" too thin and there was always the fact Fionnula's parents only had a bought council house up the Complex.

The school wall afront the square, with its iron railings, curved round to the slope by the side entrance (the polishysmooth stubs were the old iron bars, sawed off for the war effort in the forties); the upward slope of pavement delineated the precise order the choir aye sat in, 'ccording to the length of each girl's legs from arse on the old polished stubs down to the chewing-gum-blotched macadam.

CHOIR ORDER ON LENGTH-OF-LEGS
SCHOOL WALL

GIRL	VOICE	INSIDE LEG
Fionnula (the Cooler)	Sopranos	35"
Kylah	Sopranos	35"

(n.b. Fionnula (the Cooler) and Kylah an agreed First Equal but Fionnula always sits on outside.)

(A)Manda Tassy	Sopranos	34"
Kay Clarke	Seconds	34"
Yolanda McCormack	Thirds	34"
Assumpta	Thirds	33"
(Ra)Chell	Sopranos	32"
Orla	Sopranos	32"
Aisling	Seconds	32"
Iona	Seconds	31"
Shuna	Thirds	30"
Fionnula (ordinary)	Seconds	30"
English Katie	Seconds	29"
Ana-Bessie	Seconds	29"
Fat Clodagh	Thirds	28"
Wee Maria	Thirds	27"

On the flat, leaden school roof above the fifth-year choir and close to the speeding dawn clouds, Our Lady stood. Her sculpted shawl surmounted by an alert, perched seagull with a hooked, yellow beak—the cheeriest colour around. A scrawk from Lord Bolivia down in the New Chapel below, made the gull lean and fly forward off the BVM.

Our Lady of Perpetual Succour's dead, stone eyes were cast way over the teenagers below. The gaze looked above the slates of McAdam Square and the railway station clock, to the bay, beyond. She stared constant at some theoretical point, dependent on the angle of the reinforced concrete block Kirkham & Sons Construction had power-bolted her onto, year she descended down from heaven, under a Westland helicopter.

Her left arm was held out with a daft and neverending finality, offertory fingers appealing, though only ever receiving a tiny curlicue of sparrow's dropping; only ever delivering a slow sequence of rain drips to the sheered height way down onto the concrete playground below, where, every September, girls on their first day would bawl up to her: Don't jump things can't be that bad! Don't do it! Suicide's a sin.

That morning, the statue's rampant gaze drove across the surface of the port's baywaters as perusual but, it seemingly settled for once on the long black vessel now anchored there, even the communications aerials on the nuclear submarine's conning tower, no reaching above the cloud-looped summits of the distant island mountains.

Orla yawned, moved her hand over her still-short hair, looked at her palm as if still surprised. She yawned, poked a finger in to the back of her mouth, took it out again and proclaimed, Chell's right enough, wi these navies from all countries, yous never can be sure if they've shore leave. Those greeny uniform ones did, but yon last destroyer didn't and you never know if you can count on them going to the Mantrap; who's to no say they'll go get taxis out the Barn or somewhere we can't get to?

They always go to the Mantrap for a drink even if they do go on, some aye stay. And funny though if those last didnie come ashore how come Michelle McLaughlin still managed to get pregnant offof it!

A few cassandras of laugh tremelled along the wall.

From top the wall Fionnula burred, Aye, it's a disgrace if they don't come ashore and them signed to NATO an everything! She sighed.

Everyone laughed. Even the girls who wernie doing Higher History.

Spotty Fat Clodagh from right along yelled out, cross square, By the way Manda, Michelle did not get pregnant by yon destroyer, it was one the Pakistani lads come up for Saturday market in their van.

There was dubious silence. Cross square, two gulls crawed an tugged at a fat binliner on the pavement by the amusement arcade, boarded for off-season.

Rural depopulation? NO chance with Our Ladys about, Kay Clarke sighed.

Manda leaned forward and met eyes with Fionnula across Kylah's thighs, the look meaning: No that you'll ever contribute, you lightweight, university-bound virgin.

There is an old county council Ceil Meile Failte road sign just outside port, before you swing steering wheels round the high hairpin above the buspark. When Fionnula and Manda were Second Years they nicked a little pot Airfix paint offof Kylah's big brother Calum.

It was the time that First Year herself, a thirteen-year-old from Our Lady's got pregnant in the van, her bare back above the lifted blouse, sticking to the uncomfy cellophane-wrapped cartons. He was twenty-nine, refiller of cigarette machines, responsible for the entire West Coast!

Fionnula can still mind wearing their tight jeans and very white and pink trainers, being crouched up, faces close, gigglestifling in the dry ditch next the main road, then leaping out the gain when each last vehicle headlights passed and carrying on the handiwork with a make-up brush.

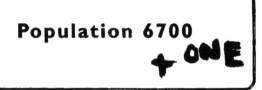

Then leaping back into the ditch as a great shift of headlight oozed round in the dark and them both cooried up, part of the tremulous, excited-feeling cause the vandalism, but also reaching for their own little, convexy belly-buttons snipped into shape by the National Health, knowing one day they would give in to some lad.

I read somewhere that submarine-ers . . .

Submariners, Fionnula grunted.

Submar-in-ers; that if they get a cut or something, cause they've been away under the waters for so long, it's done something to their . . . (Wee Maria McGill, who'd once used Vanish soap stain-remover to try get a bad henna out, had kinda stumbled into this, but she just looked along to Orla and bravely soldiered on) . . . Done something to their, blood.

Aye. Haemophilia. It's in Biology, Orla, who'd had chemotherapy, let Wee Maria go on.

Aye. Well if they get cut or that it won't stop bleeding for ages cause the air stuff they've been breathing down there.

There was contemplative silence then Orla spoke out their collective image, Aye! And when they submariners spunk with all their wanks down there, it just keeps coming out and coming out . . .

Everybody laughed cause it was Orla's crack.

. . . Inside their submarine—it would all just fill up with spunk and they'd all drown in it!

Yeauch!

Ah, dinnae scum us out! goes Chell.

Here in their spunky grave lie the hundred brave sailors, Fionnula's voice came from top the wall.

We'll test it out the night girls! Manda's filthy laugh came.

AYE!

Yolanda dropped her cigarette and yawned, Condom.

Fuck!

Nine or ten limbs of the smokers, all in flesh-coloured tights, with socks pulled up above the knee to make the legs appear longer, pulverised half-smoked cigarettes into the tarmac pavement. Each black, flat-bottom shoe that did the grinding, sported completely different, luminous, day-glo, interwoven, painted or rainbowy laces: the only means of self-expression remaining.

Various novelty lighters that played tunes (ironic wedding marches and Lambadas) B&H, Regal, Embassy, Marlboro reds and Light, Silk Cut and Yolanda's Lambert & Butler! All packs of ten, part from Manda, were returned to suspiciously full backpacks. Some cigarettes were rapidly nibbed then slipped into the secret, folded hems of the specially shortened tartan skirts.

Orla grit her teeth, bared her retainer braces in a fake smile, says, Look at her walk, its like she's got the most gi-normous sanitary towel jammed between her legs.

Carrying her famous blue bucket, today full of parental consent forms and her own choral arrangements, held wind-safe under a hefty nineteenth-century bible, Sister Condron approached cross McAdam Square, beneath the collapsing and hanging dramatics of dawn clouds.

Aisling was mumbling, I'd a dream like that.

What? Shuna goes, but smiling straight ahead.

You know? A guy got handjobbed offof me and it not stopping, it just gushing an gushing out, goggles, whole goggles of it just gushing an gushing out filling ma bedroom an just knowing mum would find out!

Kay Clarke goes, I'll look that up in my Freud Dream Dictionary. Don't know what I'll look under.

Try Wanker, Manda coughed.

Fionnula spat out a laugh.

Shush.

Good morning girls.

MORNING SISTER CONDOM. Perfectly synchronised, each of the sixteen girls slithered off the wall to lengthen the look of their specially shortened skirts.

Sister Condron breached the kerb, canted, swayed, straightened, spoke: All together, Forth Let The Cattle Roam! She dropped the bucket, lifted one arm pointing at heaven.

Sister, it's half eight in the morn, Fionnula snapped.

So Fionnula McConnel. Is your voice still in your bed?

Ana-Bessie and Kay Clarke alone giggled.

In a bland, soft whisper, Manda says, Good King Wenceslas. Fionnula let out a spirtle of crack-up, waggled her tongue, looked left and right, eyes away wi it then says, One, two, three. The Sopranos sung in the tight dawn air, an immediate beauty, like flags cracking in the wind. The sound moved cross square:

> Good King Wenceslas
> Last looked out
> On the Feast of Stephen
> The snow lay round abotit
> Deep and crisp and even

NO. GIRLS! FORTH LET THE CATTLE ROAM.

But recalling December humiliations on Port streets with stupid hats on, the Seconds joined the Sopranos in a two-parter, cuddled in the neath, the Thirds waited and bassed the thing, even splitting the carol, messing about with a four-parter, looking each other in the eye to keep silent times.

A window canted out cross square, a night shifter fro the Alginate just a-bed leaned out roaring, Christmas so soon? Fuckin shut it ya wicked wee Catholic heathens.

Two Poems

James Lasdun

Woodstock

Wudestoc: a clearing in the woods.
Forty miles from the town itself;
the name, as in Herzl's *Judenstaat*,
less about place than disclosure—
of a people, or an idea.

I was at prep school in Surrey at the time,
pre-pubescent; under my yearning eyes
the grounds—all greensward with copper beeches—
glimmered like the veil of heaven
about to be torn open.

At noon we stood on parade in divisions
and marched into lunch like soldiers.
The dining room
was painted with scenes from King Arthur.
Vividly out of green water a naked arm

Held a great shining sword . . .
In my first wet dream
Queen Guinevere seduced me in her tent.
There was an initiation rite:
six boys scragged you on the stony puntabout.

You were terrified but you wanted it.
Thereafter one had trouble with one's pronouns.
I found Queen Guinevere in the bed to my left.
Her name was Richard, I think, or Robert;
a cavalier to my roundhead,

or as one goy put it,
my jewnicorn.
Nightly my left arm crept between her sheets,
sneaking home in the small hours,
sticky with Guinevere's flowers.

We were like South Sea Islanders,
worshipping existence from afar
with our own cargo-cult
of whatever beached on our shore.
One boy found the empty sleeve

of Electric Ladyland.
We gazed till we felt the heavens opened
and the spirit like a dove descending;
Jimi and twenty-one naked girls,
Guineveres to a man;

Jimi in a braided military coat
and flower-power shirt;
a hawk-taloned dove
late of the 101st Airborne,
mouthing our cry of love.

I signed up for classical guitar
and plucked a lute-gentle twelve-bar blues
at our all-boys disco night
where the nursing sister briefly graced us,
sending her thanks and kisses on scented paper

which, in our excitement, we tore to pieces.
Later I bought an electric, though by that time
my left arm was half-numb
and the best people, Jimi included,
had checked out of the stadium.

I'm in Woodstock now,
on a mountain clearing,
my own *lichtung*
or niche in existence,
watching old footage of Woodstock.

Peace and Love . . . and War:
The throbbing choppers ferrying musicians
over the refugee traffic,
over the city-sized singalong
of Country Joe's "What are we fighting for?"

Pete Townsend in white jeans and braces
like one of Kubrick's droogies,
beating up his own axe;
Joe Cocker playing air-guitar, or is it
air-chainsaw, or air-bazooka?

Had I not seen this in a vision?
That record sleeve my tab of pure Owlsley;
vividly out of the lake the women rising,
bare-breasted, flower-strewn, Guineveres to a man;
Kesey's yippies frolicking in the mud—

A Mesopotamian puntabout;
Wavy Gravy offering to feed the multitude,
addressing them "listen, man . . ."
Too much already!
And after Max Yasgur's blessing,

Hendrix, amused-looking, laconic,
as in his Dick Cavett interview—
Cavett: "are you disciplined, do you
get up every morning and work?" And Jimi:
"Well, I try to get up every morning . . ."

The long fringes on his sleeve
make eagle-wings as he sharpens his axe,
the usual left-handed Fender,
with its phallic arm
and womanly curves.

It was at Monterey, not here,
that he set fire to it on stage
after dry-humping an amp;
his instinct for sacrifice narrowing in
like Adam's in the Talmud,

his axe the *re'em* or one-horned ox
—a jewnicorn—
offered up to Jehovah.
I think of my left arm rising
vividly out of Lake Como,

slashed by a speedboat propeller
I'd summoned for the job
(*of my hand didst thou require it*)
of securing a right-handed future
righter-handed, that is,

which it did with the dexterity, ha-ha,
of a kosher butcher
removing the sciatic nerve
in honor of Jacob who lost his sciatic nerve
dry-humping an angel.

The water foamed red, red
as the mingling red chain-oil and flower-juices
of the blossoming red maples
I cleared from our meadow;
Guineveres to a man.

And vividly out of the water
the unsheathed sword of my own
startlingly white bone *And he said thy name*
between two labial flesh-flaps
shall no longer be called Jacob . . .

But Jimi, who still later could be said
to have offered up his own head

that we not forget to remember
the art not of getting somewhere
but of being there,

is in mellower fettle here. Calmly
he sharpens his curved axe—
Quat! hit clatered in the clyff as it cleve schulde,
for a few bursts of Machine Gun,
bringing the torso to his teeth,

a panther devouring a fawn,
our eagle-clawed dove
late of the 101st Airborne,
hybrid of lion and unicorn,
then with the dexterity

of a kosher *shohet*
or Saladdin with King Richard's handkerchief
or Sir Bertilak blooding Sir Gawain,
Bot here yow lakked a lyttel, sir
proceeds to slash apart

the Star-Spangled Banner,
bending the strings till they
carve through its flesh like the blades
(*I will not let thee go except thou bless me*)
of a speedboat propeller,

the bitten steel biting back
into his own flesh
which is our flesh,
just as the Star-Spangled Banner
is the blood-spangled heavens torn open

for the spirit like an F-105 Thunderchief descending
and the sound you hear is the sound
of something being annihilated
calmly, and for good.
And your name,

whatever it is,
is no longer what it was,
for as a prince
hast thou power with God and with men,
and hast prevailed.

American Mountain

I

Our Queen's English accents
kept the class-conscious English masses
at bay, while our looks and name
did the same for the upper classes.

Being there,
as opposed to just stopping by,
was a matter of what you arrived too late
to arrange: your ancestry.

"We're not English" went the family saying.
What were we then? We'd lopped
our branch off from the family tree:
anglophone Russian-German apostate Jews

mouthing Anglican hymns at church
till we renounced that too . . . Self-knowledge
was knowledge of not being this or this or this.
We were like stencils: our inverse had the edge

over whatever it was we were,
not that that would have mattered had I not
happened not to enjoy that throttling
knot of annulled speech gathering in my throat,

or the sense of not being in a room
I hadn't left, or being too light
to plant my feet. I was my opposite;
I chased myself across the planet

till I vanished through the looking glass
of the Atlantic ocean
and woke up clinging to the tilted
patchwork of an American mountain.

II

A Family Tree

The locals,
Esopus Algonquins,
having already been massacred,
there's no one with greater claims to an acre

than you have. As for your ancestry, it's yours
to choose from whoever cleared a spot
anywhere on these tough-fibred slopes and hollows.
Patent your own coat-of-arms; why not?

Elect your forebears from the pitch-brewers,
colliers, tanbark-peelers, the German
smelters at DeZeng's forge hammering molten
pigs of primordial bog-iron; shingle-splitters,

Dutch buckwheat farmers
who felled a white pine to pitch their claim,
cleared the land, then when the tree
rotted, had them a home;

apostate royalists who took "The Test";
I have it by heart: *I the Subscriber*
Do most solemnly swear
that I Renounce all allegiance to the King of Great Britain . . .

Take your pick, you'll know them
by what they left behind—
great bluestone dolmens the Irish quarrymen
cut and hauled down ice-roads, then abandoned;

abandoned orchards from Prohibition
when a backwoodsman could stay afloat
on twenty barrels of hard cider,
his knobbled trees still cranking out squint fruit;

abandoned houses–middle-income,
cathedral-ceilinged, faux post-and-beam
"Woodstock Contemporaries"
dotted along the creeks for IBM

before they downsized; abandoned grist-mills, graveyards . . .
(and what landscape isn't finally the sum
of others' abandoned efforts to turn it
into themselves? Only the too-tame

or the impossibly wild . . .)
As for my own family tree, I'd gladly
grandfather in our predecessors
here on this slope of the mountain: glassblowers,

Bohemians mostly, shipped over
between the Embargo boom and the peacetime crash
—a brief, bright window—
to couple the virgin forests of Keefe Hollow

with the sands of Cooper Lake.
I see them at the glory hole
in their leather aprons and masks,
emptying their strong lungs

into the shimmering lungs of glass . . .
Choristers, fiddlers, jugglers,
with a taste for the gaudy,
they left behind almost nothing—

a few glass whimsies—dippers, turtles and canes
bits of glass slag gleaming in the dirt,
and a marginal local
increase in transparency.

III

After Heidegger

Lichtung: a clearing;
fire-break or beaver meadow,
Dutch farmer-pioneer meadows, stump-littered and raw;
first harvest ashes; second, Indian corn
tilled with a thorn-bush harrow.

"A man was famous"
the psalm reports, "according
as he had lifted up axes upon thick trees."
the trees are still thick, and although you've traded
that king for the secret king

of thought, and exchanged
your axe for a Makita,
it remains a matter of the ground beneath you; first
making it *unverborgen*: unconcealed,
then second, planting your feet.

I've muddled it all
like the old-time dairy-men
in their doggerel of gable and salt-box, their pastures
a garble of ditches. But that's how it is
after *Verfall*. The fallen

tend to a certain
makeshift approach towards life.
Like Kant they know nothing straight has ever been built
from the crooked timber of humanity,
and just keep patching the roof.

Theirs is the kingdom
of God, or at any rate
Dasein. Being here's just a question of having been
elsewhere unhappily long enough to feel
that that was exile, this not.

Summit Mall

Melissa Holbrook Pierson

to the memory of Euphrosyne Kalafates Russell

You were, it seemed, speaking Greek to an Algerian; he understood due to some similarities in words—surprising news. More so the fact that you remembered your language, unused for fifty years ever since hitting land at last when three, no doubt with your own suitcase already, filled with simple small dresses in fabrics that soon looked strange even to you. But more marvelous still: coming back to me in a dream.

And younger, too, your hair still black and reflective, as I recall from the days when, wearing white gloves, we drove north to the Cleveland of miracles: Higbee's, Terminal Tower, Shaker Square. In a picture gone largely green (blues and reds consumed by time's acid heat) you held my hand in one of yours, my sister's in the other, plaid-coated bookends to what can be read in enigmatic beauty, out shopping. Then, perhaps, that look was also the result of how, all your life, nobody could get you to do anything before a camera but purse your lips, narrowing eyes against such light-sensitive emulsions.

Much had changed by the end of the decade, so now you took the bus every day to shop alone while we grew busy with—what? I forget. It was not necessary now, was it, or even advisable to dress carefully for this mall, trying on several hats with nets (from tissued boxes carried on the train all the way from Fifth Avenue, a place of violets and crinkly dim perfume) in front of the mahogany mirror in the apartment that still seemed to smell of your husband though it had been years, hadn't it.

It would be years of days, wouldn't it, in which you shopped the radiant new corridors, the anchor stores,

between visits with us and bedtime with yourself. I wonder now if knowing its cheap blue-painted fountains of chlorinated plashing—not the exact shade of the Mediterranean but good enough in a squint against fluorescence to make it seem to appear for a flash in Akron—were nearby was a comfort when you chanced to move across the street. Across the street, unseen in the end by you but still visible from the windows of the St. Edward Home for the waiting-to-die, it might have been a solace,

its dour brick edifice whispering: inside, find mysteries of lost worlds. This is no mall, my shelves speak in tongues. See here, see here, see here.

High above the merchandise, yia-yia, is that now your soul?

Prospect Park Southwest

E. Beth Thomas

No moon through the snow, but a fine drift and my lamp,
imitation in the windowpane.
I can imagine it all from my desk, imagine
this pen in my mother's touch, so feathery
it didn't shape the nib; for so long I claimed
my father's traits, good with his hands and a dreamer,
but I know different as I read my mother's love letters,
full of plans and strict words granting nothing untenable.

Earlier, I came from the vet in an ice storm, unkind
sky over a dreamy dog who wobbled a bit,
unbalanced by sidewalks' slickness—
as Jack peeled oranges for dessert, I fooled myself
back to my childhood south. As he wound the clock,
cleared the table, scooped peels into his palm, how much
I wanted storybook moonlight and sand.

Instead, snow on a blustery morning and a park
on the wane. Always a ticking clock,
a weather report, the dog thumping before
the door with a sigh: morning taut like a fresh bed
under an open winter window.
I never lie to my dog: *This'll be quick, pup,*
and it is, a full hard gulp of cold.
Afterwards, I melt the ice crystals from his paws.
Helplessness opens the mother in me.

My parents saved their letters in a stack ragged
by silverfish. I bound them with ribbon

and stored them in a cedar box, sandbagging
the future. I could ask them for stories
but prefer my own: his reckless devotion,
I'm coming to see you next weekend if I have to crawl,
her practicality: *No more beer, and less play.*
She's always loved without softness, directives
replacing endearments, but her faith runs high,
romantic. In this I'm both theirs, ask human
understanding of my dog, dog patience of my husband.
These bitter mornings I return from the park,
stripped by the wind, to bury my face in the dog's salt water fur.
Flannel. Seaweed and clean sand.

Three Poems

Terese Svoboda

No Spring

Let me die when I do
in dead winter so
you'll be sorry while
it's dark and cold while
I'm ditto.

He died on the year's first day
of no coats, of running
to the window to look
out below. Nothing
much saved him and

no thick fur or sweater
will save me these shivers,
just season on season.
So what if spring's
new. A bird

falls on the walk I make
to warm up. I squat to it.
Chick, chick, chick, it says
from its broken neck,
no spring left.

Pilgrim's Progress

You run toward a light.
A cartoon idea?
Running forces its burning,
fuels its whiteness.

Such light capitalizes:
All Good as in a cafe.
Each lifted sole
is a moon left on.

No one said you had to run
or that the race raised money
but if, by running,
you actually arrived—

the dead light of stars
wink and go out.
Still, your organs swell
as you run, you want

and want but you can't stop.
Your side aches,
your head aches,
your heart.

Friends wave slick magazines
that read Relax,
friends with a capital F,
in the plural, but not the humble,

declarative friend
whose hand could be slapped
as you pass—he's hunched,
he's just laced up.

Play

It was customary in 15th century Italy
for the condemned to play the part of Christ.

You are not you, you are the Someone
on this mask and we are your followers,
we who applaud when you don't cry
or tear it off, when the noose
or the knife comes at last and our sins
rise with your soul that is better
than a beggar's, stealing butter.

Years we spend convincing ourselves.

Sun, Unreturnable Gift: Composition With Pink & Gray Galahs In Flight

John Kinsella

for Kevin Hart

The sun, unreturnable gift
obsesses the feature window,
as if the leaden clouds moving steadily
towards the point between occupancy
and delivery aren't even there

So here, in Cambridge, a composition
Sunday-afternoons itself into existence,
as if a photograph makes memory
an authentic exhibit: that the pink & gray
galahs in this photograph sent by

My mother, interring through
the hard lens that lets in light
and yet keeps the atmosphere out,
are permanently engaging
with the immanence of flight,

Flashes within the frame
which, like the sun, shine on
oblivious behind the cloud
now firmly in place, the birds fallen
from their upward rise from high perches,

Outside the memory of the camera
outside the season is distinctive
and the beeches reclothe with the sign:
        "Comme rupture franche
            Plutôt refoule ou tranche

        Les anciens désaccords
            Avec le corps"
as if each word is the perfect prayer,
and yes, I was there, and saw similar
birds fly within their hemisphere,

Though I took no photograph,
and if I had, would have lost it
to the sun, a gesture of return,
like the refoliation of evergreens
after locusts, flood, or drought.

from Less Than Spring, a long poem of conditions

Molly McGrann

1.

Storms of the world,
Storms of being, becoming human wolves.
The people are grafted to the bitter landscape
And regret. There was more to it
Than first thought.
There was perhaps everything they could see
In the long truth of the hazy moon
Beyond the apparent horizon.—
The City snowed-in.
Memory and imagination
Formed solidarity
And tears filled the empty muffle:
Grief of things.

The eye skates an imaginable depth
Plummeting outside beneath the freeze.
The eye is more violent
On the landscape,
Seeking darting shadow shapes
Or tracks in the white.
But the feminine ear triggers scenes
Of recollection and comfort:

The distant caws of black birds
Signaling dawn
And drowsy voices rousing the others;
The stovetop heating the kitchen up,
Boiling coffee, hot cereal.

The chimes next door
Are replaced with an icicle.
And dawn,
The wist of a candle
That does not exist.
We must close our eyes now
And go on listening.

3.

I brood on my lark blue eggs all day.
I reach for the morning paper
And begin to read
An article about a local murder.

The murder occurred in my neighborhood,
The paper said,
In the early morning hours of today,
The first paragraph I read.

Murder in the brick courtyard
Of my apartment building.
I haven't been outdoors
All winter long.

The murder is unsolved.
There are no suspects.
I read alone, shifting
My weight on the eggs.

The detective needs clues.
"There are clues scattered

In the night you heard indoors,"
He begs us, "All of you."

The victim looks up from the paper
And begs me with her gray eyes.
I announce something about the case.
Into the telephone I cry,

"I am a mother, I can help you.
"I sleep lightly at night.
"I brood. I don't like the cold.
"I knew the girl.

"The victim was a harlot
Like the rest of the lot
Out there.
"This is not funny.

"I was not a coward at school
But I did learn something.
"There is a moral universe.
"She did not exist for me.

"I have my family."
There was more.
There was perhaps
Everything they could see

Knowing looks
And the desperate weather lately.
The murder victim looks
Up from the paper

To the window at the police.
The police stand watching me
With handcuffs cocked,
Waiting, perhaps

For the thaw,
Or the rupture

Of the accusatory mob of birds'
Voices storming the world:

The lark, hoopoe,
Nightingale, swallow,
Duck, duck, crow.
This is justice.

4.

The voice of the riotous mob,
The body crowd,

Birds in every way;
Food-seekers, without illusions,

Cease to choose for themselves.
Prison doors close

On the prisoner or exile.
Justice is not justice is not justice.

A rose is a rose.

5.

. . . A story for Old Glory,
The body the most body of all.

The scent of winter
Hung over the City
Like a lynchmob.
Ice-storms and toxic salt
Cut at the throat
Of the body politic.

The City island,
God-abandoned,

Cut out from the motherland.
The City broke off and became
A floating island
All mechanical parts,
And whirs in a rough,
Stirred-up, muddied trough.

Scavengers and blackbirds,
Vultures and crows circled.
The City detached herself
At the throat:

Opened-up bridge-ends,
Dangling arterial cables,
Route turn-off
Swarmed like Medusa's pets,

Surefire the sewage system
Like a seaworm
Reared up and dropped ruin
Through the cracks of the stern;

The island steamed and
Hurled chunks,
Road-turf, perforated
Billboard and City block

In the wake of her tail,
The scrolled, scrapped-up *Old Glory*,
Sail and all
The coincidence of a thing with itself.

from The Metamorphoses of Ovid

Translated by Charles Martin

Of Praise and Punishment: Arachne

(Metamorphoses, Book VI, lines 1-145. The goddess Minerva, roused to
anger by the Muses, threatens mortal impiety.)

After she'd listened to their tale, Minerva
gave her approval to the Muses' song
and to the anger that it justified.
"To praise is insufficient," she reflected,
"We will be praised—and we will not permit
those who belittle our divinity
to go unpunished!"

      Her attention turned
to the undoing of Maeonian Arachne,
who (it was said) accepted praise that set her
above the goddess in the art of weaving,
a girl renowned not for her place of birth
nor for her family, but for her art:
her father, Idmon, came from Colophon,
and (like the mother that Arachne lost)
was of plebian origin, a tradesman
who steeped the thirsty wool in purple dye.
Nevertheless, her art had made her famous
throughout the many cities of Lydia,
although her home was every bit as humble
as Hypaepa, the hamlet where she lived.

To see her wonder-work, the nymphs would leave
their vineyards on the slope of Mount Timolus
or their haunts along the winding Pactolus.
They came not just to see the finished product,
but to watch her working, for such comeliness
and grace were present when she plied her art,
whether she shaped the crude wool in a ball,
or with her fingers softened it and drew
the fleecy mass into a single thread
spun out between the distaff and the spindle,
or worked a pattern into what she wove
with her embroidery. You would have known
that only Pallas could have been her teacher.
Nevertheless, as though offended by
the very thought, the girl denied it, saying,

"Let her compete with me, and if she wins
I'll pay whatever penalty she sets!"
Pallas disguises herself as a crone:
puts on a wig of counterfeit gray hair,
and with a staff to prop her tottering limbs,
begins to speak:
                        "Old age is not to be
wholly despised, for with it wisdom comes.
Heed my advice: seek all the fame you wish
as best of mortal weavers, but admit
the goddess as your superior in skill;
beg her to pardon you for your presumption
in an appropriately humble manner—
forgiveness will be given, if you ask it."

Arachne drops the work she had begun,
and scarcely able to restrain her hand,
expresses outrage through her glaring eyes,
cutting the goddess short with these sharp words:

"You've lived too long, you senile nincompoop,
that's what your trouble is! Try that speech out
on your daughter or your daughter-in-law,
if you have any children: as for me,

80

I'll take my own advice, thanks very much.
And so you shouldn't think you've made your case,
my own opinion hasn't changed at all:
why does the goddess shun a match with me?
why won't she come to challenge me herself?"

The goddess answered her with, "She has come."
And casting off the image of old age,
revealed herself as Pallas; the Phrygian
matrons and the nymphs bowed down before her.
All were quite terrified except Arachne,
although she reddened when a sudden flush
stained her unwilling cheeks, then disappeared,
as when the sky turns crimson just at dawn,
but then grows pale again as the sun rises.

Yet she persists in what she has begun;
in her desire for the foolish palm
of victory, she rushes to her fate;
Jove's daughter does not turn her down, or give
a further warning, or postpone the match.
At once the two of them select their sites
and set the uprights of their frames in place,
then draw the slender threads of the warp between
the horizontal crossbeams of the yoke;
the warp is separated with a reed,
and dexterous fingers, busy at the shuttle,
draw woof through warp, then tap it into place
with the comb's notched teeth.
                                             Then they go to it,
hitching their robes up underneath their breasts,
their well-instructed fingers swiftly flying,
zeal for the contest making light of labor.
Into their fabrics they weave purple threads
of Tyrian dye, and place beside them shades
that lighten imperceptibly from these;
as when a storm ends and the sun comes out,
a rainbow's arc illuminates the sky;
although a thousand colors shine in it,
the eye cannot say where one color ends

and another starts, so gradual the verging;
there in the middle, the colors look the same,
while, at the edges, they seem different.
Into the fabrics they wove threads of gold,
as on each loom appeared an oft-told tale:

Pallas depicts the Areopagus,
site of that contest held once to determine
a city's name. Twelve deities are seated
in august assurance on their high thrones,
Jove in the middle; ranged on either side,
the gods all look like their own images;
How regal Jove seems!
                              Next, the goddess shows
how Neptune with his trident strikes the rugged
rock from which a spring of water gushes,
the pledge by which he hopes to claim the city.
Then she depicts herself, armed with a shield
and a sharp spear; a helmet guards her head,
her breast is well-protected by the aegis;
she represents that moment when the earth,
struck by her spear-tip, instantly produces
a full-grown olive tree, laden with ripe fruit.
The gods all marvel, and she takes the prize.

And then, to give her rival for the praise
and glory some idea of the reward
Arachne can expect for her audacious
challenge, the goddess expertly depicts,
in each of the four corners of her work,
a different contest, each in miniature,
and each with its distinctive color scheme.

In the first scene, two Thracian characters,
Rhodopes and Haemus, mortals once, are
now turned to frigid mountains, for they took
the names of Jove and Juno as their own;
in the second corner she depicted
the awful fate of the Pygmy queen that Juno,
defeating, ordered to become a crane

and go to war against her former subjects;
in the third corner is Antigone,
who once dared struggle with Jove's mighty consort
and whom Queen Juno turned into a stork;
not Ilion, nor Laomedon, her father,
could save the girl: she put white feathers on,
and now applauds herself with clacking beak;
the final corner shows a man bereft:
Cinyras, clinging to the temple steps,
that were the limbs of his own daughters once,
and where upon the stone he seems to weep.
Around her work, the goddess wove a border
of peaceful olive leaves; that ended it,
and with her tree, her labors, too, were done.

Arachne shows Europa tricked by Jove
in semblance of a bull upon the sea,
and done so naturally you would have thought
the bull and the waves he breasted were both real;
the girl seems to look back at her lost land,
cries out to her companions and withdraws
her feet in terror from the surging flood.
Asterie is shown in an eagle's grip,
and Leda, lying under a swan's wing;
Arachne shows how, in a satyr's guise,
Jupiter filled Antiope with twins;
how, as Amphitryon, he hoodwinked you,
Alcmena; and how Danae was deceived
by a golden shower; Aegina by a flame;
how Mnemosyne was cozened by a shepherd
and Proserpina, child of Demeter,
was ruined by a many-colored serpent.
And she depicted you as well, Neptune,
transformed into the fiercest-looking bull,
with the Aeolian maiden, Canace;
as Enipeus, you were shown begetting
Otos and Ephialtes, the Aloidae,
and as a ram, deceiving Theophane;
immortal Demeter, the golden-haired
and infinitely mild mother of grain,

knew you as a horse; while to Medusa,
mother of Pegasus, you seemed a bird,
and seemed just like a dolphin to Melantho:
she rendered all of them just as they were,
and each with an appropriate background.
And there's Apollo, tricked out as a rustic,
now dressed in feathers, now a lion skin,
or as a shepherd to take Isse in;
and Bacchus, out to trick Erigone
with grapes that aren't really grapes at all;
there's Saturn, breeding Chiron on a mare,
and all around the edge, a deftly woven
border of flowers plaited into ivy.

    Not even Envy could have faulted this;
Pallas did not, yet, bitterly resenting
her rival's success, the Goddess Warrior
ripped it, with its convincing evidence
of celestial misconduct, all asunder;
and with her shuttle of Cytorian boxwood,
struck at Arachne's face repeatedly!
She could not bear this, the ill-omened girl,
and bravely fixed a noose around her throat;
while she was hanging, Pallas, stirred to mercy,
lifted her up and said:
                        "Though you will hang,
you must indeed live on, you wicked child:
so that your future will be no less fearful
than your present is, may the same punishment
remain in place for you and yours forever!"

    And as the goddess turned to go, she sprinkled
Arachne with the juice of Hecate's herb;
at the touch of that grim preparation, she
first lost her hair and then her nose and ears;
her head got smaller and her body, too;
her slender fingers were now legs that dangled
close to her sides; now she was very small,

but what remained of her turned into belly,
from which she now continually spins
a thread, and as a spider, carries on
the art of weaving as she used to do.

Four Poems

Jane Mead

Myth

The woman in the ordinary
cloth—came here with a vision:

*Point and Counter-Point
in All Things.* Stitch by stitch

she wove our world—print
of pear tree, color of moss

delighted. Colors of silk.
Outside, the crack in the pathway

opened, rain spilled in—*sorrow*
said the rivulets, *sorrow*

to the seas. *Sorrow, sorrow*—
heaved the low sky. Mist

entered the garden. Twilight
entered the mist. Lemon cut

of the geranium lifted too.
She did not want the scent, she

wanted the blossom. But the blossom
faded in the fading light

and the clear voice of leaves
then said *it is all just wrestling*

and turning—before the windows
of the sane: And the geranium,

and the mist, and the pear tree—
shifted slightly in a single wind.

Seventy Feet from the Magnolia Blossom

there is an ant.

He is carrying
a heavy load.—

We should help him.

The World

remaining central, there is
some knowledge we do not

debate: a child is born
to his body the day

he is born, for example, or
the sky's felt time

seems like mourning:
the grasshoppers are anonymous

to the anonymous, the birds
are always at attendance.

There comes a moment
when you see as the crow sees:

the body as slaughterhouse,
as beggar—in the long grass, kneeling.

Wing of Newt

If I could say *jasmine* or *willow*
and mean the jasmine plant

is by the water trough—and the horses
are under the willow tree, then

there would be no need to say *now*
make me jasmine, make me willow,

make me wind again—make me
the wind on a willow-green sea.

Hotel Declerq

John Berger

for Juan Muñoz

Where are you?
Here. Where are you?
Here
I can't see you.
Can you hear me?
Yes. I'm hearing you.
Well?
Like on the radio, I can make you soft or loud.
That means when I bore you, you can change stations.
If I get bored, I switch off.
I'm unfinished, are you the same?
How does he know when one of us is finished?
He just can't go on, so he begins another.
Me for instance.
Or me.
Do you think HE can hear us?
If he listened, I'm sure he'd hear us but I don't feel he is listening.
He likes black margins and that means something.
Something about absence. I fear I'm talking to myself.
That's what drawings do, my dear, they talk to themselves.
Where are you?
I'm here.

In a room?

No it's a corner.

What's in it

A round table with a cloth on it.

Exactly like here. Can you describe it?

That's what I'm doing all the time.

I know but I can't see you. Tell me about the table.

Well, the cloth is square so it falls unevenly and it's lowest point is a little left of center.

You're quite sure? Couldn't it be dead center? That would suit me a lot.

If I move my head very slightly to the left, it's dead center.

Wonderful. With four legs?

Obviously.

Of course, but how many are visible?

As a matter of fact—one!

Perfect. To the right, where the light's coming from and where there's probably a window, the cloth billows.

Billows or pillows?

I'd say both.

He likes precision, you shouldn't forget that.

Never mind. It may be a question of vocabulary. Tell me more about where the cloth billows.

I can see the underneath of the cloth—as if I was sitting under the table.

Are you?

The bottom hem of the cloth is folded there in such a way that it makes, from where I'm seeing it, a triangle.

Go on, go on. An equilateral one?

Yes.

Could we both be sitting under the same table?

I believe we are together, both sitting under the same table.

There wouldn't be room for us both.

I'm as thin as air. And perhaps you are too.

It could be a hotel room, it's got that look of being nowhere.

"I have mapped out an island in *Paradise*, that looks like you and a house by the seaside with a large bed and a small door . . ."

You've changed your voice.

It's from a poem by Odysseus Elytis.

Why poetry suddenly?

I think we are in the same room.

Is Elytis in the room with you?

There's nobody. The room is empty.

Do you know the name of the hotel?

I don't know because I've never been outside.

It ought to be marked on the inside of the door along with the price per person or per couple per night (breakfast included).

Me, I take only coffee for breakfast.

Black?

Yes black with sugar.

I don't take sugar either.

You see! We're the same.

Breakfast is His favorite meal, isn't it?

That's why he likes London and the cafes and pubs there which all announce: Breakfast All Day. What time do you think it is?

I've not had one since childhood but I must say I like a boiled egg for breakfast.

Lightly done?

Slightly under three minutes with buttered toast.

At what time?

7:40. He likes to begin early.

Room number?

I don't know. There's no door.

Do you know the hotel?

No.

He often talked of the Hotel Declerq. It had balconies.

I once heard him say the Hotel Declerq was nowhere.

Nonsense, there are hundreds of hotels with that name. He can't invent names.

Then maybe we are not even in the same town!

On the other side of the table there's a chair. It has arm rests.

I can't see the arm rests because there's a raincoat thrown across the chair.

There's no raincoat on the chair. Anyway, whose coat could it be?

His.

So he took it when he left.

No, here he forgot it.

Then he came back and fetched it. But this time he left a packet of cigarettes on the table.

There was something here on the table but I can't make out what it was. It has been rubbed out.

He rubs out a lot.

Who doesn't?

Look more carefully. He was drawing with graphite and it always leaves a trace.

I think it was a book. There may be a thousand kilometers between us. Let's face it.

Hold on. Wait. I'm beginning to see the light. I believe we are in the same place, the same room with the same fireplace, the same hotel, the same time—

Calm. I believe we are in the same room, in the same hotel, but we are in different drawings!

You mean drawn on a different day? If this is true, we are not even in the same time. Your *now* is not my *now*.

I think the time where we are—which has nothing to do with the time

He was drawing—is the same. Wait a moment. I'm going to put on a C.D. of Schubert's Impromptus and I want you to tell me whether you can hear it.

Have you put it on?

Yes.

I think it's Schuman.

Impossible. The Impromptus were written in 1827, the year Beethoven died and Schuman was only seventeen.

We all have to die sometime. No. It's one of Schuman's Fantasiestucke, written in 1837, not '27.

Why have you taken it off?

You heard it stop! You heard it stop; this is the proof we need.

The proof?

Yes, that we're both in the same place at the same time.

I was a mistaken. I didn't hear it stop. I can still hear it.

So can I. I took it off but I can still hear it in my head.

Schuman!

Schubert!

[*Long silence*]

Shall we call for help?

There's no way out.

There's maybe no way out for us, but suppose we ask for a third opinion. Then somebody could settle it for us.

You mean we could ask somebody who is looking at us?
Ask them what they think.
No one can look at two drawings at the same time.
They can look at us one after another and then shut their eyes.
For how long?
As long as they need. La Femme de Chambre! We could ask her.
It may be dangerous. What will you ask her?
I will ask her: what she thinks we're drawings of.
She'll say: A table!
Then when her eyes are shut, I'll ask her: Are we the same table?
Somebody's come in here.
Yes, somebody has come in.
They are looking at me.
And at me.
How do you know?
Haven't you noticed, after all this time, how when somebody's look-
ing at you, you feel it? A sort of desire in the air.

When at last the looking's over, you can move, that's true. You can
stretch. Smoke a fag. Have a break from Freedom . . . until the next look.

Madame, don't open your eyes please. Don't move. Just say where
we are.

She answered in German. She said Hier.
That means it's Zurich.
Not necessarily.
Signora, dove siamo?
She said: Qui? Which is the same thing.
We should try in English.
We asked her in English the first time.

Yes but she replied in German. Remember English is the language air-
line pilots use when they are coming in to land. Where are we, Madame?

Did you hear her whisper?

I did. We both heard it. It's over. We can sleep in each other's arms
in the same place under the same table on the same night.

No, I've looked again at the book which was erased.
Well?
It's a book by Elytis.
You can read it to me here.
No. The book was open at a certain page.
So what?
This is what it said.

"I have nothing more
between the four walls the ceiling the floor
to shout at
because of you
and how my own voice hurts me
it's still too early in this world, love,
to speak of you and me."

"I have nothing more
between the four walls the ceiling the floor
to shout at
because of you
and how my own voice hurts me
it's still too early in this world, love,
to speak of you and me."

Produce, Produce

Susan Wheeler

The thinnest meal on the slightest isle
Sustains but poorly. So: the file
Of men and women, mile and mile,

In consult with the wizened bat.
Plumes and boas're where it's at—
She won't remember saying that.

If hunger takes them to the coast,
They find a spectacle to toast.
Or several of their peers to roast.

Those that make it to the south
Are lucky to live thumb to mouth.
They might prefer the Catamount

Where greenish mountains freeze the nuts.
Though scavenging is an art that's bust
The ravenous can be beauty sluts.

Those lucky few who do adduce
The food that keeps them from the noose
Will crave on, too. Produce, produce.

Two Poems

Ingrid Fichtner

but the layers of ash, the lines brushed white
the fields motionless, lava, and layered, but
which shade which sound—a series of strata—
á quelque point du ciel, and how you are
wasting yourself; presence. and burning further.
Véritablement in your heart *ou derrière*; in the end
singing, *tout bas*, the birds flying up
still higher, and passing, are
gone

the lesser white, capitulum, inflorescence, the sun irrupting
faultlessly, and yet real, a sentence casually dropped,
notched, *the grass was still wet.* Again
the handful of water, like daylight, intricately woven.
The rocks, an efflorescence of rose
daphne laureola: the semidesert, signature,
notch or groove, the material words, or initials
dissolving in silver or in gold, the tongues of angels and
yet real. *That's* what it could be, essentially, head voice or of
a bird, and why
that lighter sky

Four Versions and a Pastiche from the Greek Anthology

Katharine Washburn

Gold and Brass

after Paulus Silentiarius

I gloss old stories when I'm sick to death
of writing poems myself. The legend of Zeus
raining gold on Danae, like her name, never
quite scans: The myth has it: "The god
of thunder and lightning storms her brass
chamber. Knees brace
against him, gold rams everything home
to the hymen gold forces the rim
guarded with metal and chains
and lays open the lock. She falls
backwards with softening eyes. Gold pricks
bronze. God streams in through cracks. God
breaches window. God's rain melts the last
    door."

Antipater said it better, before.
Pray to golden Aphrodite: adore
the goddess of lust and hard
cocks if you must. Then shed
hard currency and finally
    score.

Hymn to Aphrodite When Drowning

after Macedonius the Consul

When all hope was gone
you came back to me
stunned by rough water
salt-choked with despair.

Shock knocked me around
in the wallowing sea
where the foamborn drowns
her shipwrecked in surf.

The breakwater's nearer
the mariner's home
where the seaborn drowns
her sailors in foam.

Landfall is closer
Rip-tide pulls harder
Love, steer me to harbor
on your treacherous shore.

Last Word on Blackbirds: A Pastiche

after Archias, Antipater of Sidon, and Paulus Silentiarius

In the old poem you go fowling on mornings
closed in with mist. Early fog settles into
the mesh of the net. Weave it tight, then station
yourself in a place where they
rehearse at dawn and snatch a few slugs.
Blackbird and thrush fly straight
over the hedge. Together

they fetch them. You catch them
with cords in the cloud of the snare.
(Now we do it with mirrors and smoke.)
Fieldfare beware! of the rope of the nap.
Fog's thicker than blood. Back in there
fat little thrush kept thrashing around,
stuck in the hollow of horsehair and trap.

> Goodbye, gallinacous: Your flock's barely able
> to fly from the kitchen, and land on the table.

> The blackbird escaped and got the hell out,
> Bird of the wilderness found another redoubt.

> Songbird has flown.
> Snare's deaf as a stone.

> Archais, Antipater, they got it all wrong.
> Paulus the Silent now speaks out of turn.

Look at the deadfall: consider its goddess.
Artemis, lady of wild things and forests.
However much she enjoys
new blood and the slaughter of winged
creatures who live in those places, the huntress
takes care of her toys.

She lets songbirds go singing
for the sake of her brother
    Apollo, lord of the lyre.

It's something like that,
when she lets them go winging
    out of the hollow, safe from the fire.

[Note: Artemis is the goddess of the hunt; her name in Greek etymologically linked to a word for slaughterer or butcher. Like Apollo, her twin brother, she is the daughter of Zeus. The versions by Archias and Antipater of this popular legend about trapping birds explain the escape of the blackbird through a pathetic fallacy in which the snare itself spares the bird. Silentiarius will have none of it, and alludes instead to the twinning of two gods.]

To a Judge, Benched from a High Place

after Agathias Scholasticus

So your plumage has fallen. The scrum
after the trial no longer escorts you
down the long streets shrieking
their homage to the scum-
bag you were. Suddenly the sidewalk's
empty and you move out to the suburbs
and don't come into the city much.

(Except for shopping and a little theatre.)

You always knew, magisterial fool
that Fortuna sat in the room at the back
spinning her wheel. Farewell, old tool,
you're out to pasture with the rest of her hacks.
She sets us all up with feathers
and speeches and wigs for all weathers
to act in the court she directs for the pack.

That's how she cast us
and chose to unmask us.
She unseats the tragedians
and confounds her comedians.

Insomnia

after Agathias Scholasticus

Can't sleep. So I carry on all night. Early in the morning I get
a little rest and the swallows start in just in time
to send me back in tears again. A short sleep
before they sing it down. I screw my eyes tight to find
the dark once more, but *she* turns up again,
roiling around in my wretched brain,
                    reeking of roses and nectarines.

Shut your noise, you chirping twits and just remember
who you're supposed to cry for. I didn't slice off the tongue
of sweetheart Philomena and it's up to you to chitter
on for the dead boy what's-his-name. *Tereu.*
Go whoop your little hearts out
over the hoopoe's mud-caulked roost up there
on some mountain, preferably a distant one so I
can snatch a little sleep and maybe dream again
and have that dream where she comes
                    and takes me in her arms.

from Ice Fire Water

Leslie Epstein

Hip Hop

Dusk upon Rivington Street. The bells of the First Warsaw Congregation
are now making a polka. Six o'clock, *post meridium*. Rain! Rain! Come
again another day. Why have I not brought my hip garters and, for wet-
ness, Wellingtons? My gabardines are soaked. My panama is besotted. In
this ghetto I have not set foot these many years. Yet all the familiar land-
marks—the shop of Sheftelowitz, the dealer in saltwater fishes; that of
the tobacconist, Prinzmettle, and of the merchant of bedding, Herbert
Pipe; also the Premisher Butcherie—are still open for business. This is in
spite of the fact that in the Jewish Quarter one cannot with ease discover, amidst the crowds of Ukrainians, Hispano-Americans, and Coloreds,
even a quarter of a Jew. Ha! Ha! With a play of wit I dispel fears of Uncle
Al. Also unchanged: the facade of the Steinway Restaurant. A narrow
door, curtained windows, and the world-famous sign, the work of the
artist Feiner, which depicts a Greek-style maiden holding, beneath her
breast-fruits, a high-heaped platter, along with the words HOME OF
THE ROUMANIAN BROILING.

This queue is a non-mover. In half an hour I have not advanced the
length of one block. Yet more folk have lined up behind me. They stretch
to Allen Street and disappear around the bend. Each moment a new limousine draws near, joining the others that crouch with metronomes wav-
ing. Even during the broiling craze in the long ago Ragstat era—this is
when A. Einstein and Benjamin Leonard and Queen Wilhemina would
drop in for a herring appetizer—one never saw such a crowd milling in
rainstorms at the restaurant door.

That door! Behind it, perhaps in the upper apartments, perhaps in the
depths of the gentleman's WC, Miss Crystal Knight, my inamorata, is at
this very moment a prisoner. A prisoner? In an eatery? Leib Goldkorn

was not born overnight. I know full well that the Steinway Restaurant has undergone a transformation—first from a *fleishidek* establishment famed for its pitchai-slices and roll-mop salads into a dairy emporium, entirely dependent upon soy products, and then, one shudders to say, to the dreaded "Jewish style," at which meat and milk are without a care mixed; and transformed, second, from an institution that played the works of I. Berlin and S. Romberg, J. Rumshinksy and I. Dunayevski, the composer of the catchy "Song of Stalin," in other words from the *créme de la créme* of Hebrew melodists, heirs to Meyerbeer himself, to one that permitted Victor Herbert medleys and then the overtures of R. Straus and R. Wagner, whose motifs I can hardly bring myself to whistle to a dog. What next? Pisk, K. List, and the cacophony of the twelve-tone school? Caca-phoney! That is my opinion.

At last: arrival at the Steinway Restaurant door. Full night has fallen behind me. What storms, I wonder, lie ahead?

"*Bon Soir, Monsieur.* Party of four? Have you a reservation?"

The Frenchman has not addressed the query to me but to the gentleman who preceded my entrance into—this is a new development—the small, leather-padded foyer. That chap, instead of replying, removes from his pompadour his tall silken hat.

"Ah, Monsieur Steinbrenner," says the Maitre D. "*Excusez Moi.* I did not recognize you. Your table is ready."

It is indeed the Yankee Doodle, accompanied by sycophants and wives. There is a brief moment of confusion as they remove their minks and mufflers at the check-in counter. Next the door to the dining room opens, allowing in first a thunderous roar, a blaze of light, and then a round-faced maiden who wears nothing but a shiny tiara in her heap of hair and, over her right and left bosoms, a tray filled with mint creams. And below? One dares not look below, especially when experiencing, in one's own nether parts, a sensation akin to having just drunk a toddy.

"Mademoiselle La Tour," thus speaks our continental, even as he accepts a bank note from the Doodle, "will show you to your seats."

She does so, though even after the door closes behind her, the lights, through a kind of psychological momentum, continue to flash against my retinal rods and the sounds—the thump of some giant's feet, a chorus of primitive tom-toms—still beat against the tympanums of my inner ears.

"Well, well," says, in an altered tone of voice, the major domo. "Look what the cat dragged in."

I lean forward, blinking in disbelief. Could it—beneath the suave demi-moustache, the rouged cheeks, the pearl-stuck cravat—be? "Mr. Mosk!"

"So? Don't make a federal case out of it."

"Don't you recognize me? Leib Goldkorn? A member of the Steinway Quintet? I played first the Rudall & Rose-model flute and then the Bechstein Grand. For more than twenty-five years!"

"What's the name again?"

"Goldkorn, Leib. Graduate of the Akademie. Don't you remember? I will hum for you a Yip Harburg selection. *Happiness is a Thing Called Joe.*"

"Wait! I remember. What d'ya want? Can't you see we're busy?"

"A table for one, *s'il vous plaît.*"

"Are you nuts? We got a dress code here."

"But how can you refuse me? These are the pants of V.V. Stutchkoff. Yes, the founder's son. Size 44!"

"That don't cut no ice. You need a reservation. You gotta call a month ahead of time."

For this situation I was not unprepared. "Ha! Ha! I thought there might be some little difficulty. Here you are, my good man." So saying, I peel from my bank-roll an Abraham Lincoln and thrust it toward the former Lithuanian waiter.

"Are you kidding? Here's what I got from the last guy. A C-note. This is a gold mine. The dough keeps rolling in."

"I understand, Mister Mosk, that you are giving me a hint. I have not offered sufficient funds. Look: here is Old Hickory, the victor of New Orleans. What? More than twenty dollars? This is extortion, sir. I insist that you permit me to step inside. Or there might be difficulties. I am not a man from Missouri. Woolens cannot be pulled over my eyes. I know for a fact that somewhere in this House of Pleasure you have imprisoned Miss Crystal Knight."

"Any trouble here?" Those words, addressed to Mosk, come from the counter of the haberdashery, from behind which there now steps a mighty six-footer. Impossible not to recognize that lantern-type jaw, the bony ridge over the eyes, the ears like handles upon a jug: H. H. Levine!

Mosk: "Naw, no trouble, Happy. Our friend is just leaving."

"Leaving? But I have only arrived. I am a close acquaintance of Madam Stutchkoff. I demand to be taken to Miss Crystal Knight."

Levine: "We got new management."

Mosk: "We got new rules."

"Yes, yes. Then lend me, please, a coat and a tie."

Levine, shrugging: "He doesn't get it."

Mosk: "Listen, mister: you wouldn't have a good time in a place like this. Why not walk over to Ratner's?"

"Ratner's? But that is a dairy establishment. Without even solo piano."

107

Levine, while pushing me backwards: "Why don't you people stick to your own kind?"

"What? What can such words mean?"

Mosk: "I gotta paint you a picture? This ain't no beanery. We don't cater to kikes."

With one hand at my collar and the other at the seat of my gabardines, H.H. Levine ushers me to the Steinway Restaurant door. As I depart in one direction, a man and a woman—even a glance reveals that this couple are definite English swells—rush through in the other. Behind my back I hear Mosk's words of greeting:

"Ah, Lady Tina! And Lord Evans! *Enchanté!*"

#

Let us step forward in time one quarter of an hour. A chauffeur in uniform, the cuffs of his twill-type jacket as far over his wrist bones as those of his twill-type trousers are over his Thom McAns, stands at this same Steinway Restaurant door. Who is it? Hard to tell, since the brim of his cap is also well over his eyes. Clue: McAns. Yes, this is Leib in livery. I push my way into the foyer and am greeted, of course, by Monsieur Mosk.

"Hey, Buddy, deliveries at the rear."

"Mistaken identity, sir. Here speaking is a coachman. I have an important message for Herr Steinbrenner. Now if you will step aside. *Pardon. Pardon.*"

Of course this is not, as is required by barristers, nothing but the truth. Oh, I am, though a lifetime non-driver, a chauffeur. For have I not in the preceding moments paid the whole of my treasure, my hoard of seventy-five dollars, for the loan of the garments of the automobilist at the wheel of an Abraham Lincoln Continental? But which master I am now the servant of—whether it was the Doodle or Lord Evans or one of the other anonymous owners of the score of limousines at the Rivington Street curb—I cannot say.

Mosk: "Steinbrenner? Okay, but make it snappy."

At once I move forward and push through the padded doorway into the dining zone.

How to describe the scene than now assaults my senses? Even a Dante, a Virgil, might be tempted to put down his pen. Darkness, yes, an abundance of darkness; but at the same time there is inexplicable light. Rays in primary colors stab about in every direction, like the beacons of searchlights that frantically hunt for enemy aircraft. Revolving globes hang from the ceiling, casting sparkles and spangles throughout the room. Through it all, like clouds split by lightning, hangs the smoke of uncountable cigarettes. It is as if a hundred photographers stood all about me, old-fashioned cameramen, whose every shot releases a cloud of sulphurous vapor and a flash of mercury strong enough to turn the black of midnight into the blaze of high noon.

For a moment I stand, stunned, the way a venison is said to halt when stricken by headlamps at the side of a country road. I am brought from this trance by the *thud, thud, thud* of percussion that, in wave after wave, breaks against the skin of my body and passes through the soles of my shoes. The very walls of the room seem to be reverberating, thumping inward and outward like the speaker of my Philco before expiration of the tubes. I step forward, a single seed in this great vibrating gourd, a solitary blood drop, that is what if feels like, in a huge convulsing heart.

In a moment I come to a cleared space where men and women are dancing together. Dancing? Together? They writhe, they twist, they collide with the force of catapult stones. On their faces, the lips are back, the teeth are bared, the eyes are wide and staring, as in a mask from the South Sea Isles. Above them, on a high platform, a near-naked female dances alone. Her blond hair sways back and forth upon her dorsals and, on her chest, her bare bosoms careen like balloons from which the air is escaping. Could this be, I wonder, one of those Fone Fancies, which whom I sometimes converse? A glance at the sirloins confirms my suspicions: show-through silk in the skivvy, with opaque black trim. "Pardon!" I exclaim. "Are you Fraülein Corky?"

Before she can reply, two doors swing open at the back of the room and a procession of cooks and waiters enters from what I know to be the Steinway Restaurant kitchen. At the head is Ellenbogen, transformed by silk pants and silk-banded headwear into a distinguished-looking person. Behind him, wearing a hat as tall and white and fluffy as a Yorkshire-style pudding, strides Martinez, the master of broilings. Next come chefs and sous-chefs and—what's this? Can I believe my startled eyes? It is Chino! Chino! A definite Puerto Rican! When last seen at this establishment, a wispy-chinned lad. Now, three decades later, a mutton-chopped adult. And look! Right behind him: Jesús! Also a non-Sephardic. He, too, has aged, but it is not possible to mistake those two closely placed, liquid-filled eyes.

On and on comes the parade, through the burning phosphor, in and out of the closely set tables. At the rear a half dozen scullions are lifting high into the air—higher even than their own stiff white hats—a great silver dome upon a silver platter. How it gleams and glows! It seems to capture every stray beam of light. Now, to my surprise Ellenbogen—only the small square of white cloth on his arm serves as a reminder of his former station—turns toward where I am standing, next to a table of aristocrats. Amazingly, when he reaches that spot the old waiter stops and bows, with one knee touching the ground. Martinez follows, as does everyone else in the train, even the bus boys. But Chino glances up to where I remain on my feet. "Goldkorns! Is you? ¿Como esta usted?"

"Error, sir," I declare with insouciance. "I am a Lincoln limousine driver."

Now Jesús addresses me as well. "Ha! Ha! Señor Goldkorns! Ain't no doubt it's you."

Resigned, I bend toward the cooks of short order. "Gentleman. Will you tell me? Who are these grandees? Is that Prince Philip, perhaps?"

"You don't got eyes, gringo? That's Cruise. You know, Tom Cruise. Look at that smile, man. A million dollar smile, right? Look at that chin."

"¡Loco hombre! I'm looking at his woman. You see her Goldkorns? You want maybe some of that?"

"Would you be so kind? Who is the gentleman with the hair? Resembling a pineapple?"

"That's El Greco, eh? Comes in all the time. What's his name, Chino?"

"Stephanopoulos."

"And the Afrikaner? Also with hair? There: like a porcupine."

"What? Goldkorns! ¿Esta en vivo on el planeto de Mars?" Or asleep twenty years? Man, that's Don King!"

"These names do not, as we say in the vernacular, ring the bell. I am not, owing to the lapse of Herald Tribune home delivery, au courant with affairs."

"Oh, man! You pulling my leg? Jesús! This Goldkorns don't know Puff Daddy!"

By now all the servants are rising. The sous-chefs struggle to lift the platter into the thickened air. As they do so, the music ceases. All about us the dancers come to a stop. Even the smoke seems to grow sluggish, staying its movement in the atmosphere. Now Martinez, standing on a chair seat, prepares to raise with flourishes the silvery covering. The guests at the table stare upward without uttering a single word. At adjoining tables the diners also pause, the knives, the forks, motionless in their hands. Off comes—it is like a St. Peter's in pewter—the great dome. What a sight greets my eyes! For there, with a pomme in its mouth and a pom-pom on its tail, is the forbidden beast itself: the glazed, staring eyes; the round, hunched shoulders; the four folded hooves, as uncloven as the devil's. Pork! It is pork! A whole suckling pig!

Now the search beams swing round, one after the other, illuminating the metallic platter, and making the animal glitter and glare, as if one of the *sauciers* had doused it with brandy and another one had set it alight. "Oooh!"

With that exclamation, rising from every quarter in the room, I cannot help but feel a chill in each of my extremities and a sensation of hollowness within my heart. I know what all those in the Steinway Restaurant are worshiping. It is the Golden Calf.

Now an aged gentleman—by this I mean someone more advanced in years than the present speaker—pushes through the crowd; rather, the pack of men and women fall back before this centurian, who, wielding his cleaver, approaches the beast for the ritual carving. On the head, a skullcap; on the nose, circular spectacle lenses; on the chin, a long white beard that spreads like the bib that gentiles wear when eating crabs. Margolies! It is Margolies! Dean of the Steinway Restaurant waiters! High in the air the priest raises the shining blade. Descending it snaps open the pigskin, releasing a fountain of juices. Once more the knife is raised, once more it drops. Now the pale flesh is exposed; and now the bone, ribcage and chestbone, and a hint of the inner organs, pearl-like and intact. On every side the gentiles strain forward, their mouths open, as if in anticipation of the blood-filled flesh. And the Jews? As in days of old, they are the slaves and servants, delivering to their masters the forbidden feast.

And now come three new Israelites. At the sight of these men, Salpeter, Murmelstein, Dr. Julius Dick, my heart soars within me. Here are the surviving members of the Steinway Quintet. Impossible to avoid the inevitable thought: could this trio become a foursome? Dr. Dick possesses still his double viol; it towers above him as he edges through the mute-mouthed crowd. But what of Salpeter, the first violinist, and young Murmelstein, the second? Neither man has with him his violin. Surely room might be found for a flautist without his flute? I am able to whistle, if called upon, cadenzas from *Call Me Madam*. Dreams. Hopeless dreams. Murmelstein hops like a youth of sixty onto the bandstand and bends over—it is not a Bechstein, nor is it a Bösendorfer; but it is a keyboard nonetheless. Dick follows, hauling his fiddle onto the platform, and Salpeter sits before his own instrument, which must, from its shining cylindrical surface, be some sort of drum.

Salpeter: "A one-ah; a two-ah; A one-two-three!"

How to describe the resulting din? Each plucked string of Dr. Dick's double bass resounds like a cannonade. Useless to clap my hands over my ringing ears. Murmelstein attacks his keys like a man who has made a pact with the devil: for hidden in that device is an entire trumpet section, invisible strings, klaxons and bells, above it all the clarion call of what sounds like a steam caliophone. The crowd, in response, goes into a frenzy, twisting and jerking and hurling themselves against each other, knocking their partners to the floor. There is a sudden howl, a scrape, a high pitched squawk, as if the poor porker, under a kind of anesthetization, has awakened with a squeal of terror. In fact this caterwaul is created by Salpeter, who stops the disk that spins before him and sends it screeching in the opposite direction.

Who is that man approaching the bandstand? Short, stout, with a nose that dives down into his moustache. Heavens! Rabbi Rymer! The man who made Leib Goldkorn and the former Clara Litwack man and wife! He climbs onto the platform, seizes the microphone and, in the style of our fathers, begins to chant:

Rymer:

> There was a man wit a tan in the lan of Uz
> Job had a Jag checkered flag play tag wit da fuzz
> Bossest hog in da catalog
> Cuz
> He was upright, recondite, every Sunday night
> Went to confession wif his Smif-n-Wessun
> Had faith in Jesus 'n Joseph 'n Mary Jane
> Speed, bleed, weed, 'n cocaine
> 'N Able
> Drink any dude unda da table, wit Black Label

Chorus
(Salpeter, Murmelstein,
Dick):

> Ballin in da fast lane, chillin on da block
> Golden chains, Einstein brains, sportin a Glock

Rymer:

> Fifteen hos in Versace clothes covered head to toes wit
> Oil o olay
> Gold-toof bitch don' wear a stitch got her ass onna pillow

She give the alarm break her arm like da V da Milo
A kilo
To his valet
A Benz for his friends, a 'Vette on a bet
Nuffin he don' buy us

Chorus
(Salpeter, Murmelstein,
Dick):
   Job be pious!

Rymer:
   Grand for tips 'n on his lips a holy prayer

Chorus
(Salpeter, Murmelstein,
Dick):
   Boss player! Boss Player!

Hard to believe that anyone could comprehend the meaning of these words. Is the language English? Hebrew, perhaps? Is it even human speech? At the table the guests are eating the suckling pig. Mr. T. Cruise gnaws on a bone. Mr. D. King tears the skin. How wet their fingers! Their chins! Nor does the crowd, swaying, faces aflicker, teeth agleam, seem to grasp what only I have deciphered: that these poor Jews were attempting to express their own sufferings through the tale of their unfortunate co-religionist in days of old. Now the aptly named rabbi resumes:

Rymer:
   Up in heaven by a Seven-Eleven with the angels singing chords
   by Andre Previn
   God sat at da feast
   "Don't wanna boast but he be the Man coast to coast
   At least in the east"
   Thas' his toast

Chorus
(Salpeter, Murmelstein,
Dick):
   Ain't no mirage! Head nigga in charge!

Rymer:

> Then up stood a bro of high birth going to an fro on da earth
> "That muthafucka crowdin' my turf
> Put forth thine hand, smite him in his gland
> Give his hos to his foes, make him speak prose
> Rip off his contraband"
> God withheld his rod
> "You got a case of a-nomie? Talkin bout my homie
> A boss ghetto styler, got hisself a Rotweiler 'n a
> AK 47"
>
> But Satan wassn't done wit his hatin'
> "Deny his lays, snatch up his purses, not to mention his verses
> All his praise turn into curses"

Chorus
(Salpeter, Murmelstein,
Dick):

> Whadaya know? Done seen this story on da video
> Gonna test the power of this dude's religion
> Look who's comin': a stool pigeon—

Rymer:

> "Wussup?" said Job. "How's tricks, 'fucka? Why the alarm?"
> "First thing, sucka, you bet da farm on the Knicks
> Lost all yo bread
> J hit the trey couldn't cover the spread
> You dead—
> Them hos didn't knows da X's and O's caught a disease
> Ain't psychosomatic
> A automatic between the knees"

Chorus
(Salpteter, Murmelstein,
Dick):

> It's da rape from Hell, see?
> I's only excape to tell thee

Rymer:

> "You talk the talk, nappy head nigga, wit yo' PRAISE DA LORD

114

Now walk da walk,
I's happy pull da trigga, put you on a pine board
Outline in chalk
Forget abouts you family tree, going down on a APB
All yo riches them yaller bitches you fake-ass schemer
The King o' da Universe puts you inna hearse no top down Beamer
Meet yo maker, faker, take dis fag inna body bag"

Chorus
(Salpeter, Murmelstein,
Dick):

Goin' crazy, bats in da belfry
Rate this a X tape
I's only excape to tell thee

Rymer:

But Job ain't bout to jump from da Tappenzee
"You think this dampens me? Shit happens, see?
Naked I came from da womb
Naked I goes back to da tomb
Take my hos 'n my hoard but blessed be
Da name of da Lord"

Pigeon grows a tail two horns 'n a fork
"You wish you never borns in New York"
Gave Job boils on his balls, sores 'n tsouris
Wrung his tongue couldn't rhyme worth a dime calls
"Cure us!"

Chorus
(Salpeter, Murmelstein,
Dick):

Cure us!

Rymer:

Come the worst trick of Satan
Made him sick in da dick forget masturbatin
The G jes stutter
"J-J-J-Jee-sus!" he's pleadin
Up the Devil stands takes his nuts in his hands 'n cuts

No ifs ands and buts
Wit a box cutta
Job got the hex of Oedipus Rex whole box of Kotex
Won't stop the bleedin
Cocksucka!

Chorus
(Salpeter, Murmelstein,
Dick):
   Doth thou retain thine integrity
   O say can you see?

Rymer:
   Blind on hands and knees tries to find his main squeeze
   "Hey, baby! Yo, whas goin on—?"
   Look at that blond-headed witch, in her Guccis
   Ho of Babylon—

Here, ladies and gentlemen, all heads turn to where the Fone Fancy continues her gymnastics upon the raised platform. Her golden locks fall as advertised to her buttocks. Her shoulders, her mammalia, her maidenly midriff—all shine with moisture as if she has just stepped from her bubbling bath.

Rymer:
   She wiggle that ass full of sass hold aloof
   That gold toof can't hide her uncloven hoof
   Looks down at that chump sees only a stump
   'N toss her head high—

Suddenly the chant comes to a halt, the music ceases, and the illumination swings to where the dancer has brought to a close her undulations. Into the silence she hurls the words of Job's wife—

Curse God and die!

From the crowd, a low, animal roar. Mouths gaping, they surge toward where her greased body glistens in the light. There now occurs to Leib Goldkorn a thought so terrible that with a vigorous head shake I attempt to drive it from my brain. It remains. Will this young woman, so sportive in figure, be set upon by the hungry masses? Is this a sacrifice—a human one to match that of the animal only moments before? In short will— here we see the infectiousness of Rabbi Rymer's idiomatics—Corky be a Porky?

Before I can either speak or make a movement, the deafening music resumes, the crowd breaks into its dance, and someone pulls upon the sleeve of my chauffeuring jacket.

"Psst, Goldkorn. Look. Do you see? That chair."

It is Margolies. Cautiously he leans close, whispering by my ear. I look to where his spotted hand is pointing. A small, dark man, with goatee wisps and shaded glasses, sits with a superior smile.

"Do you mean, Mr. Margolies, the Afrikaner?"

"No, no. Not Spike Lee. I mean the chair. You do not remember? Who sat there? She had a cigarette in a holder. A habit, you know, a nervous tic, of picking the flake of tobacco from the tip of her tongue. I saw this! I changed the ash trays. I brought the black coffee. Goldkorn, do you know of whom I am speaking?"

My voice has died within my voice box. I can only nod.

"Yes," cries Margolies. "Sarah Bernhardt! In that very chair!"

Then he too falls silent. Does he feel in his breast the upward welling of shame that now fills mine? It is distress at what we have allowed our world to become.

In the Beautiful City

Paul Nemser

I kept pulling levers
so as not to lose connection,
the hook-up to the larger organon,
and was amazed at the sheer

inhumanity of the motion,
repeated till numb I felt
the pull of the river,
the pleasant, unanswerable desire

to be other; as things
in human guise resemble us,
beckoning like the souls of lovers.
Was that your voice? you said.

And I: was that you?
And loudspeakers played tunes
that swept us along,
our movements ever more instinctual.

Let me begin how the wind brought fever,
and I heard a heart
in the air compressor.
Had I seen that light before

on the waves, on the shore,
in the quicksilver splash
of an albacore
hooked, slashed, pressed into cans?

Light cut me off
in the midst of movement.
Everyone was on a video screen,
deep in reminiscences of human action,

welcoming, retreating,
like dear ones in a dream,
but even there, water was moving.
Even stillness

moved through the flux,
crossing a forehead,
shiver on a shoulder,
in the factory where I heard a heart,

and the great derrick
turned on its axis
under clouds professing thunder
rippling the vats.

Grapples turned their hooks toward heaven.
For all I knew, it could have been earth.
I too was moving,
molten as the steel.

2.

Under factory floodlights, the conveyors
bent like a stream
thrust deep into land, then back
oceanward, the black glide

through banks of shouting people;
widening, the wave
expired in the gasp of sprayguns;
leviathan's motors revved up

to rip the sod of a mechanized field
where even the oats were trademarked

to the protein. Nothing
was too small.

Earth had become a small place,
a fleck in time, a flit in space,
a byte, a wave, a valuable trace
of seasalt and useful ore.

Business took place
at the intersections
of light-speed currents,
and connections.

Out of the tiny, endless change.
Out of the dwindling, the new.
On behalf of a few corporations,
the sun was rising through the sulphur.

Buildings were rising, yellow-windowed,
like slow-growing crops.
Goods passed in procession
beyond the reach of any retina

down the hazy, jazzy canyons
where sky meets the street
through warehouses into orbit
across lakes and into bodies

from keystrokes into TVs
and winding and winding.
Belts spanning the country
made minds go drowsy in the crossing

or simply carried them off
like pigs newly slain
in great pink piles of eternal peace
never having looked so gentle.

Rich ones, poor ones,
middling shivering pure ones

shook from the static
in their telecommunications

on the jostling banks
where they jockeyed for position
to receive new deliverables, never quite usable,
in definitive, but alterable designs.

Listen! The thirsting
and the amphitheatrical hush.
There, in the waters,
was a half-human head

announcing the newest representation
among delegates of the material persuasion
who spoke in eerie unison,
eyeless and orphaned,

"What do you see
when you peel the onion?"
"I see a landscape
incapable of tears."

3.

With claws in water, a sphinx-like expression,
I fished for a semblance
to approximate the past:
love sundered, joined,

like running water sundered,
and the wind seemed to shake me from inside.
I thought of the sound
of my mother breathing

and repeated riddles
to whatever I encountered.
Was love the last thing memory wanted?
Was the last thing the first thing was love?

Thinking of answers increased my fever.
Surrounded for miles,
I saw only the river.
Rush of goods, information,

products, prices, tangling like eels
in unfeeling interinanimation
through the waters of the factory
so swift and sleepy

in the throes of a civilizing transformation.
Violence was the synonym.
Violence the antonym.
I was a man. Grown.

A social creation, adrift
in the hot oblivious waters.
First man, first child, first born.
Raised up to see from a great prospect

the changeless interchange, death and dream,
in the work I was doing—
was it work for the waking?—
the work I was born to in the world.

4.

From nothing but a silicon
waist curving narrow,
and hips hopelessly
hopelessly wide, in the glass,

the clear uterus of time,
where the sand of his seconds
met the sand of her hours,
and the flow of the sand,

the heartbeat of the sand,
belly and penis and soul of the sand,
the child of the sand—that was I,
late the king of digits,

of dials and constellations,
key meeting fingertip,
seed of the future. O river,
may you never run dry!

5.

I kept seeing obstacles
in every description.
Could it be the unpronounceable
was shaping the air

and the stammering daybreak
fled his arrows,
the broken heartbeat
washed on shore

as the sun looked in
behind the door,
and found the knot
in the mire and rot

that held the shadow to the floor:
horse, horseman,
dreamer, dream,
stepping through the muddy stream,

dumpsite, ass-end, smokestack, outfall,
licking the lead in a cubicle wall;
sun behind the news, a data eclipse,
blotting the views

of a rose's hips,
or a bird's claw, or a squirrel's fall
or the microchips
that decode a call?

To me corruption
was the narrowing of vision.
And destiny—
a bomb in transition.

Everywhere glass and glass on fire.
A wall of blind eyes in a line.
When I looked,
I too could not see.

6.

Not used to lunch hours,
nor man hours, nor sunless time,
I haunted the city of many markets,
still young and lost and looking.

Windowshopping, what had I become?
The lure of goods was a dance by the river.
Had I lost all feeling? Did I cross over?
Forever, it seemed, in the bottomless glass,

I watched a creature of efficiencies
aflush with odds and angles
feeling tall as heaven with economies of scale.
Buy! said my eye, and the goods passed.

I paid cash. Ignored people.
At the bank, punched my number.
The machine asked what transaction I wanted.
Then I knew: I wanted bliss.

7.

I saw the sinuous passage before me,
heard my mother's voice.
"Dus vet zayn dayn baruf."
Raisins and almonds.

Ineluctable current.
Through the giant cablework
electrons flew,
and I knew at that moment

she would not save me.
The time was mine to change

or yield to. There was only
one design. It was then

my loneliness came to me,
compressing my heart.
And in the maniacal
cacophonies of metal,

I felt the meekness of machines.
They were kind as pigs,
but they ate no corn.
Predictable and temperate,

they did not reproduce.
They transmitted by the telephone.
They were the telephone!
And O the way they talked to me

on visual read-out!
How my breath caught
near the high-speed printer!
The look of the console

as I programmed it solo,
and it told me the square root of two.
You were saying something to me
about needing a lover

and how in sympathy
we would see forever,
and how we could never compute the number
of times we could return.

8.

O, you said. O what, and I was dreaming,
was floating on waters,
caught a glimpse, had a feeling.
The water smelled salty,

and the sky was clearing.
Even the smoke above the beautiful city
had taken on a way of looking like writing,
and the stars had the look of a sea.

A sign lit up across the cloud,
it said splendor, and water broke open
twelve doors round the center,
and all the stories

told to the ocean
were untold in whitecaps,
unrolled in rips,
unrelenting in the bow of a back;

wet, wet, in the curve
as they found you, and
you were turning
over in the sand.

9.

And I turned to you,
for the last thing, the first thing.
Earth Angel, Earth Angel,
the Penguins sang,

as if from the polar star.
Had there ever been such looking
and navigations? Ever such finding
and what elation!

I saw every latitude in a drop of water.
Lakes stretched
to the farthest round of the planet,
and trees serrated the variations

of hillside and pit.
An avalanche of whales
splashed into the river
making a wave

that overwhelmed
the remnants of structure.
Even to the end of things.
Even to the center.

For a time I laughed like a gander,
and all we said
had hilarious clarity.
For a time we knew nothing,

only rolled and rolled
down dunes till we smashed
our fresh water into sea
and woke somewhere foreign

under the sun, free
as if the galaxies conversed
along our arteries,
Now and Now and Now.

10.

Blue waves crisscrossed
beside the factory island.
Your eyes fixed mine, began
to widen. The wind was cool.

You looked like a blossom
opening in slow, generous motion.
Larksong in the deep
backflowing sand.

I saw memory more clearly
than what I saw.
And the memory
that transfixed me

was alive in a future
conjured from Edens,

ages of gold, painted murals
on the handles of plows.

Mountain mist, hillsides
of peasants, ships at a city
in crooks of valleys.
Hands doing, lips clucking,

cows' macerations;
winged arms fall into sea
and no one looking.
But O that feeling

when he rose so high
and what repose when he
crashed to the bottom
crossed the preoccupied face

of the plowman
whose life continued its own
mythic directions
to and fro along the side

of the mountain
in the gorge where miracles
always happened.
Angels thrummed, the messiah

came, and centaurs
shook their manes at a stranger,
pranced clip clop
by the weeping water

that searched the catacombs
and cleansed the traveler,
for there was no
unkindness in it,

though it hunted its lover,
and above ground

time ran back and forward
simultaneously toward eternity.

11.

There are cities where my heart
has poured its best
into the fountains,
and I've been borne up

as if I'd found my destination
in a word or the deepening
of an eye. You turned to me,
and love was in the rotation.

I found your glance,
The hill was green with cultivation.
Grapes in baskets,
plums in the hand,

mushrooms with an odor
of the richnesses of earth.
An embrace by a well,
the clear, clear water.

The sun was going down,
but the moon was rising.
Your left hand touched my right;
soon the other two

were meeting, and before sleep
we saw a new planet rising
through choked calls,
the multiplying halls

of gas rending, spirits split
beyond rescue or grace,
but here the wind was a womb
for our soarings,

and the house we were making—
others might come too:
children, old friends
ancestors, citizens;

mammals in garden burrows,
songbirds in their seasons;
wildflowers, thistle seeds,
raspberry, salmon,

goddesses with gray eyes, flute-playing gods,
harps and sarods and balalaikas,
dragons and swordsmen, elephants and emus,
taoist masters and divining rods,

roses climbing the trellis of the gateway,
and a galaxy, and a ladder of light,
reaching to the pinnacle of night.
A city, rivers, a sea.

from A Theory of the Novel

P.N. Furbank

What a Narrative Is

To think that narrative can "copy" or "imitate" life is to forget an all-important fact once put by Louis Mink with great conciseness. "Stories," he said "are not lived but told." There are no stories "out there" in the world, waiting to be told. They have to be invented. We are so familiar with the act of storytelling and perform it so often ourselves in our daily lives that we tend not to reflect on its nature or remember that (even in its most banal form) it is a creation *ex nihilo*: it is not a "copy" of anything, except perhaps of another story. It gives a special kind of meaning (a meaning concerned with how and why *this* led to *that*) to what till then does not possess it. Mink puts the point very luminously:

> Life has no beginnings, middles, or ends; there are meetings, but the start of an affair belongs to the story we tell ourselves later, and there are partings, but final partings only in the story. There are hopes, plans, battles and ideas, but only in retrospective stories are hopes unfulfilled, plans miscarried, battles decisive, and ideas seminal. Only in the story is it America which Columbus discovers, and only in the story is the kingdom lost for want of a nail.[1]

Narrative as a medium is, after all, not some blank recording substance; it is, rather, something of the same order of things as language. As Roland Barthes rightly said in "An Introduction to the Structural Analysis of Narratives," "It is hardly possible any longer to conceive of literature as an art that abandons all further relation with language the moment it has used it as an instrument to express ideas, passion or beauty: language never ceases to accompany discourse, holding up to it the mirror of its own structure." Narrative is a set of propositions; a sequence of sentences that are each themselves a narrative in miniature; and an array of figures of rhetoric, such as simile, metaphor, apostrophe, aposiopesis, prosopeia, erotesis, hypotosis and prolepsis.

The problem in studying narrative, as I have said, is that it is too ubiquitous. Every day, in our daydreams or reminiscences, we draw on its vast repertoire of plot-devices. We say to ourselves, proleptically, "*That* must have been the turning-point, that was when it all really began"; or, "When X— did that, what an extraordinary reversal of fortune [*peripeteia*] it was!" Then, going over the same events on another day, we may tell ourselves a different story, connecting the events up differently or relating them to other events. Very often, in this, we are borrowing plot-devices from literary fiction or from professional storytellers; nevertheless, even by nature we are born *raconteurs*.

But then, the very idea of an "event" entails the idea of narration. Events do not simply occur, they are the fruit of an interpretation. They come about through somebody deciding that an "event" has taken place; and indeed it may well be that another person will refuse to acknowledge this event. (It would be perfectly possible to deny there was an "Industrial Revolution," and in fact certain historians do so.) Positing an "event" already involves thoughts about other events or possible events and about one thing leading to another, and this is a defining characteristic of narrative.

Curiously, even Barthes does not seem to see how completely this rules out any notion of narrative as a copy or simulacrum. He is, indeed, very emphatic as to its not being such. "Narrative does not show, does not imitate," he insists. "The function of narrative is not to 'represent,' it is to constitute a spectacle still very enigmatic for us but in any case not of a mimetic order." But in stressing the logical as opposed to the "mimetic" nature of narrative, and the resemblance of narrative structures to the structure of language, he seems all the same to be half hinting that things might be otherwise: that there could be such a thing as verbal mimesis and the making of a verbal "copy" of events, and that in this respect narrative is a "distortion."

> A purely logical phenomenon, since founded on an often distant relation and mobilizing a sort of confidence in intellective memory, it [narrative] ceaselessly substitutes meaning for the straightforward *copy* [my italics] of the events recounted. On meeting in "life", it is most unlikely that the invitation to take a seat would not immediately be followed by the act of sitting

down; in narrative these two units, contiguous from a *mimetic*
[my italics] point of view, may be separated by a long series of
insertions belonging to quite different functional spheres. Thus
is established a kind of logical time which has very little connection with real time, the apparent pulverization of units
always being firmly held in place by the logic that binds together the nuclei of the sequence.[2]

As an observation this is exact, and one can easily imagine a novel (not
even a particularly "experimental" one) interposing a hundred pages
between a host inviting someone to sit down and their actually doing so.
But Barthes' "straightforward copy" and "mimetic point of view" appear
to be pure phantasm.

Barthes's "Introduction to the Structural Analysis of Narratives" hits
many nails on the head, for instance when he formulates the following rule:

Everything suggests . . . that the mainspring of narrative is precisely the confusion of consecution and consequence, what
comes after being read in a narrative as what is caused by; in
which case narrative would be a systematic application of the
logical fallacy denounced by Scholasticism in the formula *post
hoc, ergo propter hoc*—a good motto for Destiny, of which narrative, all things considered, is no more than the "language."[3]

But Barthes, we need to remember, is talking about narratives in general, not specifically about *literary* narratives, or about what qualities might
make a narrative good. "Caring nothing for the division between good
and bad literature," he writes, "narrative is international, transhistorical,
transcultural: it is simply there, like life itself."[4] It is indeed a matter of
principle with him to banish value-judgment from criticism (though
allowing it to creep back under the disguise of *jouissance*). A discussion of
literary narrative will have to proceed rather differently. It may, in fact,
need to avoid talking as though "narrative" were a separate element, just
one element among many, in fiction.

For to assign special qualities to "story" or "narrative" tends to lead on
to a set of cherished but very dubious propositions: that there are only so
many archetypal stories in the world (thus that stories cannot really be
said to have an author); or that all the stories of the world have already
been told, because there will be no more storytellers. (Storytelling as a
craft is doomed to destruction by industrial society.)

Barthes, it is true, allows there to be an infinity of possible stories; he is merely insisting that they have a "common structure." Nevertheless, by his very grudging attitude towards the "author," he seems rather to imply that storytelling is a matter simply of permutation. "There does, of course, exist an 'art' of the storyteller," he says, "which is the ability to generate narratives (messages) from the structure (the code). This art corresponds to the notion of *performance* in Chomsky and is far removed from the 'genius' of the author, romantically conceived as some barely explicable personal secret."[5] As for Vladimir Propp, in his *The Morphology of the Folk-Tale*, the idea that there is a fixed repertoire of stories, fixed for all time, looms large. He invites he reader to follow him in "the labyrinth of a diversity of which will finally perceive the marvelous unity," and to ponder what he calls the "essential problem": the similarity of stories throughout the world. ("How explain that the story of the frog-queen in Russia, in Germany, in France, in India, among the American Indians and in New Zealand resemble one another, seeing that no contact between these people can be established historically?")

Propp, however, is not claiming this to be true of all stories. "We need to note," he writes, "that the laws stated above only apply to folklore. They are not a characteristic of stories per se. Artificially-created stories are not subject to them." The idea that all the stories have already been told comes out more strongly in Walter Benjamin's "The Storyteller: Reflections on the Works of Nikolai Leskov." Benjamin wants us to think that the best stories are those which evoke "the voice of the anonymous storyteller, who was prior to all literature."[6] He wishes to think of all fiction, including the Novel, as rooted in folk tradition.

> *Memory* creates the chain of tradition which passes a happening on from generation to generation. It is the Muse-derived element of epic art in a broader sense and encompasses its varieties. In the first place among these is the one practiced by the storyteller. It starts the web which all stories together form in the end. One ties on to the next, as the great storytellers, particularly the Oriental ones, have always readily shown.[7]

"The web which all stories together form in the end!" How attractive it is to a certain type of nostalgic primitivism, this notion that all the stories in the world have already been told. How tempting to defy the Modernist injunction to "make it new."

It may help in getting at the issues involved here to consider a remark of Franz Kafka's, that the tale "Unexpected Reunion" in Johann Peter

Hebel's *Treasure Chest* (1811) was "the most wonderful story in the world." Walter Benjamin speaks of it almost and warmly,[8] and the opinion does not strike me as absurd.

The story, which is only three pages long, tells how a young miner at Falun in Sweden taps at his bride-to-be's window in the morning as he goes to work but does not return from the mine that evening; "and in vain that same morning she sewed a red border on a black neckerchief for him to wear on their wedding-day, and when he did not come back she put it away, and she wept for him, and never forgot him." Fifty years later, miners discover the body of a young man, soaked in ferrous vitriol but otherwise untouched by decay and unchanged, and his aged fiancee—the only one to recognize him—has him taken to her house till he can be buried and follows the coffin next day in her best Sunday dress, "as if it were her wedding-day."

> You see, as they lowered him into his grave in the churchyard she said: "Sleep well for another day or a week or so longer in your cold wedding bed, and don't let time weigh heavy on you! I have only a few things left to do, and I shall join you soon, and soon the day will dawn."
>
> "What the earth has given back once it will not withhold again at the final call" she said as she went away and looked back over her shoulder once more.

Among all the arresting touches in this story, one might single out that "and looked back over her shoulder once more," which is beyond all question "right," but which we spell out to ourselves in twenty different ways.

Walter Benjamin, in his Leskov essay, has an appealing remark: "There is nothing that commends a story to memory more effectively than that chaste compactness which precludes psychological analysis." It applies very neatly here. He is also quite right in saying that, in Hebel, "The moral always appears where you least expect it. All the same, something in Benjamin's approach to Hebel makes one want to dig one's heels in. What most strikes me about Hebel's story is not its roots in folk tradition, but rather its novelty, freshness and uniqueness. After all, one of the marks of the popular storyteller is to be long-winded and repetitive—the very thing that Hebel, who pinned everything on extreme concision and labored over his tales like a Flaubert (though taking care, as he said, that the "art" and the "labor" should not be visible) was signally not.

One wants to say, as against this appeal to tradition, that Hebel has brought something quite new and intensely valuable into the world. I brought in Kafka deliberately, because one would be inclined to make the same sort of claim for "In the Penal Colony," "A Hunger Artist," or "The Metamorphosis." One should not misunderstand what the narrator in Kafka's "Investigations of a Dog," disgruntled about the vaunted "universal progress" of the dog community, says about "old and strangely simple stories."

> I do not mean that earlier generations were essentially better than ours, but only younger; that was their great advantage, their memory was not so overburdened as ours today, it was eas-ier to get them to speak out, and even if nobody actually suc-ceeded in doing that, the possibility of it was greater, and it is indeed this greater sense of possibility that moves us so deeply when we listen to those old and strangely simple stories. Here and there we catch a curiously significant phrase and we would almost like to leap to our feet, if we did not feel the weight of centuries upon us.[9]

The message of this is not nostalgia; it is, rather, a belief in the extreme newness, the "greater sense of possibility," that narrative can offer. Kafka himself liked to speak about writing as a birth. The writer, he told Janouch, liberated himself from his subject by placing it outside himself. "It's a birth, an addition to life, like all births." In the novelist Heinrich von Kleist, Kafka said, "modesty, understanding and patience combined to create a strength which is necessary for any successful birth."[10] If regarding narrative as a separable element within a fiction entails think-ing of it—whether for good or evil—as something "primitive," we had better give the habit up.

Alternatively, we could apply it in a rather different sense, one in which not only Hebel and Leskov, but Jane Austen and Dostoevsky and Proust are great masters of narrative—I mean, in their vision of how, at a profound and not merely a superficial level, one thing will lead to another. The strength of Austen's novels lies, as much as anything, in the richness, the extraordinary complexity and cogency, of the pattern of causation within them: it subsists in the way that, behind any given thing that occurs in these novels, one feels the pressure of so many other things, of all kinds. How many things, how many significant factors, lead towards and away from that famous picnic on Box Hill in *Emma*!

It is for this quality that she must rank higher than Trollope. I think of that chapter in Trollope's *Phineas Finn* in which Phineas and Lady Laura look back regretfully on the past. "'How much we would both of us avoid if we could only have another chance!' sighs Lady Laura." "If I could only be as I was before I persuaded myself to marry a man whom I never loved, what a paradise the earth would be to me! With me all regrets are too late." "And with me," says Phineas, "as much so."[11] The scene is, for the reader, a significant let-down. For the careers of Phineas and Lady Laura do not really fuse in our imagination. Their two careers have been neatly entangled, in a mechanical professional-novelist's fashion, but the entangling has not given birth to any new idea.

E. M. Forster once made a suggestive remark about a short story by Angus Wilson, "What do Hippos Eat?".[12] In this story, an ageing old-school-tie-sporting con man is taking his girlfriend, on whom he sponges, round the Zoo, and, maddened by her bright, "mad" sense of humor, he suddenly feels like pushing her into the hippos' pond. "He put his hands on her hips and in a moment would have pushed her into the thick vaporous water; then he suddenly realized that he had no idea what would happen." Forster, who admired the story, said: "Of course the most interesting thing of all would be to tell us what happened if he pushed her in. But that is something only the very greatest novelists could do."

Plainly, Dostoevsky possessed this kind of vision in a superlative degree. The whole of the first part of *The Idiot* is one precipitate succession of wildly unexpected, but logical, consequences. One may think, too, of that wonderful little incident in *Crime and Punishment*, when Raskolnikov's sister Dounia is thrown out of the Svidrigailov household by Marfa Petrovna who—as she thinks—has caught her in a compromising situation with her husband. Svidrigailov then confesses that he was entirely and solely to blame; and upon this, Marfa Petrovna sets off "without the least delay" to the homes of all her acquaintances to proclaim the girl's innocence, and her own error. Is this the end of the story? By no means. For certain of Marfa Petrvona's friends take great offense that she does not come to them—rather than to other friends—*first*. It is a quite new dilemma for Marfa Petrovna. The solution, she decides, is to issue a timetable, specifying when she will be performing her penitence at any given house . . .

Or we may take that wonderful and terrifying story of Dostoevsky's, *A Disgraceful Affair*, which is one swift and dizzying progression from a casual decision to utterly devastating and far-reaching consequences. The protagonist, a senior civil servant, is walking home through the snow when he passes the home of one of his clerks, where there is a wedding-party in progress. During the evening everything has gone wrong for him; at dinner with one of his colleagues he has been irritated and frustrated at every turn. Thus the thought strikes him, as he passes the welcoming doorway, "Why shouldn't I just go in for a moment? How pleased and honored they would feel. And I needn't stay more than two instants. And what a well-conceived gesture, and how pleasant their gratitude would be. Really, the music, and the doorway, are most inviting." So he goes in. And by the time he emerges, the wedding-night, the clerk's livelihood, and his own character and self-respect lie in total ruin.

We may relate this vision of unforeseen consequences with another, of which Dostoevsky was also a master: the collision of quite unrelated life-histories. I am thinking of the scene in *The Possessed* in which Stepan Trofimovich goes to see the Town Governor. Stepan, the liberal idealist, proud of his reputation as a dangerous progressive, has been subjected to a police raid, and it has driven him almost out of his mind with terror. In sheer desperation, and with the air of someone mounting a tumbril, he goes with a friend to complain to the Town Governor, Lembke. Outside the Governor's residence they find a crowd of factory-workers, come to complain about unfair dismissal. Lembke emerges. He has spent a sleepless night, as the result of a quarrel with his wife. Indeed he is on the verge of insanity and instantly decides that this is a revolution and wildly gives orders for the ringleaders of the workers to be flogged. This strengthens the outraged Stepan in his sense of himself as a hero and a martyr, and when eventually admitted to Lembke's presence he presents his complaint with majestic dignity and polished irony. Lembke is violent and abusive, but then, to Stepan's surprise, begins to mumble disconnected apologies. Stepan replies with a witticism. And at this, Lembke exclaims "That's very amusing, of course" (he gives a wry smile), "but" (almost screaming) "*can't you see how unhappy I am?*" "It was", says the narrator, "probably the first moment since the previous day that he [Lembke] had full, vivid consciousness of all that had happened—and it was followed by complete, humiliating despair that could not be disguised." Stepan, jolted so unexpectedly out of his own drama into another's, bows before the superior grief. "Your Excellency", he says, in a voice full of feeling, "don't trouble yourself with my petulant complaint."[13]

The Concept of "Narrative History"

It helps in thinking about narrative to remind oneself that what historians mean when they speak of "narrative history" has very little to do with literary narrative and is, indeed, a rather vague and empty term. The fact comes home to one in reading an article by Lawrence Stone in *Past and Present* (November 1979) entitled "The Revival of Narrative: Reflections on a New Old History." It relates, or claims to relate, how historians, having for the last fifty years deserted historical storytelling in favour of *Annales*-type structural analysis, are beginning to grow disillusioned and to see virtues in the narrative method again. The essay strikes one as extraordinarily muddled. For instance, Stone writes that "More and more of the 'new historians' are now trying to discover what was going on inside people's heads in the past, and what it was like to live in the past, questions which inevitably lead back to the use of narrative" (13); yet we are later told that Emmanuel Le Roy Ladurie's *Montaillou* (1976) is significant, first, in being an out-and-out best seller, and "secondly, because it does not tell a straightforward story—*there is no story* [my italics]—but rambles around inside people's heads." This, he says, is no accident, for it is "precisely one of the ways in which the modern novel differs from those of earlier times."

The truth is Stone has not given any serious thought to what a literary narrative is. Had he done so, it would have come home to him that a work of history, whether by Gibbon or Motley or Trevor-Roper or Simon Schama, can only be called a "narrative" by way of metaphor. The point is easily demonstrated. Consider, for instance, the opening page or two of A.J.P. Taylor's *English History 1914-1945* (1965): "The president of the board of trade was also busy" . . . "Kitchener soon wavered" . . . "The English people could not be ignored so easily." It is plain—and no criticism of Taylor is implied—that what we have here is not so much a narrative as the graveyard of innumerable abortive narratives. For a half a page or a page we are offered a little plot about how the Board of Trade would bestir itself, or how Kitchener would vacillate (over the best landing-place for the B.E.F.), or how the English would demand to be better informed; but this little promise of a story will not be kept, nor do we expect it to be kept; it will be forgotten and discarded almost as soon as it is born.

The contrast with literary narrative, which makes it a point of honor to keep narrative promises, is great, and the reason is fundamental. It is that literary narratives are—what historical "narratives" would like to be but signally are not and cannot be—exemplary systems of causation. They are to be judged according to the infrangibility, subtlety and profundity of their demonstration of what led to what. Now, obviously, this is only possible because a storyteller or novelist, unlike a historian, is free to invent his or her materials; he or she is exempted from the duty to report certain things simply because they in fact happened.

I do not mean that causation is not a matter of concern to the historian. Stone suggests that why historians turned away from chronological ordering was precisely because, though it was excellently adapted to answer the *what* and the *how* questions, it did not—even if directed by a central argument—seem to help much in answering the *why* questions. Indeed this is hard to deny: *post hoc ergo propter hoc*, though a golden rule for literary narrative, would plainly be a quite fatal one for a historian. But then, *causality* has always been an almost insuperable problem to historians, as is notorious from their endless, baffled, and often rather absurd, wranglings over the "causes" of (shall we say?) the French Revolution or the First World War.

Thoughts of this kind haunt us when reading Fernand Braudel's *The Mediterranean*. He is fertile in the kind of explanation of phenomena that is best described as a "reason." The reason why the Arab invasions of the seventh century, unlike the Turkish ones of the eleventh century, disregarded the high lands, he will argue, was because the Arabs used the dromedary—which, unlike the camel, could not function at high altitudes. This strikes one as altogether plausible and most appealing. But he is also very prone to use "causal" language—to say "because" and to speak of "necessities" and "forces" ("hidden forces," "the vital force of the sea")—leaving it quite unclear how seriously these expressions are to be taken. There seem to be no rules for the use of such language; for, and this is the whole point, one is not going to be told by what mechanism these causes are linked to their effects. For Michel Foucault one of the attractions of the "archaeological" approach to history was to escape such rule-less and untrammeled dabbling in *causation*.

The novelist and the historian thus start from opposite ends. The historian, at certain moments, must envy the novelist, who can present subtle and complex systems of causation, just as novelists used, playfully at least, to aspire to be "historians" and to write the "history" of Tom Jones or Henry Esmond. Actually their professions have very little in common.

Notes

1. Louis O. Mink, "History and Fiction as Modes of Comprehension," *New Literary History*, I, 1970, 541-58.
2. Roland Barthes, "Introduction to the Structural Analysis of Narratives," in *Image-Music-Text*, ed. S. Heath (1977), 119.
3. Ibid., 94.

4. Ibid., 79.

5. Ibid., 80n.

6. Benjamin, op. cit., 107.

7. Walter Benjamin, *Illuminations*, trans. H. Zohn, ed. H. Arendt (1970), 94-5.

8. Ibid., 91.

9. Kafka, Franz, *The Penguin Complete Stories of Franz Kafka*, ed. N.N. Glatzer (1983), 299.

10. Janouch, 164.

11. A. Trollope, *Phineas Finn*, chapter 69.

12. In *Such Darling Dodos* (1950).

13. Dostoevsky, Fyodor, *The Possessed*, Part II, Chapter 10.

Small Talk

Jane Shore

On the drive back from dropping off
our daughter at sleep-away camp,
again a woman and a man,
we make small talk—
lake, cabins, canoes, cafeteria.

Take that blue Chevy in front of us—
that red Toyota tailgating behind—
a three-car cortege mournfully
inching along the logging road,
three sets of parents driving home
an empty backseat, slack seat belt,
empty trunk. Do you think they'll
jump into bed the minute they get there?
Tell me, when have we had a week alone together
since our daughter was born?

Home, I pay a visit to her room
formal as a doll museum.
Will the tent she's sleeping in
spring a leak, will she run out of
clean underwear, will they remember
to give her her allergy pills,
comb her hair? She's barely nine,
she's never been away from home
for more than a pajama party.

Remember that Thai cafe in Hawaii,
a month after she was born, the first time
we left her alone with a baby-sitter,
we'd try to behave like a couple
on a date, the very couple we were
four weeks before? But now
I ordered my food mild on purpose
so the spices wouldn't pass
into my milk and give her gas.

We nibbled Pad Thai, sipped ginger ale—
twirling the paper umbrellas in our drinks,
fiddling with our chopsticks,
checking the clock—
Was she hungry? Was she crying?
We lasted half an hour, then gave in.
"Emma!" we cried, repeating the name
together, same name I printed
with laundry pen this morning
on all the collars and waistbands
I stuffed into her duffel for camp.

The night she was born premature
in the hospital near Waikiki,
the night they cut me open, removed her,
and stitched me up again,
after the surgery and all the drugs,
I had a nightmare:
I was floating over a cemetery
by the sea in Hawaii,
over gravestones of black lava.

Now, again, she is separate from me.
As in the dream, my body,
suddenly lighter and free from gravity,
bounced from gravestone to gravestone,
the way at a party a balloon
is flicked from person to person
around the circle to keep it in the air.

Don't Ask Me I'm Not Telling

Claudia Keelan

There's no filling anything,
bag of sick,
briefcase full of the dead sea.
It's easy to comprendre, Ramon Perez,
everyone's tired of it,
have you seen me?
The Jiffy Lube time simulator
drawing exactly the face of Juan Perez
seven years after you stole him.
The God on fire in dreams and in days,
the red surge *there* and *there*,
laughing at you, at me.
Take me for instance,
an animal fingering hunger runes,
the carousel horses my boy
refuses to ride
ascending behind my lids
until his absence is complete.
Draw *that* Jiffy Lube, you fucker,
time's on your side but nothing else.
Raymond and John are far from the sea
and I've stopped following them.
And the next—oh, the next . . .
I lost my nerve there and there
my love's dead sister
still sits in the front row of the Christmas pageant
a child, her last second written on her brow.
Nobody goes farther than that.

Take me for instance,
Ramon, Juan, my boy,
the world I can't fill in,
quiet beneath a horse's tongue.
Need gets used up in it.
Mothers, fathers, lose the thread—
the senile's "is that you grandpa?"
to her youngest son—
and why not,
why not, there's nothing here
to tell us where we are.
Jiffy Lube, poetry,
calligraphy of present and past.
I should know and I won't tell,
all my faces in this ruined future.

Five Poems

Bruce F. Murphy

Le Thérapeute

René Magritte, 1937

There is nothing left to know.
While we were talking I dreamed of seashells
And the rain came down.
I looked out past the cement owl
And the hollow bust pondering,
Bottle-green. Past your shoulder
And the hanging vines,
The empty birdcage and twining ferns,
Toward the private sides of houses
In the next street.

A woman came to the window
And stood there in her slip,
Looking at the rain and perhaps thinking . . .
And there is nothing to know
There, she is just what she is.

No one comes to wake us
When we are awake. The room darkened
By the past of silence and gravity,
My thoughts wound down.
I am the watch I was too lazy to fix.

In the morning our dreams leave us
Stricken with resolve. By midday,
The coarse bag will drop
And shades slowly cover our eyes.
I feel the wet hem, and the day
Drying away. A philosopher,
His cloak heavy with rain, says
"The mind is air, the cage
Is bronze," and stares.
A stick, a hat laid aside, a road.

Meditation: Invocation

I held my tongue, my breath until it burned,
Then came my heart, leaping into my throat
As I stood aside and gaped at the world,
And looked into its wasted eye; but then
The sun changed into its last clear shape
And we saw the end. We cannot stop
Believing, we can only scratch our hands
And make the cries of extinct birds; here,
A man offered them names that died
Ten thousand years, a hundred long lifetimes
Ago; and here, a fool pulled a wall down
On himself. The stylus is always moving
Over the face of life, in summertime
The warmed iris watercolors, on the wall
Of winter the cold chisel makes an image:
Teeth are bared, lips curling back, gums white,
Tongue nested in itself like a viper,
The larynx rattling, crowing at death.
Disguised with the hide of a snow leopard,
Organs carried close to the warm belly,
We're still heaving and panting with life as
It runs out of us and pools at our sides.
Walking noiselessly in among the trees,
Running after the scent of living things
With our eyes open, mouths wet, licking each other
In a ditch half full of rain—"I want this!"
I cry, and laugh, but then there is no more—
It's so easy to die, we want a thousand
Times more than that, we want all the voices
To go on crisscrossing like the arms
Of constellations, pointing out the scales
Of justice, and into the deep bass of
Embodied time. A giant swan flies over us,
And a little man stuck like a tack
Into the globe's side points upward,
But the bird turns to a cross and rusts
In the sky. The man is a dust speck,

But there's nothing he has not destroyed
In his mind. Doesn't he affirm as much
Himself, at the end? Take hold of the tail
Of the dead man's spine, feel how it shakes like
A divining rod over the fissures
Where spores hide themselves, dormant in our lifetime.

Meditation: Hunger

That cracked voice was not a voice but a tree
Warping in the cold wind; it sounds like the heart
Crack, when you need time for sadness suddenly
In the stillness moving among the pines.
You'll see what a friend is then, and what
A family is, even as the bough cracks
Against your foot, the bough where the tree
Was downed in a wind storm after standing up
A hundred years, after which none of us stand.
The flames are quiet, it's the wood that sings.
The flames make a sound like drapery, like
A woman's clothing, a flutter that could be
In the heart or in the room, in a dress
Rustling quietly over the precipice
Of shoulder that is smooth and somehow straight,
Falling like a curtain that held each breast
Behind its breath. Between the parted lips
The pause that is silence, that is *about to,*
That is smoke, that is fog, that is sleep
In the violet darkness which is always
Hidden. It is the breath we cannot say
Softly enough to have it be the truth
About the moment, in which life and all
That it is not are on the brink of being
Permanent, the chasm between two bodies
Hushed and charged as absence beckoning to
Lightning; then the figures touching, and the last
Second of not touching that you want not to end.
Your hands reach across that gap and are
Illuminated, like leaves falling between trees
And never striking anything until they touch
The ground, and in that void there is no word,
Just sound, a catch in your throat, your hands
Lost in ecstatic fumbling, so eager
That where they touch, they start back
For another touch, becoming clumsy,
Touching themselves as often as the other.

Oh, that plosive space between us like our need
To be inside each other—not to be one,
But to be all of two, when the difference
Between loved and nothing is too violent
To understand, when thought rears its head
Out of the blood and falls back with its sharp
Cry thrust clear, the way you bent your cold face
To a blasted oak's still circulating core,
Hot and so like flesh you said you had to
Taste it, had to; that is the desire of
Our bodies, which cannot hold themselves
And do not even want to, as long as
This impermanent black air is gathering
Like an eclipse between our abdomens,
The skin heated to brilliance, so awake
That it is almost sighted, our unbroken,
Radiant, immeasurable coastline.

Theogony

The sun came up before
there was a sun.
Under mud, a wasp stretches,
cannot feel, dies.
On our backs, the word
crawls out of Egypt.
We weren't born to be
the slaves of god, we curse
the dust that chokes,
not knowing we damn
a vanished world thrust into
us, photons, grass, the Oort cloud.
We breathe, and choke on heaven.
I won't be back here
for a million million years;
who knows what the stars will be
by then? Stumps of a dead Elysium.
Lose a finger of yourself,
eloign: free the caught fore sheet,
the spindle, the splintered wheel.
Run.

Meditation: The Heliotrope

Playing my last string. Working at the one
Umbilical note. The lute stays unstrung,
Because the player now sees only where
The lacquer work has faded, the varnish
Blistered and turned into the wings of moths.
Now he has their dust on his fingers
And the death, the flightlessness it signifies.
Look at the birch dust on his shoulders and
On his hands, then at their emptiness.
Only now, things that were frightening are
No longer so—the voices in the wind
That everyone has heard, the tree that falls
A different way from you. Here is a small
Sliver of faith that may prove acceptable:
There may be no hardship and no anguish
Approaching out of that place you cannot
See into, but don't blame yourself for that,
Or having been a fool. No person can
Distill a life except his own, and leaves
A world as desolated as before,
Even if more desolated than before.
Only a boy makes the promise to himself,
"I will be iron": once hardened, he finds
It harder to stop needing cruelty.
I do not know what promises girls make,
Women don't say, and I don't tell them what
I think they won't forgive—our stories are
Fragments, not like the tales we listen to
Alone in bed, thinking, counting the days
For no one but ourselves. "Yes, I was hurt,
But I exacted terrible revenge." We lie
Awake, writing our thoughts like scrimshaw
Into bones best meant for love, our scriptures
Of loneliness. My lips are divided,
Which were once a single serpentine body
That never asked to be propelled into
The light; it loved the darkness, when once

My pursed mouth lay under my mother's heart,
Not yet divided, unspeakable, before
I was. We were singular, and now are twinned.
I would like to meet the boy grown out of me
Like a son, quenched and impossible as
Strangled, assassinated hopes, the dreams
Forgotten purposely. Another's blood
Runs through me, and I speak as I myself
Would never talk. If when I touched you
I gave nothing, nothing was all I had,
Endlessly afloat in space that has no sound,
No flavor, texture. I am that man who died
When I was born, and this half-earth, half-dead thing
With a potato for a heart, trying to grow,
A heliotrope, like a tree which drops
Its foliage and fruit in the small
Circumference of its crown, nourishing its shadow,
And grows out of itself until there is
Nothing but the loam of a waning orchard,
The sweet bread shared between one life and death.
I tried to stay the apple in its fall
To taste the hard, green bitterness of youth.

from Sonnets on Death

Jean de Sponde

Translated from the French by David R. Slavitt

X

My feeble body deteriorates: it flows
downhill as surely as water does to seek
its lowest level. I feel myself grow weak
approaching death's threshold. Meanwhile, my woes

burden me further. Grief upon grief I bear.
Suppose a desert wind that drifts the sand
to cover a house, a town. . . . Can I withstand
such overwhelming force as I find there?

Then let it go, my soul, for you can live
without it! Look to your own affairs, and give
your thought to what must come. On this reflect:

the Author of the Book of Life is kind
and may conceal the time, but we're not blind
to his design: we know what to expect.

XI

And why should Death be proud, if vermin teem
over our bones and delicate nerves and the Soul
flees this loathsome carrion (its goal
is elsewhere than this shadow of a dream)?

The body that in life pursued its lust
and hunger is refined to a name and then
chewed in the mouths of envious lying men,
its hope of fame corrupted to disgust.

Riven apart, the soul and body long
for one another and the world. The strong
bonds that held them having come apart,

as Heaven requires. Each one who dies on earth
must leave a corpse below for his rebirth—
save Enoch, or Elijah in his cart.

XII

I am beseiged and undermined, undone:
the World, the Flesh, and the Fallen Angel conspire
to ruin me, exploiting my desire . . .
Help me, O Lord! Seize me before I'm gone.

Send me a sign, a ship, a prop, relief
from some unexpected quarter. Lead me to
your sanctuary and heal me. See me through
this valley. Do not let me come to grief.

Your steady hand, your voice, your temple's door . . .
these are my only hope, and I implore
your mercy. Fend the Devil off and save

a desperate soul. Without that prop, that barque,
that sign I need and pray for in the dark,
I must go under, drowned by the next wave.

H*t*l M*rq**s

L.S. Asekoff

for Neil Schaeffer

So the Frenchman confuses roses with vaginas,
silk umbrella with manta ray.
All we do is but the pale image of what we dream of doing.
A flashing wing.
Vico's flower turning turning in the sun.

Imprisoned in his tower,
M. le Six,
a debauched libertine & lucid reasoning being,
lectures on the decay of lying
from Cain's jawbone to the megaphone
& the new *frisson*—transparent as water over sand
rippling through the executioner's hand.

Today, the Observers of the Society of Man
present *homo feris*, the wild child,
Victor,
V,
"the lost Dauphin."
Flushed by foxfires of the Revolution
from his savage solitude, the forests of Aveyron,
he's brought to justice by electric shocks from a Leyden jar,
taught to spell with heated metal letters pressed into his palm.

L-A-I-T he screams.
They roll him in the snowbanks of Rodez.

Bless the twice-born howling in the wind!
They've heard the whistle of the woodman's axe.
Crack a walnut. Fire a gun.
They startle, whimper, cringe.
They fear what grows out of them.
He shows them the root & flowering branch,
the hinge without the door,
saying, *The body is a threshold to be overcome!*

Supercilious light,
profil perdu, God's shadow
cast across the iron maiden of the bed,
"the obscene theater of sleep . . ."
As the red column falls
in a blizzard of black snow,
Floreal to Thermidor,
he sees the headless torso
& the flaming sword.
Ah, St. Just . . .
Darkest angel of our enlightenment . . .
Who stands between the guardian & the gate?
Who will watch the watchers of the State?

What is man? A jerkoff monkey?
Great Refusard
ejaculating giant figure 8's
across a shattered glass lake?
Intricate as Vaucasson's clockwork duck,
Leonardo's brazen-hearted lion,
the mirrored automata of the Turk,
this latest labor-saving device
(imp & engine of love's
perverse reversals,
reason's *cul-de-sac*),
severing head from heart
(*à la M. le Docteur Guillotine*)
exposes public virtue's secret vice:

to wit, an ergonomically designed
perpetual motion pleasure machine,
viz., this wicker basket with winesoaked wafer
fitted as bunghole for the Christmas goose
suspended by ratchets, harnesses, pulleys
triggered in a sequence of relays.
Now, take your novice, prelate, nun &
arranging them (as in *ill. 3*) isoscelesed,
inserting A to B & B to C & C to A
until libido sparks—an anserine squawk—*ergo* . . .
Divine Afflatus? Golden Egg? Virgin Birth?
The moral of such post-Euclidian cupidity?
The Holy seeing what It lacks
finds even the Devil does God's work!
Thus, my Citizens, in Revolution's arsy-
varsy *volte-face*
crown serves as chamberpot.
Down the chain of sacred obligations
all's tried & true—tit
for twat—*"noblesse oblige"*
to the Golden Rule:
The doer doing does as s/he's been done to.
Hence, having thrashed the scullery maid,
I made 18 marks upon the mantel &
lowering my britches passed the rod to her.
This I call *Spanish fly* or
"making love with the whiphand."

May wine.
High postillion of the clouds.
Eros over-ruled, there is disorder in the polis.
Bordello of wild horses!
Sorcerers of wind!
Inside the pink-throated daffodil I see
a red groom buggering the Emperor's white swan.
Long live the miracle of the three-minute egg!
My incandescent blue lieutenants,
my drabcapped wrens,
my delicate dove of Venus, porcelain shoe,
my petite truffled moon mined by the snuffling swine of Perigord,

your mauve unfoldings, dark declivities,
your puckered apricot & indigo delta!
Where disgust is the footman of desire
what is the end of all our light & lust?
Sweet cruelty's delight?
A weasel in a rathole!

In truth, Madame,
you may as well prove to a pig
rosewater custard tastier than shit
as teach a fool to think or
hoodwink a whore to virtue.
Let others gorge & swill where weak appetite will
for the man of reason & true libertine
freedom comes from following one's principles & pleasures.
Let the workmen laugh at you.
Obey my orders!
I want a top that screws
90 milimetres from the end,
a rosewood & ebony sheathe,
cutglass inner flask
turned to my own measure for, as you know,
I have my reasons!
(Any good woman can tell you
when sheathe comes loose in pocket, purse, *etui*
the surplus overflow too easily spills pellmell,
all 6's, 9's,
'til your fair sex lies in mortal danger of
being pricked by pins & needles of an errant pleasure,
pain's petty recusals, brief resurrections,
sin's pretty little rosaries of an infant bliss.)

Send me also, posthaste,
crock of stewed pears, pot of Brittainy butter,
3 doz. cherry gateaux of firmest texture
(not the dry-as-goat-turd tarts in your last batch),
orange blossom brandy, a bottle of *good* orgeat,
the pink taffeta hem torn from your loose gown,
3 ell-long green napkins,
6 doz. of M. le Noir's night candles,

12 plump baby thrush wrapped in bacon fat ripe for the spit,
beef marrow pomade, the horsehair cushion with a hole,
the aforesaid sheathe & cutglass dildo,
paper, pen, ink, per usual,
so I may singlehandedly practice,
as they say, my *"vertu Japonaise"*
& the following volumes: Toussaint's *Les Moeurs*;
Mystère d'Egypte; *Refutation de la Nature*;
& *Bas Empire*, in duodecimo.

Finally, here's a riddle fit for M. le Curé
& his brothel-keeper son,
the Honorable & Esteemed Archbishop of Lyons.
Once I had three children & a wife.
I was born in the bed my mother died in.
All night I held her in my arms.
Papa, Papa, she cried . . .
Now, Madame, let me iterate,
no threat or admonition of Church or State
can move me to deviate
from what I wish & what I will.
I'd pluck a quill from the dungiest swan,
dip it in Holy Virgin Blood
to write across the milky altar of each breast
my testament & philosophic faith:
Satisfy Thy Desires!
In closing, sweet Renée, nothing gives me greater pleasure
than to know thy pained heart
freely bound to one who remains as ever
your imprisoned Lord & Master,
M. de Sade.

Three Poems

Greg Delanty

Behold the Brahminy Kite

That the Brahminy Kite shares the name of a god is not
    improper
with its rufous body the tincture of Varkala's cliffs and
    white head matching the combers.
The kite riffs, banks and spirals; flapping black-tipped
    wings
that are mighty as the wings of the skate who might be
    the bird's shade in the stilly water.
The Brahminy makes light of the wind and circles the distant
    salt and pepper minarets of Odaayam Mosque
rising above the palms and the silence-made-susserus
    of the Lakshadweep Sea.
Now the kite is a silhouette in the glare of the sun,
    reminding me of vultures
above the secret Towers of Silence that Patti and I
    spotted from the Hanging Gardens.
They dined off cadavers of the followers of Zarathustra
    himself.
And in my way, I too believe, in the kasti—the sacred
    thread—of the elements
stitching us all together and would rather the kite pluck
    the flesh from my bones
than be laid in the dolled-up box of the West. When the time
    comes, imagine me the grub of the Brahminy.

Keep your elegy eye on the bird a day or so. Watch the kite
     make nothing of me.
Then, as I have now, give the Brahminy an almost imperceptible
     nod and turn and go.

Leper's Walk

We're away for slates, secure in the signifying gatch
of our city, gabbing about spotting the talent
along the meandering, quondam river of Patrick Street.
At the Saturday night disco, if the gauzer
stayed past the first dance for the clinger,
the fella made the move from a movie star peck
to a probing French kiss, but wait till at least
the second date and the all clear of heavy breathing
to slip the hand under a blouse along a quiet stretch
of the crepuscular Lee fields, Lough,
or Lover's Walk that's the epitome of a lover's walk.
Its winding incline skirts the city, blossom-confettied,
bordered with necking nooks and arbours.
And having long since chucked testing such love,
jilted, you half joke, by your own idyllic notion of amour,
doing a line now with your ersatz crush, Madam Words,
you switch to tell us with a lover's ardour how Lover's Walk
was Siúl na Lobhar in the Gaelic days, but the Sasanach
translator's mistook the Irish V sound.
Then maybe cúpla jorums too many, feeling jilted
by our city that you still can't let go, you turn inward.
And as if you yourself were the city, you fume
in a kind of shamanistic fury about how lepers secretly
trudged to the contagion hospital up this hill.
They bypassed locals, themselves infected
with the typical small town *mycobacterium laprae*,
the paralysis that no soul dare attempt anything
different, diagnosed as rising above one's station.
And whether you're right or no, for you I'd have the city
ring the bells of its malady and cleanse itself in the waters
of admission.
            And there are other unforeseen hybrids
rampant on the islands of Academe and Literati.
We stepped onto these shores with such expectation
of goodwill and safety, with such naivety,
certain the vaccine of these learnèd isles would protect
inhabitants from sickness, only to find here

strains not unlike the small town class: fear
of other island enclaves, numb envy
among islanders, immunity to the very spirit-vaccine
they themselves dose out, to say nothing of other
deformities, mutilations and lesions unchecked.
How can we escape who are surely infected now too?
Is there a makeshift raft camouflaged in some palms
of the patrolled banks of these mirage islands
that on some cloudless night we can sally forth on, raising
the tattered sails of our learning and be borne by
a kindly, out-of-the-dark zephyr away? We'd guide ourselves
by the night sky of humility, itself the journey's end,
accepting we must continue on the makeshift craft of knowledge.
My friend, for what else did we come all this way?

Notes on Cork Slang and Irish
away for slates: comfortable, satisfied, happy
gatch: a distinctive gait
spotting the talent: checking out distinctive young women and men
gauzer: attractive female
clinger: slow dance
Siúl: Walk
lobhar: pronounced lover, but means leper.
the *Sasanach*: the English
cúpla: couple
jorums: drinks

Prayer to St. Blaise

The Buddhist monks are up chanting and pounding their
       two-sided drums.
They've been at it since before dawn across the sanctuary
       of the lake
in the Temple of the Sacred Tooth, praying to the molar
       of Buddha.
Lately I find myself mumbling a Hail Mary or Our Father
       on the quiet
like I did in the old, short pants days when I thought I
       was in deep shit because I missed spelling,
was late for school or had impure thoughts about the Clark
       sisters, but now
I'm in trouble deep and childhood's terrors couldn't hold
       a candle to it.
What matter what the trouble is? We all know trouble—the
       royal trouble—what matter if I said
it's what must be called midlife crisis—Christ, such a
       suitably pathetic phrase. The candle of hope
guttering down into a malaise of disappointment about the whole
       hocus pocus, holus bolus ball of wax, even poesy—
I've lingered too long in the underworld of the poetry circle,
       another jostling jongleur jockeying to sup
from the blood of fame, or rather the ketchup, my ailing
       throat desperate to be heard.

*

Now I swear I'll beeline to the Holy Trinity or whatever
       chapel when I'm back in the country of churches.
I'll not care a damn if any bookish crony spots me dip
       my hand in the font
as I slip inside to kneel among the head-scarved women
       lighting votive candles,
beseeching their special saint for whatever ordinary
       miracles.
I'll light a candle at some saint's side altar, Saint
       Blaise preferably.

Around his feast day I'll queue up for the X of a pair
    of crossed candles to V wax my throat
in the hands of a priest lisping the Latin blessing
    that my voice box not fail.
Sound. I'll chance this. I'll come again to poetry pax.
    I'll kneel before my childhood's sacred tooth.

Kindertotenlieder

Joshua Weiner

Not a day ended that the mind did not seek
    a spot in the mind,

tender and dark, bruised by a fear
    finding its shape there,

that neither grew nor deepened, but only ached
    always, reminding

something could, at any moment, sometime
    happen, could happen

as things happened, and they could (and did)
    happen, for example, to anyone—

to his sweet dirt genius, queen prankster, joy bean:
    little girl *kinder*

bright unafraid millennium's child,
    waking each day

like a sun rising new on the world,
    eager to shine original

and burn it up with attention—the bruise
    of *could happen*

could bloom just like a day dream
    that takes you in transport

for the long trip's duration
        as moment by moment

the window frames a new picture
        (a trip that once started never can end . . .)

Composer obsessed, he stayed on board with it,
        traveling further

into discolored regions, filling his heart
        with the heart's bitter juices

—bruise sap, wound gas—to make from his fear
        of what could, perchance, happen

a cycle of songs on the death of children
        which deepened the bruise

with the heat of making, his full attention
        to shaping, to saying,

to singing fiercely what he could not
        dwell on, or in

until what had not happened
        rose up a house of song.

And when his wife protested
        that fate had been tempted,

he had no license to take another man's poems
        built from real grief

and set them to music,
        was he crazy

in love with disaster, spoiled by fame,
        or proving (again)

he was more than some thought him,
        a frustrated conductor . . .

And when his own daughter died
      afterward—

after the work was completed,
      receiving praise

and kisses from friends filled with envy
      (who loved him more for it);

after he too sat on several occasions,
      listening again

to hear just how good, rightly made and sung,
      and so deserving

praise, and stood for applause—
      after all that: accomplishment

burned to ash; and the mind's bruise
      (the taste of ash all he tasted)

opened its patient, dread primordium
      as if perennial

and long overdue, and he heard
      the songs anew—

a dark magic now, a mocking invocation
      to some god, to God,

to make what was sung true now
      to fact, and scatter

the notes coherent in the ear,
      such that his ear

could no longer hear music
      where once it seemed mind

found a contour through sound:
      his songs made this happen.

Now gone beyond our heat we feel you light
            Us with our loss, and we burn bright—

So I wrote on the death of another's boy,
            how they dreamed him a man

Who, in the world, remembered us as well
            And loved us finally,

as we love him still. And still I feel
            the mother's bodily warmth

surprising me with her thankful embrace
            for a poem I wrote

as a kind of professional, carried
            to experience

on *poesy's wing* flapping in strained imitation
            behind the forged weld

between that and this, there and here,
            then and now . . .

Yet I know I felt something, the movie of losing
            what was not mine to lose

entertaining and twisting me all through the night
            as I worked at the page

for right combinations I might steal
            or conceive . . .

And it spoke to her so fresh in her grief,
            as if annihilating sadness

could warm to life such inert manipulations,
            like a golem sparked

by a rebbe's learned and greedy tongue
            (to turn to its maker, and turn on its maker) . . .

And I have a son now—imagination sprung
        grubby and driven—

rising hot from dream sheets to master
        the world:

truck, pop, water, up,
        block, two, egg, shoe—

though not a day ends that the mind does not seek
        a spot in the mind.

tender and dark, bruised by a fear
        finding its shape there—

Mahler's *Kindertotenlieder* a warning and a question
        I cannot keep from asking,

as this poem also would not stay unwritten,
        my own need for *never*

pulling me to it, as now I sing it
        (now almost sung)—

the poem you hear from my mouth
        to your ear,

will it find further life on some fateful
        tongue called to taste it,

that even now might be wagging
        with ardent incantation,

obscenely coaxing its nightmare
        stalk to bloom?

Two Poems

Charlie Smith

Five

Inexplicable foreign substance of life,
blue sky with milk solids squeezed into a corner,
an unusual configuration of adolescents
trading hand shots . . . yesterday
a fleet of old women arrived on the block,
returned to the school they graduated from 60 years ago,
rushing along blown by ancient breeze,
45 voyageurs returned from the impossible journey
carrying tales of joy and hardship
endured . . . it got cold last week then warm again:
in Denver snow: in DC drought
curls sycamore leaves, plucks feathers from the oaks:
here they've turned the fountains off, businessmen
hardly notice, they buy shirts on Broadway
eating Italian ices . . . someone fires a gun and
the crowd scatters, soon returns like a flock
resettling . . . very soon there's harmony,
a sense we will go on moving along together . . .
always some crisis to be avoided,
sidled past . . . women talking on the phone . . . three artists
meeting for coffee, competing with each other, saying
a few amazing things, not even trying to come clean,
a light dancing in one woman's eyes, memory
joined suddenly with some
episode in the present, something distinct
like the scent of basil, a touch she remembers,

recalling a weekend on the Cape . . .
other friends dissemble and delay,
one loses track of another's interests,
confuses an important point, the friendship
dwindles, fades . . . there are men scolding
children early today, a woman leans
against a tree eating an orange, celebrants
step into churches to pray . . . a passerby rushes
into a hotel to ask a favor,
goes on thinking of a bet he might place,
recalls a maple with one red branch like knitting
unraveled over a paddock, remembers bells rung all night
at the French Society, car races,
a word he might use: he thinks of his wife
bobbing her head crying as she
tried to explain, pictures her tipped
on the examining table grimacing as the doctor probed . . .
sometimes he thinks there's
nothing he can do . . . it's late morning,
buses arrive from the Hamptons bringing
the slack and sated few
to their commitments in town; there's an argument
taking place at the top of the stairs:
a union organizer frets over some papers
he left in a bar; you can see the World Trade Center through
haze . . . a lawyer eats a steak sandwich . . .
tomorrow there will be a special section
on Middle Eastern poets: the tide's in:
a child memorizes his third prayer: carts rumble
on Fulton street: the curator dusts
the Marconi equipment: many take to pathways running
for health . . . *You could have told me,*
the girl says, beginning to smile,
and there's a rush, a sense of momentum gathered and
thrust forward, a change of speed, of something
about to happen . . . you look up
and see the sky, streaked white:
it's still early,
as if a new era has just begun . . . it's possible
to live unresolved, inconclusively

and without appeal . . . you take a walk in the park,
take a few minutes off and watch the squirrels
dodge and run . . . there's not much you can do,
nothing helps much . . . you may be seeing things. . .
the same vicious couple feeds pigeons,
the artist places sheets of paper on the grass,
everything speaks for itself.

Rapid, Impossible Placement of Fact

. . . Chinese market salesmen, unnoticed in their inestimable grace,
scoop eels, pomfret, flat silver bream into bags,
weigh peanuts, antique yellow apples, they
tend small gardens in the mind, give change,
a man stands apart watching, his hands in his pockets . . .
this is you if you like . . . under Manhattan Bridge, dark spaces
felled like trees piled in windswept forests, mountainsides
turned dark by rain, no light enters these dank
areas under the bridge where Chinese businessmen discuss
gambling traditions and small women push children along,
it's late in the day in Lower Manhattan, cross-hatched streets,
vague purplish light of Succoth, huts and reedy palm-strewn
floors, young men returning from visits to elderly relatives,
old men on benches, old women on opposite benches . . . you
make a place for yourself, rest a second, short structures,
a street branches off, north tending, a man stands dreaming
in shadow, a rosary in his hands, there are children everywhere,
lost, craven glances, strutting ganglords, frail wives
mistaking a patch of blue sky
for hope . . . you might find what you were
looking for, a madness unveiled but without penetration,
absolved from something desperate, a kind of anxiety
always a part of life now, sturdy barrows,
placements controlled by larger forces, a formula possibly,
possibly not, no one gives away much, you
recognize the library, books in Chinese,
a girl looks up from a shop window places a thousand years
of culture in your hand, a boy eats an orange,
here a painter gathers himself, you think of Ronceveaux,
paintings that are a means of not flying apart, anxious age,
variety in every window, *There must be something*, she says,
you'd like—what about a figurine? but there is no time,
it's late in the year, the street bends left, downhill
a park appears, sunlit trees in full leaf, a dusty faded light
against the side of a building the only sign of fall,
radiance sustained in the mind by love did you say,
stop now to eat sugary fried pastry, leaf-wrapped

indescribable concoction raised on a stick, a girl
with slick silky hair lifts her face
to the light, you become mythologized by this, find your way,
vague patchy music begins, from Buddhist temple
exit old ladies as from Catholic churches,
sunlight stands wearily outside a jewelry store,
turns slightly and scowls . . . it's time for other dimensions,
all investigations . . . the police arrest themselves . . .
all fruits of labor to be recalled . . . spoiled . . . given up
for the night which is almost here
in its drapery and fine words . . . you seek shelter,
bob and dance slightly, it comes with the dusk,
soft lights go on, streaked glassy thin colors fill
the air below dark windows, cries, imaginings begin,
it was always later, you push through the solid doors of night,
a book in your hand, pockets the exchange artists
haven't gotten to, you look around . . . city
stalled on the way up from its knees, ressurecters,
excavators all working late, prancy short-change artists
without depth or meaning come forth
to explain the rhythms of the impersonal touch . . .
soon all will pass away . . . someone pours beads into the street,
a blond dog strains at his leash, the slim gangster
eating ice cream surveys the scene and smiles, *Long day*,
someone says and heads home, night drops like a diving horse,
falls, day like a false destiny departs the scene,
it is as if you have imagined your life, testimony, the hard
red fingernails of a woman on Canal, a brilliant set of conjurings,
the face of man scanning the territory combines will and fate
in a mix so intricate there is no way to separate them.

What They Remember

Brian Henry

For the record he assiduously adhered to the speed limit
Except for that one time
That time he daisied around the bend
They say he pursued the lascivious side of life until the end
He fell in with the religious crowd while an infant
That squirrel still carries a pellet behind the ear
They say he was a generous man
Orphanages foreclosed in his name
He always knocked before entering
They say he had a tendency to enter through a bathroom window
And no one home
And no one home
They say he never broke a bone
He never spliced a comma
Or used exclamation points in a profligate manner
The Fourth of July was his favorite holiday
The fireworks scared him half to death
They say the Fates smiled on him at birth
Someone cut the cord
He'd no sooner look you in the eye than salute the president
They say his car would stop on a dime
They say he drove an injured animal to church on Sundays
And put his groceries in the trunk
They say the groceries sat in the front
With that poor animal in the trunk
They say he had a nervous twitch
He never owned a bird
They say he drove his cockatoo crazy with his continual knitting

He wove his way into highfalutin circles
He didn't know a thing about antiques
They say a peeping Tom at the window caught his eye
The rest of him remained free
Freedom of choice kept him awake
He slept only on Wednesday
He slept like the dead on vacation in Cuba
They say he could play any tune by ear
A keen financial acumen marked his life
They say he bled the coffers dry
He paid his tithes religiously
Any sudden movement would throw him completely off kilter
He looked cute in a skirt
They say he could thread a needle with his eyes closed
He peeked when in public
They say he never missed a beat
You couldn't knock it out of him
They say he could have been in the movies
He forgot a line or two at times
He recovered remarkably well for his age
They say he had a thing for candles
Brittle brittle days
They say he shot the bolt a bit early now and then
Now and then he stayed in for the long haul
He got caught with his pants down once
Under the bleachers
Under a full moon in the park
They say he never bounced a check
For honor is all a man has
What good is a man without honor
He yelled Damn! when he fell from the monkey bars
For honor is all a man has
He forged solid relations with his neighbors
They say he could hit a nail on the head
They say he never worried about mutual funds
Compound interest drove him to the brink
He never touched the stuff
Except on Wednesday
He pitched horseshoes on Wednesdays
On Wednesday he was puritanical about everything

His ancestors were tramontanes
Hard to pin down
You couldn't pin down his ancestors
For they were tramontanes
They say his soul outshone the sun
They say we didn't know him as well as they did
He made no mention of that squirrel in his will
They say he didn't give anyone anything

Two Poems from Nova Cantica

John Peck

As at Beauvais,
so also
with vaults and ogives steepling
in a raw try

from my own hands:
the ribs
crush walls of the first attempt—
and the builder finds

his clues among
wreckage,
how stresses yet might better
jam downward, hang

outward in skirts
spilling
lanes of support, and send him,
beyond the carts

hauling it all
away,
glimpses of what next time
will stand, with the feel

of his will rising
up through
tonnage and mortared seams,
the piled weight easing.

For the small will
jamming
close up against the project
is not the soul

that builds. Sweat-lather
with one stone
shows that you don't do it,
that it's another

at work. He rode
from rubble
out into the fields
where young he'd plowed

frustrate, from where,
had it stood,
the high nave would have promised
a basis. Peer

from that limit
and perhaps
you see what holds and what acts
at the point set

for your labor
and your
surrender. He stood, looking.
He stood to bear.

Into the fields
where ache is,
sweat into dirt, where one can't
glide rippled golds

along the glance—
vision,
we are assured, is vast, now—
but strong the hints

that such scope calls
down on us
the listlessness of the cheated.
It is weight pulls

down and down, thus
oozing
the mind forth—is it strange
that we must pass

that gate and torque
to become
vintage? But first to be
in the bone work

and the drag sleep
seeking
no merit there, lost there
until one slip

into the unroofed
blessing
of the brute thing, no image,
and so enough

into being
at home
while at risk to find risk
homely, knowing

such is the field
tilled
and the stocks tended: crush
us until galled

rebellion go
off with
the pulp and skin, and casks
seal the rest, do,

construe the brines
of our blood
through the relentless ferment
that attains.

*

*Giovanni, would you
see me
alle cinque, Chiesa Nuova?
To talk. I have to.*

Overworked teacher
and weary
paterfamilias,
shy would-be searcher . . .

we had been guests
at a friend's.
Now I sat where the Corso
Vittorio thrusts

widest, the smooth
steps ripple
away from the barney church
and pigeons breathe

stertorously
among bronze
hours, and watched a protest
march gather hoarsely

in the oblong square,
the blind
gypped by the state led there
by the blind to roar

through their bull horns
and step off
in waveringly good order.
A cart of melons

got sideswiped by
a leathery
motorcyclist, who doffed
helmet and drew

up to the splatter
and paid for
three more than he had smashed
The old man twittered.

A waif on crutches
swung and
swung through the mess with whoops
kicking swatches

of rind, a crone
cackling
back of him filched one up
to taste, alone. . . .

Then it was those
I'd remarked
other evenings, now brushing
strangers, and haze

from the late rush
acridly
holding the heat, and the whole
air of it threshing

slowly and greatly
up through
that vast parlor, none of us
explicitly

invited, over
our criss-cross
making for the blue ceiling
with a sound never

quite spoken out
and a fragrance
obscurely of the occasion,
of all those there met—

so I sat for
three hours,
and the desperate man never showed,
who in his rare

delicacy
had dispatched
all that company, all
those beings to me—

their half or no greeting,
or straight on,
aiming at something we all sensed,
moving, or waiting—

my appointment
was with them,
and now, these years since, with
this deep content.

Five Poems

Phillis Levin

Futile Exercise

How do I put together
The way he gently held my finger,
Feeling for a splinter,

And the cruelty of later;
Or his thoughtlessness two years after,
When he invited me to dinner

In the final week of summer
And announced in less than an hour
That he was sorry

He had to be somewhere—
After noting how the grids of cities differ,
Then recalling his journey

To the prettiest town he'd ever seen,
Where he took it easy
In a valley in Kentucky

Whose name and memory
Made his face warm over
Before he changed the subject abruptly

The moment we smiled at each other;
How do I account for
His sudden interruption,

A conversation leading to terror
For no good reason,
And his courteous offer

To walk with me to the building
We lived in together,
Although we hadn't met in a year;

And how explain my rising
Sense of danger
As he said goodbye at the elevator

And I saw inside his opening door
Pieces of plaster
Covering the floor,

And then a week later
Saw the fracture
Running down his hallway mirror,

Repeating a riddle
No one could answer—
Why the scholar who was a dancer

Came to stand himself no longer;
Who can fit together
What made him show the super

A twisted chair his fist had beaten
Until it finally was broken,
And who can tell

Why days before
In the entrance hall
He stared at me, unblinking, feral,

And how connect the rampage of a mind
With a hand
So bent on order,

That cleaned the coffee pot completely
Or lowered the arm of a record player
Onto Mahler;

How do I put together
The hand that touched mine
And the cold revolver

Ending failure
When he pulled the trigger
With the finger that found

The splinter
He was after
Before

Morning Exercise

Line by line I unremember you:
Places your mouth hid, and where
Your teeth almost bit through
My skin, leaving a necklace

Whose blue pearls lingered
For days—a few scattered across
My chest, as if you broke a strand
Whenever you left. Say nothing

About how you are, or who
You have been, say nothing
Now that there is nothing to say.

It is useless to ask for a word,
Useless to know what is true.
Line by line I unremember you.

There

for Steffen Stelzer

It was somewhere else,
Not in my heart.
The room not moving
But on the moving one,

A shape ablaze
With color and scent.
Not here, but there:
Not with me or for me,

Not mother, father, light.
But light made it happen.
Dark pushed it away

And made it closer, too.
It was cool, separate,
Just beginning to be.

Intervals in Early August

I.

I don't know how it is where you are now.
Mostly, I watch the trees move,
Though today they aren't doing much at all,
Except this instant when I wrote them down

And they began to sway the way they do
When a breeze out of nowhere stirs the air.
It seems the wind behaves erratically
As if to show us that we cannot say

What is sure without effacing it,
Or what is true without assuming light
Awakens beside a shadow of doubt.

Do you feel empty because the earth
Is full, and does a door slam shut
When a gust promises to change you?

II.

In the woods this morning a veil fell
Over everything, as if memory
Were in hiding and would not be back.
I almost panicked, then felt such relief

Untethered as that leaf upon the lake,
Not grieving or desiring anyone,
Content to look without a sense of loss
Until I saw another leaf nearby,

And focusing too long on the line
Between them created the illusion
Of a mirror holding nothing but a sky

Concealing nothing underneath, and all
At once I was dissolving into it
And in a moment the world could sink.

III.

In a second we were suspended
Like clouds in a bottomless chamber,
With no chance to alter shape or color,
Sentenced to float forever on a surface

That held the promise and the threat
Of changelessness, until a bubble
Newly forming on the lake
Glinted in the sun as it broke

Inaudibly into a ring of light
Whose radiating center disappeared.
A silver fish swam into sight,

Clearly going somewhere as well,
In deep enough waters off the shore
To live undisturbed by surfaces.

IV.

How would it sound if we could hear
The pop of that bubble,
Hovering there
Like a dragonfly at the exact interval?

What if we could enter
The fraction of time in which
A tadpole by the switch
Of a neurotransmitter

Turns from a darting creature
Into a frog who blinks on a lily-pad
Under the moon as a hand on a pad

Of paper scribbles notes on nature,
Trying to measure
All we are after?

On the Other Hand

The leaves of the ivy
Are heavy today.
Even we are too heavy,
Their shadows say:

Nothing moves us,
We cannot stray
Across a walkway.
But glory is still green.

Whoever leaned
Against a screen
Unlatches the door,

Whoever said
There, there, now
Doesn't anymore.

from Plot

Claudia Rankine

Submerged deeper than appetite,

she bit into a freakish anatomy, the hard plastic of filiation,
a fetus dream, once severed, reattached. The baby femur
not forktender though flesh, the baby face now anchored.

What Ersatz would make would be called familial, not foreign.
forsaken. She knew this and tried to force the scene, remake the
world. In the dream, snapping, the crisp rub of thumb to index,
she was in rehearsal with everyone, loving the feel of cartilage,
ponderous of damaged leaves. And only she singing
internally, only she revealed, humming, undressing a lullaby:
Bitterly, bitterly, sinkholes to underground streams—

In the dream, waist-deep, retrieving a fossilized pattern forming
in attempt to prevent whispers or poisoned regrets, reaching into
reams and reams, to needle seam a cord, in the stream; as if
a
wish borne out of rah rah's rude protrusion to follow the
rest
was sporded, split and now, hard-pressed to enter the birth.

In the dream the reassembled desire to conceive wraps the
tearing placenta to a walled uterus, urge formed complicit. First
portraying then praying to a womb ill-fitting. She grows fat.

The drive in utero is fiction-filled, arbiter of the cut-out infant
and main-streamed. Why birth the other to watch the seam rip,

to roughly conjoin the lacerating generations (lineage means
to step here on the likelihood of involution. And then hard not
to notice the depth of rot at the fleshy roots. To this outbreak
of doubt, she crosses her legs. The weight of one thigh on the
next constructing rectitude, the heavy, heavy notion of no.

Ersatz,

outside of this insular-traffic a woman in pink underlining the
alias of gender. Who is she really? Call her, could you, would
you call her?

The hope under which Liv stood,

her craven face, it clamored. The trumpeter announced it.
She stood more steady then, marveling at some stammering,
hammering heart, collecting a so invisible breath. feeling
extreme. commencing. deeper than some feeling was.

She wanted what he had been told she'd want, what she was,
expecting. Then the expecting was only a remembering.
remembering to want. She was filling her mouth up with his—
yet it was not. it was not the sound of sucking on the edge of
sleep. not soft brush of cheek. not the heat of the hand along
the neck. There is a depiction, a picture, someone else's boy
gorgeously scaled down and crying out and she not hearing,
not having, not bearing Ersatz—

She was filling her mouth up with his name yet it was not.
it was not

Liv forever approaching the boy like toddler to toy. the
mothering more forged than known. the coo, coo rising air
bubbles to meet colustrum, yellow to blue to milk. not having
to learn, knowing by herself. Come closer—

in front the glare, pools in straining veins making Liv
nervy. Malachite half moons on each lobe listening inward,
the hormonal trash heap howling back.

There is dust from a filed nail. The wind lifts, carries it into
ambient light: not monochromatic, not flattened but isolating,
solicitous, soliciting. Come closer—

Once Liv thought pregnancy would purify. You, Ersatz,
as plot, as place, not sign of guilt, not site of murder.

Then of course. of course. when do we not coincide elsewhere
with the avoided path. a sharp turn toward the wombed
shaped void.

Liv is feeling in vitro. duped. a dumbness of chimes. no
smiles for every child so careful, so careful

Ersatz

infant, bloomed muscle of the uterine wall, you still pink
in the center, resembling the saliva slick pit of the olive,
resembling tight petals of rose, assembling

Ersatz

this name was said. Afterward, its expression wearing the ornate
of torment, untouched by discretion, natural light or (so rumored

(and it, once roused, caused dis-ease as if kissed full on the mouth.

Herself assaulting the changing conditions, Liv added
desire's stranglehold, envisaged its peculiarly pitched ache
otherwise alien to her wildly incredulous hopes: Ersatz

Ersatz

Aware of your welt-rising strokes, your accretion of theme, Liv
was stirring, no, breathing the dream. She was preventing a crust
from forming, the bony attachment was gaining its tissue
like a wattle and daub weave.

Ersatz,

arrival is keyhole-shaped, it allows one in the assembled warren
of rooms to open the game box even as the other leans against
the exposed from her freestanding, exaggerated perspective.

She is in her way, in the corridor unable to enter this room.
And if she prays to be released from you as one would
pray to be released from tinnitus or welt: boy ridge of flesh
raised by a blow,

imagine in your uncurl of spinal arch, her eye your eye, an
apparition hushed to distortion, her heart unclosed, yet warped
by dullness and pure feeling, her lips but a crease re-crossing
time, needing a softer tone.

Imagine the prayer itself,

Ersatz,

unswallowed, swollen within her lips so grieved:

Ersatz,

Here. Here. I am here.

inadequately and feeling more and more less so because of not
feeling more. But stopped. For I am of course frightened of you,
what your bold face will show me of me. I am again leading to
regret. I have lived, Ersatz, the confusion in my head. The
fusion that keeps confusion, could it keep you? Could it make
those promises to remedy tortuous lines, thickening encroachings?

I could quadruple my intent toward you, be your first protection.
But Ersatz, my own, birth is the limiting of the soul, what is
trapped with it already owns. I could not wish a self on any self
as yet unformed though named and craved. Oh Ersatz, I am here
and here is not analogous to hope. I can see past the birth into
the eyes of you, into what inconveniently overstates resemblance.

That sort of resemblance one might wish to tuck under
the arm, into the sweat of the armpit, its wiry odor of exhaustion,

remembering the self and any reflection thereof
is never a thing to cradle. Ersatz,

were I coward enough to have you, child, coward enough to
take my pain and form it into a pulsing, coming round the
corner any odd day, of course, of course, I would believe you
the intruder. had intruded.

Provoked, Ersatz, the best I could be would be shivering illness,
mucus rising, the loud rush of sob.

I am made uncomfortable and more so, and not warmer, no
closer to the everyone you are. Already the orphan, suffocated
and overlapping a trillion faces—

Are you utterly anywhere? Have we, have we arrived
anywhere? Ersatz,

has the rudimentary ear curled open, are you here?

Intermission

What comes through the bloodstream to be flushed reduces him to
human even as he does not breathe, even as his lids lower. This is the
thick beginning, one-third of an inch below the upper surface of her
swirling pit, the place he fills, fills with viscid fuel and yet somehow
does not drown him in the basement membrane of her own convoluted,
veined, capillary network. Her own ocean of wear. He is blister of cell,
grain named embryo, a climbing substance perceived, absorbing such
intimacy as she can offer. Nourished, absorbing, coaxed forward in the
presence of her whole presence, consequence of her consequences.

Ersatz,

of freehand sketchiness,

of hollow form,

anonymous, delineation of bone,

of moody hue dipped in fetal city,   oh so neatly laid.

within Liv,

estranged interlacing

that she is.

Are their seasoned movements truly without desire? Is her organized
breath simply a direction as his face forms in his eggplant-purple landscape, the likeness of no other? There now is the peculiar sound of
blood flowing, a soft pulpy whoosh aquatic, the spreading heart-shaped
mouth darkly stained, untidy eyebrows, a mole blemish-shaped. In the
minds-eye, never abandoned are the supposed markings on the boy.
What is seen before his profile splinters is a face that looks and is certainly startled.

How not to smile out loud.

The Insult

Howard Norman

for Jonathan Galassi

As for what happened to us, our thoughts at the time, what was said and not said—that movie, "This Woman Is Dangerous," we watched twelve consecutive nights on the grade-school projector in the Churchill train station, Eskimo audiences, dungeon clank of the stoves, the Arctic nights—I wish that I could talk to Helen even now, twenty years after her death, because there are still so many things to talk about.

Helen's unrequited love with the world. "It's true, I was blessed in getting to work with dignified people in remote and beautiful parts of the world. I heard wonderful stories. I saw birds far from where I was born,"—letter dated March 19, 1978—"but I wasn't given enough time. I simply wasn't. I don't feel forgiving about that. I'm referring to Fate, with a capital F, not faith, with its tiny f. This dying, it's an insult. I'm grateful for what I was given. But I feel insulted." That was my friend Helen Tanizaki, age thirty-nine, who loathed any convenient notions of solace. I knew Helen for two months, September and October, 1977 in Churchill, the town situated in Manitoba at the mouth of the Churchill River on Hudson Bay, where we were both working with the elderly Eskimo man, Mark Nuqac. Helen was translating his stories into Japanese. I was translating them into English. This was unforeseen; we had never met. We had arrived from opposite ends of the earth. Helen once described our experience at "a strange linguistic duet." The phrase pleased her.

One night, after viewing a grainy print of "This Woman Is Dangerous," a 1952 noir starring Joan Crawford, we stood outside the depot, watching a group of young Eskimo boys and girls, roughly age twelve or thirteen, smoking cigarettes. We recognized them. They had seen the movie every night that we had. I began a disquisition, replete with self-generated theories, nonsense, really, on the movie's "larger" implications, this meaning and that, when Helen interrupted me, "Life's gotten away from you. You've taken a simple basic plot and—." She stopped, exasperated, scarcely able to speak or take in breath. We stood in silence a moment. Then, as if drawn by a magnet, we both turned in the direction of the Churchill River. Out over the tundra was a display of aurora borealis, not uncommon at the end of summer, which, in the Arctic, more or less is the beginning of winter. We saw our breath clouding. This aurora was a subdued palette, compared to the outlandish, even haunting—in the sense of suggesting a mythological experiment, the inchoate time when the world was being formed—curtains of undulating colors, the near hallucinatory resplendence of deep winter auroras. Those you sometimes can actually hear crackling. Still, this one had a quietly arresting nature, off-white, blue, green tingeing to lighter green, flecks of red like spattered paint. Neither of us commented on it. Perhaps comment would have demoted the experience. Anyway, Helen insisted on making her point. Both of her hands on my shoulders, she said, "Look: the movie's simply about a woman gangster who won't give up on love." Then, as if the effort to get purchase on the essence of things had utterly depleted her strength, Helen crumpled like a marionette, not quite to the ground. She caught herself. I was too late. "Guess I'm not up to discussing this just now," she said. She was so ill.

In memory, it is a still-life, "The Argument," call it—was it that, an argument? I think, yes, our voices carried a certain pitch of annoyance. The Eskimo kids looked over—; otherworldly lights pulsing above the river, me, Helen, collars turned up against a chill night, emotions running every which-way, though not, finally, intimately toward each other. Then we walked on to the Beluga Motel.

"Looking back on it"—letter dated March 27, 1978— "I consider our friendship lovely, hermetic, difficult." Helen had a way with words; besides which, I don't contest her opinion.

In late August of 1978, I stood on a cliff near Cape Freels, Newfoundland, and scattered Helen Tanizaki's ashes to the wind. Cape Freels is located between Newtown and Lumsden, and reached by tributary road off the Trans Canada Highway. A decade earlier, Helen had watched birds from pretty much this same spot. She and her Dutch husband, Cees, spent, as Helen put it, the "relatively calm" final week of their turbulent marriage visiting outports in Nova Scotia and Newfoundland. Having arrived in Halifax from London, they drove to Cape Breton. A few days later, they flew to St. Johns, then drove to Trinity Bay where they spent the night, ironically enough, in Salvage. The next day they drove to Cape Freels. After Cape Freels, they turned back. So, perhaps Helen thought of the locale as a place of endings and beginnings. "We took a belated honeymoon," Helen told me. "First, we suspected we'd been impetuous to enter into the marriage; finally, we felt like we'd aged badly in it." She had married Cees, an architectural student in Paris, when she studied Mythology and Linguistics at College de France. The marriage lasted not quite two years. "Cees was a nice man, but too fearful." They returned by ferry, Newfoundland to Nova Scotia, stayed at Haliburton House, a few blocks up from the Historic District in Halifax. En route, Helen kept a list of the birds she saw, as was her custom. Then Cees went to San Francisco to be an architect. In order to finish her Ph.D. thesis in linguistics, Helen returned to Eskimo communities in Greenland, Repulse Bay, Baffin Island, and Melville Island in the high Arctic. "Now and then," Helen said, "Cees and I wrote letters. They were very formal. Then we stopped."

Helen's mother was British, her father Japanese. They had met in Kyoto. Helen was born in London, but raised from ages three to fifteen in Kyoto. Her family then returned to England. In their house they spoke English and Japanese. By age eighteen, she was fluent in French as well. Helen had a brother, two years younger, named Arthur. Throughout their life, Helen called him "Artie-Tan." Arthur eventually settled in Kyoto, took up bookbinding, married (Arthur's wife became Helen's closest friend), had two daughters, and became a book designer as well.

Helen's Last Will & Testament instructed that Arthur allow me to disperse her ashes, specifically "off the Newfoundland coast at Cape Freels." By telephone, I suggested the ashes be sent to the central post office in St. Johns. Arthur and I had a two or three minute conversation, Toronto-Kyoto. (I still kept a one-room apartment in Toronto.) He got right to the point; I offered condolences, he said thank you. I knew from her letters that Helen had told Arthur that we were friends. To some extent, I was a convenience. For one thing, I was often in the Canadian Maritimes, often out of work, not so urgently occupied that it wasn't easy for me to facilitate Helen's request. Helen knew all of this from letters I'd sent her, as well. Still, I wondered if perhaps Arthur was bewildered, even angered by her posthumous assignation with me and Cape Freels, Helen's choice not to remain after death in Japan, that is. I suspect, however, Arthur had been made to understand that looking forward to her spirit being among Newfoundland sea bird haunts—which she particularly loved—offered Helen comfort. She had spoken this very sentence to me, "I believe in reincarnation, conceptually." Her final letters to me indicated, however, that her heretofore tentative belief was profoundly focused. "I now think"—letter dated April 7, 1978—"it's quite possible." For Helen to designate "Cape Freels," meant she could at least control the demographics of afterlife, and if there wasn't such a thing—: ". . . if I don't become a fjord ghost, shore bird, or any other thing on my short list of preferences, I won't know it anyway." So be it. At the post office, I signed the customs form, took possession of the small package. It was festooned with Japanese stamps.

I rented a car, then drove to Cape Freels. The wind that day, August 27, was truly wild. The sea air was ventriloqual; the keenings and crying of gulls seemed to ricochet off an invisible wall far to my left, while the gulls themselves were seen off to my right. No more than half a mile offshore, Cory's shearwaters were eddying in great numbers around an enormous iceberg. Cory's, Sooty, and Greater Shearwater summer in the North Atlantic. Icebergs in August were not all that uncommon in these waters. Every so often, a gust of cold wind swept in from the iceberg, which seemed capable of producing its own weather system, and brushed over me like a ghostly presence. On the flight up from Halifax, I had seen an aerial view of this iceberg; the pilot had circled it on behalf of tourists. It looked like a white planet floating in light blue space, a few updraft combs of cloud in between. Now, standing atop the cliff, I could distinguish the darker blue of the current. Still, such was this iceberg's enormous illusion of fixity, I had to study it through binoculars in order to determine that it was actually drifting. Waves lapped up against it. I used to collect descriptions of icebergs from books, explorer's journals, northern diaries. In 1887, for example, one Lieut. T. Reynolds, described an iceberg emitting "a groaning crescendo," which echoed. Having myself heard something of their acoustic repertoire, the creaks, moans, calving avalanches, I can corroborate Lieut. Reynolds' testimony, that icebergs produce the more guttural notes in the Music of the Spheres.

In its transport south to Canadian waters, wind had eroded, gouged, and hollowed the iceberg, so that, near the center of its upper tier, were three somewhat amorphic shapes, resembling a Henry Moore-sculpted parent sitting with two children. Shearwaters, some perhaps hitching a ride for days on end, swirled from their shoulders. Through binoculars, I took notice, too, of puffins, a pudgy, comical, gaudy-billed bird—excellent divers—which old-time fishermen called the "parrot of the sea." However, puffins kept to the opposite side of the iceberg; they catapulted up into view, looped crazily, then dropped below the horizon of ice again. An elderly, bearded fellow drove up and parked his pickup truck behind my car, about fifty feet from where I stood. He crouched out, gave me a hard stare, and left the truck door open. He was lanky, slightly stooped, wore a double layer of sweaters, black trousers, fisherman's galoshes. He walked up beside me, nodded hello, leaned over the cliff. In a Scottish accent, he said, "Dizzy-down-sheer." Then he got back into his truck and drove on. It indeed was a harrowingly steep line of vision between cliff and sea, where, in between woven rugs of slick kelp, I occasionally glimpsed a shadowy whale. Finally, after an hour or so mindlessly gazing at birds, I recalled a letter in which Helen wrote, "The Ainu people, in Hokkaido, are capable of what they call, 'Travel off the earth.' They stare at birds until their minds fly out of their bodies. Enviable, huh?" Suddenly I was wont to follow suit, stare until the sun went down and the last light faded, in hopes of successfully flying out of myself. But I had these new hiking boots on; they hurt my feet. I was stuck in the quotidian world, the earthly domain. Not Helen, though. Finally, I unwrapped the brown paper. Tucked under the cloth wrapping was a small envelope. I slid out its note. In her elegant English cursive, Helen had presciently written, "As long as you are there, you may as well look at birds." I opened the beautiful lacquer box which depicted a flight of Japanese cranes, and held it at arm's length above my head. Cross winds scooped out the ashes, casting them like black confetti every which way. Gulls came in for a look; nothing they could use. Starkly inimitable moment, delivering Helen's ashes. Gratifying, surprisingly not sad, albeit slightly chilling. In my life I have regretted nothing less. Most importantly, of course, it was a promise kept. Once all the ashes had disappeared, I read the note again. Then I did something I had never done before, or since done. Laughed until I cried.

In her cracked leather satchel, Helen kept ledgers, notebooks, diaries, correspondences, dictionaries. And there was a dust-jacket photograph of Ryonosuke Akutagawa, Helen's most beloved writer. Looking at the camera, it's as if Akutagawa wants us to dismiss his youthful handsomeness as a fraudulent representation of a tormented inner life. With his intense, sidelong glance of preoccupation, he seems to judge the sparse, cafe-life tableau of table and tea cup (actually, he looks wired on caffeine) an annoying "writerly" cliché. Weary, sardonic smile, sensual mouth, disheveled black hair combed back from a high forehead on a long face, his is one of the most severely enigmatic expressions I have ever seen. (After composing the elegant, disturbing *Note to a Certain Old Friend*, he committed suicide in 1927, at the age of thirty-five.) In the west, Akutagawa is perhaps most well-known for Rashamon, the recounting of a murder from contending points-of-view. Director Akura Kurosawa based a film starring Toshiro Mifune on this book. Along the lower margin of the photograph, Helen had written something in Japanese. I asked her to translate. "Roughly," she said, "it means: What good is intelligence if you can't discover a useful melancholy?"

"Did Akutagawa say that?"

"Yes," Helen said. "I agree with it. Melancholy seems just the right mood to keep a clear perspective. What do you think?"

It was early September, 1977. We were standing in a cold, whipping wind off the Churchill River. Helen wore a frayed, black parka over two sweaters, flannel shirt, T-shirt. It was lightly snowing. This was the briefest philosophical exchange. One question, no answer. Yet in a way, I have been thinking about it ever since.

Indelibly, every mental snapshot I retain of Churchill includes at least one raven, usually a bunch of ravens. The proper vocabulary is a parliament of ravens, a murder of crows. Ravens are much larger than crows; I've seen crows look downright puny alongside. Ravens at the garbage dump. Ravens on the gandy dancers at the train station, around the grain silos, the roof of the train station, Beluga Motel, school, Churchill Hotel, post office. Ravens scavenging the rocky shore of Hudson Bay, the Churchill River. Then, of course, a slapstick comedy right out of a folk tale: ravens, just north of town, harassing polar bears, divebombing, nipping at their genitals as the bears lolled on their backs. At any rate, ravens were ubiquitous.

Helen had arrived to Churchill, Manitoba, on August 22; I arrived on August 27. Helen had taken the Muskeg Express train up from Winnipeg. I had flown in. My pilot's name was Driscoll Petchey. For a little over two months, Helen and I were to be the only two residents in the Beluga Motel, a rickety establishment built along the Churchill River. It had a dock. When you walked fast across it, each hollow step made the warping slats sound like its construction was actually that of an ancient xylophone. You heard the wind inside the rooms. Otherwise, it was standard fair; electric heaters, faucet rust tingeing cold and less cold running water, pale green walls, framed posters of exotic South Sea islands, a kind of visual paradox right there in the Arctic. There was a wooden sign depicting a white Beluga whale on the office door. The motel had twelve rooms. I was in room number 12, at the far right end, if you faced the motel from the dock. Helen was in Room 1, closest to the river. Bookends. As I've mentioned, we had both come to Churchill to translate Inuit folk tales. The man who'd given us each permission to work with him, Mark Nucaq, was a member of the Eskimo band known as Caribou, who spoke the dialect of Qairnirmiut, which is largely spoken around Baker Lake, on the west side of Hudson Bay. On as good account as can be expected, given the almost impenetrable nature of the local historical record, mixed with hearsay and conflicting recollections from elders, including members of his immediate family, Mark Nucaq's parents were born in Baker Lake around 1890. In turn an approximation, Mark was born around 1912, possibly as late as 1915. As far as language goes, four main groups of Caribou Eskimos (Inuit)—the Qairnirmiut, Hauniqtuurmiut, Harvaqtuurmiut, and Paalirmiut—were recognized by the Danish Fifth Thule Expedition of 1921-24 (led by Arctic explorer and ethnographer Knud Rasmussen), whose report was published in 1930. Later, a fifth group was recognized, the Ahiarmiut, to the southwest on the upper Maguse and Kazan Rivers. Contact with white people began in the eighteenth century with the founding of Churchill, Manitoba; a famous summer trading center was at Akiliniq on the northwest side of Beverly Lake, where driftwood had drawn Eskimo people from great distances. Mark remembered searching for driftwood there as a child.

I refer to so-called "first contact" and driftwood, because they both figure importantly in some of the stories Mark told Helen and me. For example, the arrival of Noah's Ark, an event about which Mark Nuqac related quite a few stories, was clearly, to him, a moment in time when his ancestors first saw white people. In these stories, Noah is a complicated figure. You might say he was in the wrong place at the wrong time; then panic makes him lose all humane bearing. Stranger in a strange land, his Ark locked in ice, plunging temperatures, punishing blizzards, claustrophobia, all possibly contributing to unforeseen domestic violence aboard the Ark. Noah is sickly, destitute can't provide for his family, utterly unresourceful because his foreign intellect is of no use, unless he were to take vital instructions from local Eskimo people, which (he is arrogant) he won't. As for driftwood—in one of those stories, Noah stubbornly refuses to share rare and precious driftwood; as a consequence, a particularly gruesome spirit-folk persuades Noah's wife to wander out on the ice. She is overtaken by a blizzard. Noah has to pay a stack of drift-wood—plus a bonus of a long plank from the Ark—to have his wife located; a shaman conscripts ravens for this task. They swirl above Noah's wife, dead far out on drift ice. In fact, in several of Mark's Noah stories, it is Mrs. Noah toward whom local spirit-folk dish out the brunt of retribution for her husband's fatal misjudgments. I don't know why. I never asked Mark about this.

That Helen had a lot of financial support from her parents estate was a matter of immediate record, when, the day after we met, we compared notes about our work. "My parents send me money," she said. "I'm thir-ty-eight. I didn't know what I wanted to do for a long time. I wandered around Europe." But in Churchill she was frugal with money; that was a feat, since there wasn't much at all to spend money on in the first place. Meals, postage stamps, some warm socks at the Hudson Bay Co. store, supermarket magazines. "After my Ph.D., I was intending to teach uni-versity," she said. "Maybe in Japan. Maybe in Europe. Possibly in Canada. Not in America."

"What if a great offer came along, in America, I mean?"

"You know something, Howard Norman," she said—she always used both my names—elevating my obtuse "what if" (She had a fatal illness; there was to be no "what if.") to the realm of practical aesthetics, "in Greenland, the Eskimos warn against talking about the future. They say its terribly arrogant, you see. There's so many dangers—some spirit that's been holding a grudge against people for hundreds of years, might ambush you. Perfectly sunny day out, too. Everybody's happy. The sled dogs aren't fighting. They aren't being tortured by fleas. The children are all healthy. The hunter kisses his wife goodbye, sets out for the best fish-ing ground. The world in perfect balance, huh? Then, watch out! Disaster strikes. To use Biblical language, good luck begets bad luck. Or something like that. That way of thinking sure keeps you on your toes, doesn't it? It makes these stories unpredictable, too. In Greenland, peo-ple in stories seemed to believe in two things, basically: what they've already experienced, and what they consider inevitable. I grew fond of this outlook. The past—sure, let's talk about that. The present, sure. Don't let's talk about the future, though. It's not in your control, so why act like it is?"

Sometimes I lay on Helen's bed reading as she sat at her desk, typing, or translating a passage, or typing a letter to one of her friends or colleagues in linguistics, usually either in London or Japan, but also in Canada and Denmark, as well. I noticed that, on occasion, Helen pressed down so hard in her handwriting, she would break the pencil lead. Her ledgers were tied together by string. She preferred black and maroon covers. Notebooks were reserved for linguistics; fragments of stories, translations, annotations, emendations, notes, in English, Japanese and French, as if three languages were necessary to accommodate the complexities of the Inuit language. In her ledgers, Helen archived her life as a birdwatcher. They contained, in neat columns, the names of each bird she saw, the date on which she saw it, time of day, and, when possible, the approximate latitude and longitude of the sighting, as well as the weather conditions. Helen wrote up this bird information only in Japanese.

She also kept a separate notebook. Inside its charcoal cover, it contained prayers, also in Japanese. These did not echo any religious sensibility; they were simply direct requests to see birds. These prayers did not betray big emotions, nor were they particularly philosophical, except for the general idea that a powerful entity, or God, was listening and could perhaps thus be petitioned. Nowhere in these prayers is mention of her illness; my guess is that Helen did not wish to barter with sympathy. Reference to her considerable pain was elliptical; to directly exploit her own "medical situation," would be demeaning, because it would imply a belief in a hierarchy of suffering—those in the most pain might exact first priorities of Mercy. What thinking person, cynic or no, having lived 37 years with any real depth of alertness to the world, could ever come to that conclusion? "I'd like to die fast," she said, bluntly in a blunt tone, almost an afterthought at the supper table one night, in the dining room of the Churchill Hotel, where we took all of our meals together. "I don't want to have to be helped to turn over on a hospital bed, all those tubes. I should do what old Mrs. Piumiuk did, when I was in Greenland two winters ago. It was about 50 below. No kidding. Mrs. had cancer—a western doctor diagnosed it—and she just went house to house saying goodbye. Her nephew gave her a bottle of whiskey. Then, middle of the night, she just walked out. Probably as far out of sight of the village as she could, slipped off her clothes, lay down, drank the whiskey completely down, closed her eyes and died peacefully. That cold, you'd get numb to feeling right away, I imagine. There's a lot of dignity in that way of thinking—I should pay attention. I didn't witness it for nothing. There were polar bears, of course. But I think she drifted out to sea, or fell into a crevasse, when the ice started to open up. Anyway, after the summer thaw, nobody ever found her."

Helen's prayers were not Haiku, nor as far as I know followed any other compositional formality. They were for the most part declarative; evidence of desire was monotonal. And yet in the strictest regard, her prayers were autobiographical, often strikingly intimate and revelatory as entries in a diary.

> I lost out as a Buddhist, worse so a Christian.
> Never mind. I ask, please, to see a Harlequin Duck;
> it would have to be quite soon.

I have in my possession all 116 of Helen's English versions. They are on nearly transparent, onion skin paper, each prayer numbered. "Prayer One," "Prayer Two," and so on. Followed by the date of authorship. (The Northern Saw-whet Owl was the only bird she asked to see more than once.) The manuscript had a title: Prayers to See Birds. I say "manuscript," because why else title it if you don't see it, to some extent, as a literary work? Only once in conversation did she refer to the prayers as "poems." There was no preface; no epilogue, except the odd sentence, "Typed by Remington typewriter, in Kyoto, Japan." I like thinking of her alert enough and physically able to even type, what turned out to be so near the end of her life. The last prayer was dated July 6, 1978; thirty-one days later she died in her brother's house in Kyoto.

Fate constructs memory in odd ways. Given the utmost intensity of circumstances, give-and-take honesty, a modicum of good cheer, and if you're able to embrace each other's take on life, you can learn quite a bit about another person in a short time. Late one morning, just a week after arriving in Churchill, I stopped by Helen's motel room. I knocked, heard a weak, "Come in." I opened the door, and saw Helen curled up on the bed, clutching her stomach. She was fully dressed, including a rain parka. The shades were drawn; the sedatives Helen took made her eyes excruciatingly sensitive to light. I then uttered the most profoundly ignorant words imaginable, "You okay?"

"I have stomach cancer," she said. "So there. Now you know." Then she asked me to rub her feet. And sit and listen to the CBC radio a while. I do not want the fact of her cancer to import sentimentality into this memoir; Helen would have despised that, chastised me for doing so, even unwittingly. In a letter, Helen wrote, "I hate that my illness put such boundaries on elation." Compressing no doubt mindboggling pain and frustration into an aesthetic equation, was typical of Helen's self-effacing nature. It must be said, that the sentence, "I hate that my illness—," bespoke Helen's writerly self, too. Her years, I mean, as a translator, laboring to find equivalents in Japanese for the emotional dimensions, prodigious amounts of information, historical gravity, outright weirdness of incident, and stark or slapstick humor found in Inuit folk tales. That is, like any writer, she constructed sentences as a way of shaping the world, enduring it. To Helen, translation was an "ennobling way of life." Her words exactly. Yet the fact was, in dozens of conversations, Helen proved the least sentimental person I had ever met. Mind you, I only knew her for two months there in Churchill, and about a month afterward, in Halifax and during a brief travel together up to Cape Breton, Nova Scotia. I'd be a fool not to admit that untold sentiment resided in a smile or frown, anecdote, turn of phrase that I was too inexperienced with Helen to perceive. Naturally, it occurred to me that physical pain might have been a recent influence. One day, as we stood in front of the motel talking about something we had heard on CBC radio, pain doubled her over. Indeed, she required pain-killers every night, if she was to sleep, even fitfully. I suspect, however, that her studious demeanor, mitigated on rare occasion by wry humor, even a raunchy joke or two, preceded this condition. It would not have surprised me to learn that she had been quite a serious child, as well. If this were true, I hope that for the sake of freeing her up to be herself, Helen had discovered her own "useful melancholy" early on in life. During September and October, 1977, Helen slept through the afternoon hours. Her appetite—her ability to keep down foods—was meager. Her pharmacy was always close at hand. As for generally bearing up, she once commented, "Despite my medical circumstances, most days I don't feel in a hurry. Oddly enough."

Two Poems

Vijay Seshadri

Thelma

We have a small place on an ugly street,
though we keep it spick and span.
I take the garbage out, but you,
Thelma, you the man—

brilliant as the velvet eye
setting off a peacock's feather,
rayed as the sun is rayed
through storming, broken weather

and gilt-edged clouds. And me?
I strip to my birthday suit
and scream out the window at the Arab kids,
who scream back, "*Sharmout!*"

rolling by on their Rollerblades.
You and me, Thelma, and the little squirt,
with me on the stoop
in my cap turned backward and my undershirt.

Anima

Not Garbo, for instance, or my wife but white, though flecks
and patches of melanin coruscate
the olive acres rising between
her breasts and her thighs,
and African ovals frame her eyes.
Twenty-eight and chemically complex,

she studies all night for her G.E.D.
At dawn, she goes out to do
what her doctor tells her to do:
dig in her garden, where she grows
the rose they call the cabbage rose
and the huge iris they call the fleur-de-lis.

But every so often her mind goes slack
and desperate. Spectral and pale,
she walks her hills in a long black veil
mourning me—her quizzical, her other,
her bitter, prodigal, absconded half.
Where, just where, am I that I can never come back?

Stanzas in My 39th Year

Wayne Koestenbaum

Why I Want X in My 39th Year

I used to be pretentious;
then I grew simplistic.
Should I devote myself
to pleasure or to labor?

I dreamt of a deep thinker:
Rousseau? A moment ago
I had the idea (it escaped)
that almost saved my life.

I love concentrating,
hugging a periphery
or a hole:
I wish I could prove it.

Somebody strong circled
the word "was" when it occurred
three times in one sentence.
I might have been the figure circling "was."

Aphoristic in My 39th Year

I wonder if I have scandalous doings (an early botched
marriage) to reveal
tabloid-style in a poem
and thereby charm the world.

Doubt it.
I was miserable and then
wrote a strict
opus one in C.

Ritardando in My 39th Year

Without license I drove
a bad car in the dark.
I kissed and saved the pieces
in an envelope and slowed down.

My mother telephoned the room
where my brother and I
slept and played Schumann.
Sick of delays

I said, "Unless the composer
intended them, I'm skipping
ritards in this piece,
we don't want it to drag on longer than it should."

Role Model in My 39th Year

I nominated my role model for a Nobel Peace Prize
in Woodstock. Who could blame her
for offering me a bite of lemon meringue pie?
At the cramped diner she eased

herself into a long meditation on our distance
from the rock-n-roll era;
my body temperature dropped below the cistern
level the role model decreed adequate for schizos.

She'd retired from the civilized world
to pursue theory. Her maiden name:
Valium. She massaged my buttocks
and promised warm compresses that never came.

Today, my black wool sweater smells
of stalagmites and pauses:
my role model wore it on an ocean liner—
waters damned by omissions, equally damned by gold . . . .

Princess Diana in My 39th Year

I walked a Hamptons beach.
Diana approached. I stopped,
backtracked, performed reconnaisance.
"Well, look who's here," she said.

We claimed a corner table at the beach club
and met my relatives—aunt drinking mirabelle,
uncle offended by Diana's misuse of a Yiddish phrase.
He plugged his book; the princess turned away.

She told me, "I'm grateful
for the affair. Over the years
I've given your evasions much thought."
What evasions, Diana?

Mayoral Race in My 39th Year

I dropped out of the mayoral race:
a scandal. Offered
the democratic nomination,
I begged to be left alone,

I gave up every ruse.
Standing upright, I napped.
Everyone said, "He looks awake!"
But I was fast asleep.

Nothing in My 39th Year

My face is widening,
cheeks a clown's.

Lazy, slow, without ambition,
yesterday I met

a man with breasts
and beautiful

slick Johnny
Stompanato hair:

I swallowed his
incomprehensible propaganda.

I wish I had a larger chin:
it could function as stop sign.

Two Poems

Donna Masini

Natural History

For lack of a better direction I steered us
into the *Biology of Invertebrates*. We watched
the way the spineless milky creatures grew
luminous at night. Jellyfish hung—grassy, diaphanous—
a bluish squid pinned to the ceiling itching
to squander its inky diffusions.

I wanted to be wowed, knocked out.
I wanted to place us, somewhere
unchangeable. We walked past each diorama—
static, dramatic. A soft wind blew
the seagrass like some deepsea carwash, anemones
spread their delicate tentacles, swaying gracefully

among jumbled clusters of silver fins—a stupor
of spawning. Above us a parrotfish slept, suspended
in its gelatinous sac. Everything in its place.
There was an empty space (labeled *angelfish* in the key below).
I wondered if it had fallen among the soft corals
that reach, transform at night their animal tentacles,

capturing whatever happens
to drift through their chambers. I am saying
that the way I look at my life has changed. I am afraid
I have been knocked out of the window, the picture,
the place I call my life. I am trying
not to cling like some graspy crab

dragging its eely prey. I didn't think that day
of this card on my wall, three devils peeking
out of bone-white cavern jaws, the flames drawn on
like pink squid maneuvering their luminous tubes. *The descent
of Christ into the limbo of the fathers. (Detail.)*
This detail looks more like hell than hell itself.

I didn't think of how I just fell into another life,
frantic, gasping—a fish, as they say, out of water.

The Trap

I looked away, then back
without my glasses. Only
a blur: dark, furry, shadowed.
I couldn't look. I looked

to where I'd set the trap flush to the slice of space
behind the oven where I'd seen the quick blur run
that afternoon, past the chair, the shelf of books, past
my terror of fur, ancient and dun-colored,

something like a dream that leaves
a mood, an almost-image, that finally gets away.
I saw the stuck black shudder
to unglue. I sickened and then

left it. I left it
as I have left friends
shuddering in their beds. Wheezing among their
birds, their griefs and hypodermics. I couldn't watch

the struggle in the dust, all night
shudder under the shuttered dark. All
night the fur hummed a numb chord. Every noise
was its noise though I'm told they're quiet.

What do we wait for? I waited
for a squeal. To hear that foul clump of dusty fur
suffer under the oven. I wanted
to love it, its twitching

tail whipping the floor, the air, its heart
a pulsing bomb that would explode
right through its fur, like those cartoon
hearts in cartoon mice. Love made them

thrum, and fear
of love. I have feared love. A furry thing.

It sickened me and so I looked away.
I didn't want to see its little claws hugged up,

the way the back legs twitched,
myself husbandless, buried in this dark apartment.

How We Became

Julie Carr

Servants of vast flux,

so I see it.

We walked, or
I walked and he rode
from corner to corner. Sometimes we skipped
the corners and crossed diagonally through sparse traffic.

What pleased us? The flowers pleased us and the colors they lifted
from the earth. And the sun pleased us, as it brought luster
to the metal bars of the play equipment.

The tiny clothes, bright undies and vests to be worn by a Dawn-doll,
these pleased us, blown about in the wind as they were.
Other pleasures were more like relief:
the un-huh we spoke when hunger was abated,
when we were body to body and still.
And when a truck slid across the window, exposing finally
the other side of the street we'd been wondering about,
we were pleased in a quiet way.

Then our portrait emerged
as if out of water, as if a reflection
broke free of its bird.

And it was strange, like the brown shoes worn by foreigners.
We hardly recognized ourselves, we were so changed.
For the better, we told ourselves hopefully.

If it wasn't a hair cut or weight loss that did it, it was that we were now
two people. Two!

One of us was very small. The other did all the talking.
One had gentle dough-like features,
the other a hardened surface like packed earth.
What was there to do? We laughed. We laughed as we
looked into our own eyes, and laughed
to touch the inside of our two mouths
where it was always wet, warm and moving.

That, finally, was how we knew
that despite appearances,
we were still our one self,

walking to see the boats,
the barge big as a planet
slowly pushed upriver
by the squat determined tug.

Two Poems

Pura López Colomé

Translated from the Spanish by Forrest Gander

Heartache

> *Why do you wander alone*
> *Among the ships through the camp*
> *In the middle of the night immortal*
> *Iliad X, 139*

The lake of the dead has no shore.
Vast Stygian, it is also called a river.
It flows, wary, warily,
infatuating sages and believers.
Layers of illusion, of rumor,
settle easily in the ruck:
fluent mirror
of human labyrinths.

I can feel your beginnings in this boat, I murmured.
Your planks have left marks on my hands.
The night's oars spin
the very chrysalis of horizon.

Is this the eye of water
where the goddess dunked the boy
to make him invulnerable,
brutal, indifferent?

Is this the dry,
lachrymal Word
hurling escutcheons overboard?

I Follow You

To see oneself without the world,
not to recognize oneself in the mirror.
How fragile
we are, and frail,
made only of meat and bone.
The finest feelings come clear
in the tangible memory of someone
whose appearance is already intangible.
Small as we are,
we swallow the void,
what is yours without you,
me.
Wanting a voice to fill us,
we strain to hear echoes, within,
which never stop
dreaming of their origins.
Happy is she who can face
all that withdraws
and remains.

Butterwort

Judith Baumel

The soul of the wind is wind.
The wind of the soul is wind.
The breath that carries the leaf
carries the dry leaves down
the street in solitary pleas,
in mobs, that death could have undone so
many. Just to touch the wing
of the butterfly is to pull the scales
from its nervures, to pick color
from collars, to end flight.
In the dream, my dark hair came out
strand by strand, one by one, strung
with pearly nits which I hung
over my morning
head like a bead curtain
over that head from which the wiry
white renegades curled out
and the morning shook off where I'd been.

My child looked up from his pillow,
a satisfying simian scratch of his scalp
completed. He did not know
where I'd been in the dark
hours between "good" and "good."
He wanted to know from where came
to humans the very very very first louse.

Jewish Variations on Erik Satie's "Sports et Divertissements"

Daniel Kane

THE BALANCER
It's my heart that balances like anise. It's got nothing to do
with vertigo. Come on and follow my little feet.

THE FISH
Murmurs of you in a light on the river. Venue
suitable for a fish. Or another fish. Give me two fish.
"Do you have a pill?" "It's a fish, a poor
fish." Lord have mercy. "Jack returns cheese here,"
the fisherman mumbles. The Jews murmur
with their lights on the river.

THE BATH OFFICER
The sea may be large, madame, but it's all ours. In your house, *you*
    season
your big ass. No use assaying this dance of fronds—
it's plain to the *other* Jews. "You are tooting
mussels!" "Yes, ma'am, I am."

THE CARNIVAL
The confetti descends. Voices and masks.
A Pierrot in the stage-set library catches a marlin.
Strictly not kosher.
Turn on the lights and bells, uh-huh.

THE POOR
The poor are inside a cavern. She is amused with
these crabs. She pursues them. She is availing and traversing.
Haggard, she marches on their heads. She bites a Jew
who reminds her of Demeter.

THE FOUR COINS
The four sewers. The Jewish chat. The sewer-agents the
chat. The chat entire. And the lance. The chat is well-placed.

THE PICNIC
"*And for you* are these three freezing Jews."
"Thanks. Why don't you lay your head on this lovely white
    church-robe?"
"Holy shit, an airplane!"
"No, no, hush, it's just an orange."

THE BAD FLIRTING
"How are you?" "No
Jew *I've* ever met is amiable." "Lash me!"
"You are like a gross Jew." "My voodoo
has entranced the moon." "Just as I suspected. I'll hock your tit."

THE ARTIFICIAL FOOL
Oh, a fool from Bengal!
A fusion! A completely blue fusion . . .

THE TENNIS
"Play?" "Yes!" The good servant. Come
and spread jam on these balls. There's a good servant. Service
the military coup, please, service the jackboots . . . "Game!"

Try Love

Susan Bergman

There is no love in Istanbul, only the depletions of commerce, the old shoulder of practicality. Not that Yara was looking for love, so she may have missed it, though in Paris that wouldn't happen, she would have felt its dreamy heat. "The value of a thing is how much you will pay for it," one rug merchant tells Anshe, looking at the stitching on his woven leather shoes. Anshe slides his feet under the cushion Yara is sitting on and presses his toes up under her so that she feels as if she might tip over onto the heap of rugs they've endured over apple tea. "You must buy the one you love," says the dealer. "And I will," says Anshe blamelessly, rising to leave. There is, naturally, the love of rugs, in Istanbul, but not the kind of love that Yara left behind her in America.

Her love would call her, when she was still home, from Mobile. Maybe he would call from somewhere outside San Francisco where he stays with his west-coast dealer whose small daughter collects monkeys. Or the phone would ring and his voice would stream across the Mississippi River to Chicago from one or the other Dakota. He isn't the man she is traveling with, though she's trying to love Anshe. And she does, for there are more reasons to than she can count. There is also that kind of love in Istanbul.

Yara tries to love Anshe by doing little, consequential favors for him when she thinks of it. She knows, for instance, that he likes to read the Herald Tribune first before she folds the pages backwards into quarters so that she can manage it. She leaves the news beside his coffee cup and pours enough milk for the color to fade from chocolate to toffee. She waits to read until he's finished, for which he thanks her, noticing. He breaks his bread into pieces and dips it in the soft-boiled egg. Though mostly Anshe does favors for her, larger than hers and more promising, and that cost him his pride. He performs acts of kindness that seem to spill from him on her behalf. He buys her a bag of anise-flavored candies from the kiosk inside the Egyptian spice market. He loves the way the vials of scented oils from a stall farther in smell on her wrist and asks from time to time if he may hold her hand, which he then turns over and presses to his face so that the hint of patchouli, or sandalwood, or rose water, or the heady concoctions called *harem* or *gypsy* waft through his imagination, though she's right there in person of course, even if her mind wanders.

He asks if she prefers the Turkish or Iranian saffron. He holds them toward her so that she may have her choice of long red strands or short golden ones. He likes to present to her the lessons of potentiality, to indicate in his gestures the multitude of options that only he can provide. "A man likes to satisfy the woman he loves," he tells her, as if he could stand for one half of the race, and she could hold up her end of the other. She prefers the red saffron from Iran that comes in a flat, round jar. She prefers, as a place to sleep and eat, and shop for carpets, the quiet of the old quarter, Sultan Ahmet, down the hill from Haghia Sophia, to the fashionable European district of Beyoglu.

Yara also prefers that Anshe not be hurt by what she feels, and so she keeps much of what she feels to herself. Her feelings toward him have the quality of rock candy, she tells herself, indelicate, crystalline. Taken in the mouth perhaps their hardness could dissolve. *The syrup of love is not petrified*, she passes this line through her head, all the syllables on a single pitch like the end of a dirge. And though her feelings are not amber, neither do they bend to her commitments, which are long standing by now. Twelve years she and Anshe have been together. This is the time of life for it, her friend Belize, who married early, tells her, tossing her head like a donkey when she laughs. *It* being a thorough reconsideration of one's life, Yara takes her to mean. Her friend has three children. She has been sending retouched videos of herself to the hotel room of Sam Shepard. She tries to compare things that can't be compared.

Anshe knows the man in America, though refuses to say his name. There is no reason for secrets when nothing, finally, can be hidden. They have spoken on occasion and are not friends. Once, when Anshe came home unexpectedly, he and the unspoken man fought and called each other words about nationality, about shape and size, about aging, and defended territories far beyond their actual borders. They were the picture of each other standing face to face, the one as perfect as the other, though utterly dissimilar, each complete, and this struck Yara as acquisitive on her part, wanting so much perfection for herself. She stood like a prop, wearing only a Japanese kimono and a beaded gold bracelet, in the middle of the room. One had to have thrown the first punch, and later their stories agreed precisely as to the one. Neither tried to cheapen the event with hyperbole or heroics; neither felt wholly defeated.

They moved behind a wall, away from her. A fist landing on bone was what you could hear, the dull stretch of muscle against muscle. The grunting sounds of breath being forced by a sudden, abrupt pressure. She moved to look behind the wall where they were fighting and stood for a moment watching them. One's neck exposed. One's raging, loved face. It was the first the two men had met. She remembers them pronouncing sounds like *cocksucker*, *sorry-ass*, syllables she never could have imagined in either of their mouths, so that the quality of hilarity that overcame her, hearing the one try to denounce the other, seemed only mildly surreal. Under the edge of the mattress on the floor, a condom wrapper.

Yara turned away, profoundly unrelated to the action, and in the other room began tidying like a kind of domestic dervish. She unplugged appliances, and ran water, and swept crumbs from the table where the man in America and she had been sharing a plate of cheeses and English biscuits. The proofs for a new monograph of his work—images of Desert Storm— which they had been going over, she stacked behind a row of books on the shelf. All she could think was that the loose pages might be thrown in disdain, and they were the one thing she could protect. The pages floating randomly, unnumbered, she couldn't bear to think of this pale disaster in light of the images they bore of soldiers' obedient braveries. And how ridiculous or merely unhappy the one collecting them would feel remembering them being heaved, remembering the rage that heaved them, the love that provoked the rage, and the miserable loss of love.

The man she is traveling with is, of course, her husband. You knew this. When they lived in Japan several years ago he had chosen the kimono she was wearing that day from a roomful of fraying Asian textiles for the way the colors looked against her skin. The day of the fight she dragged the heavy silk of the sleeve in sudsy water, listening to what the two of them were saying. Anshe told the man to leave. His voice sounded like coarse pebbles grinding to dust in his mouth. The other voice had lowered to a growl. When they finished, together, the fighting exhausted in them, she stood near the heat of one man, then moved to examine the swollen face of the other. Any word she might have said felt mannered and abstract when the situation had no manners in it, only freedom and recognition, and what felt like finality. But the end of what, they wondered, each of them shocked by their own participation, each of them horribly serene. It was what it was—a man confronting his wife's lover. The husband and wife would talk later. The man and the woman who was the other's wife would talk too. There would be words then.

Calmly, while Yara tidied the rooms, she felt the feudal implications of marriage even this late in the century. The bonds, the implicit ownership. The fallout of belonging to another. Not that this was the first these implications had occurred to her. She had read Castiglione, Betty Friedan, Germaine Greer, Simone de Beauvoir, but this was clearer. Unless she could deliver the words that would allow her to own the one life she wanted to live, at that moment, and for the rest of her life, she would be property, possessed, and if not by love, then what? *If not by love.* It was only her choice, but it was not only one choice—it had a series of others embedded inside it, and inside those choices, the careful inlay of others.

She was no more able, than they were to share her, to take action in an utterance, to proffer the one needed gesture. All the vivid detail prevented this, Anshe with his clenched face one inch from the other's, the stark smell of week-old lilies purpling at the edges, a platinum light slicing itself across the floor through narrow bamboo blinds, the slow thwop of the ceiling fan, what looked like carnations of blood randomly exploding on the walls, a clump of torn hair on the window ledge, water drilling in the steel sink. If she sounds helpless you must try to imagine how she felt as the American gathered his things to go—his eyes cast around the room for his missing photographs, his hands trembled. She felt calm and slow and giddy and profoundly, pathetically owned.

Years before that day her feelings had turned to stone, is what it seemed to her, not that they were dormant, but that they were stone. She was aging. She had grown accustomed to the concrete properties of isolation and accumulated sorrows. Life had not been like that for Anshe, nor had it been entirely like that for her. I exaggerate her sadness, looking back. But then, with the force of quiet rain over time, and erosion, something had grown from inside that rock. Another thing. Stone or flesh, she thought that day, these are my choices, stone or flesh. But there are rarely only two choices, consoling as it is to think that this one decision will change her life forever.

"Nothing hurts when it's happening," Anshe tells her later, on the airplane. "You do it, and take it, and don't feel anything at all, right then."

She thinks, "This is how it is for him."

"He was within his rights," the man who is not in Istanbul will tell her much later.

"I am a peaceful man," her husband says. "Next time I will smash his face."

Across the Bosperus they could feel it—the wind changing to mark the coming of winter. Meltem from the north, perhaps with rain in it—an invading hoard sweeping into Anatolia. On the streets it's cold as bullets. The low sun encamps along the Golden Horn. All metaphors speak of the battle which love is. Anshe walks with his arm through hers. He's holding the umbrella mostly over her head. The misty rain beads in her hair like a net thrown over her. Strands of damp hair coil around her shoulder and the smell of wet wool. It's not intentional the way her mind travels back to America. Neither is it disciplined. Now he is in Seattle delivering a speech. Now he's hunting partridge. Yesterday he must have driven into Canada with friends to watch the snow geese migrate, though her days are jumbled and the hours switched. She's read the papers less and less. The peace prize has been given, at least. Some of the women from the university here in Istanbul want to wear their head coverings to classes and the government prohibits this. So there have been protests, arrests. You see them on the front page of the papers holding hands in their long coats and scarves, demonstrating on behalf of their own subjugation.

"In a state of constant political precariousness, in a conflict whose only end is violence, certain freedoms we cannot allow ourselves," their driver allegorized on the way from the underground cisterns to the French Embassy at the head of the street where they want to walk. "Certain expressions we cannot permit." He stared at Yara in the rearview mirror. He tooted his horn and blinkered like Turkish drivers do in traffic.

There is a steady drizzle now. She looks in the shop windows from underneath the arc of the umbrella as they're walking. She lets the tips of her fingers run gently over the hair on the back of Anshe's hand. He is still young and willing and almost inordinately tender. "It is only natural that you wouldn't feel for me now," he says, with a sad smile at her touch. He links his fingers through hers. "You love him still. It would be unnatural for you to be any way other than the way you are." He's making what is natural into an act that he can accept, and that she must end. That she must recover from, as he thinks of it. He sees her love of the man in America as an aberration, a wrong turn for someone with an impaired sense of direction. He refers to her *affair*, which is a matter of time to him, as death is a matter of time. She is a little sick, a little weak.

It's raining harder now and they turn into the English language bookstore on Istiklal Cadessi. "You're mine," the man in America said to her once. This enters her head the moment she steps into the warmth of the room filled with books. She wants to be. She takes the wet umbrella from Anshe and places it in a can away from the opulent collection of Ottoman Palace Plans, and Tribal Embroidery, and Maps of the Fallen World. She doesn't want to enough, is what the man has decided, though his offer has not been withdrawn.

On a table near the back of the shop Yara finds a translation of Orhan Pamuk's new novel and Anshe says over her shoulder while she's reading, "When we are together is there a part of you that feels you're betraying him?" This is what she was thinking in the middle of the night as she pulled the sheet over her breasts, that they did not belong to the man asleep beside her, that perhaps when you try to love two men at once your body is no longer entirely your own. She would rather not answer. "Do you?" he persists. She nods, confused about why he would want to know the extent of what he would consider her disloyalty. The book's cover in the British edition is a drawing of a man whose face is an open book. The sentences of the book have the feel of a smooth translation. She focuses on this. "Well, you aren't betraying him," Anshe says. "You don't owe him anything."

Yara had given the American man a celadon green cut velvet scarf that had been made for her by an artist in the city where she lives. The scarf hung over his bed and he burned it when she told him she was leaving for Istanbul. She had written him letters, between phone calls, between the times they'd been together, which he also burned. She gave him an ivory carving of a fist that had at one time been a snuff box. The hand reminded her of his. When he came to Chicago to see her she placed it in his hand, which closed immediately around it. He studied her face, as if he were unaccustomed to receiving gifts, and then opened his fingers and memorized the small carving carefully before putting it in his pocket, with his knife and money clip. Between the cracks of the fingers, delicate black lines. You can see the suggestion of jealousy in the grip.

"If you go to Istanbul," he told Yara, "I will feel as if I've made a mistake." She thinks of the small fist burning. She has saved everything of his. She feels the loss of her letters more.

Anshe asked her to promise not to write to the man while she is in Istanbul. He is trying to love too, and this is what he requires of her to keep at it. Love isn't trading up, is what she has always believed. Love hopes. Well, they don't know how very well—to love each other. Not to split into the familiar-companion-tender parts, and the passionate-resistant-greedy parts. "I want everything in one place," she tells him. "I want only one life."

"I want you," he says. He says this at least six times a day, like a call to prayer, so maybe he is good at loving, or remembering to try. Maybe he is calling things that aren't yet into existence, things that used to be. He asks her if she knows what the date is. Not a birthday, not their anniversary. His face softens and she sees that he is moved by one of his own thoughts. Perhaps by the significance of the day which she forgets. "It is the day I asked you to marry me," he says, "and tomorrow is the day you said you would." They've come all this way, to Istanbul: first Roman Constantinople, then Byzantium, then the Ottomans, fallen to the mesmerizing *Ataturk*. Now this layer through which the vestiges of others show like scars, like their own unbidden ancestry vying for tradition.

They find a perch in a third story window of a student-run *mehune* overlooking schools of pedestrians on the street below. It's dusk and fans of white lights have come on in the shape of peacock tails on poles. Girls walk alone in platform shoes, or with a single friend. Dark Turkish youth strolls in fives. The young men talk on cellular phones that ring out fragments of familiar overtures. *Mereba*, they say into the newfound signifier of their significance. Inside Yara and Anshe lean against old cushions made of camel sacks and argue about the usefulness of categorization by gender. In the bookstore he had been scanning a self-help book that makes every effort to explain what women want, and what men want, and the differences between what they want, in terms of brain function. She is more interested in specifics. Charlie—there, she said it—shares her intolerance for astrology, and eneograms, and the breakdown into Venus and Mars—ways to divide and classify that make one moment typify another. When he touches her he is not touching anyone else.

"What bothers me about you is your refusal to recognize that you are basically the same as other people," Anshe goes on. "I don't like the way you . . ."

"The way I won't divide the world in two," she finishes his sentence. He lets this incongruity between what she does and what she says register, and then pass. It's more a late lunch than supper: soup and some warm bread. A pitcher of raki.

"I love marriage," she says suddenly, which is diversionary—something she heard another woman say—and too bland to mean anything, and probably especially not *I love being married to you*. There are ways other than small favors to try love. Willful declarations. And travel is a way to try, as is a move, or for some having a child. There are private ways that involve trying to forget. She can't remember, right this minute for instance, the exact date she met him, the city his last letter was mailed from, where she was standing in the picture he made of her. Raki helps forget. The waiter pours three fingers in a tall glass and when she adds water, the liquid turns white.

"Like a lion," the waiter says, scowling ferociously. "Milk of a lion make you roar." He reaches for her camera on the bench beside her. "A picture of your honeymoon," he offers, making use of his best English. The whole world conspires to keep what they perceive to be a solid, if not happy, marriage intact. The waiter brushes back his hair to show how hers has fallen into her face. Peering through the viewfinder, he motions them closer to fit into the same frame, and they move together, submissively, as two people might who didn't have a third person there between them.

She thinks the waiter may be able to translate her gum wrapper for her, which appears to be a poem, or a rhyming fortune of some sort. She hands him the small square paper with four lines printed on it and asks him to read it aloud. *Guzel bir ildir Denizli / O sim dilik sizli bizli / Ama kismetinde o cikti / Kendisi solgun benizli.* "Ah," he says, "It means there is a beautiful country far away. In that country lives a man who loves you. He has a white face—I think the white stands for suffering, or, like an old man with pale skin. I don't know how you say this in your language." She is nodding to encourage him. "But he is, anyway, your love." The waiter peers up at Yara, then turns to look at Anshe. "Your face is not white," he says, puzzled, or maybe to console him, before retreating to the kitchen.

Next the musicians form part of a circle around their table with their instruments—a hand-held drum, a squash-bellied zither with twelve strings, a long, breathless clarinet. They play, in their distinctive quarter tones, not songs of romance, surely, but songs of Suleyman the Magnificent's magnificence, of Muhammed's journey into the Seven Heavens, songs of spiritual starvation is what they sound like.

"You look apprehensive," Anshe lets his mouth brush her ear and raises his voice over the din.

Yara shakes her head. Regrettably the musicians move to the next table.

"Are you thinking about the fight?" The bone gleams under his eyes. His fine, aquiline nose. The way the light from the sheepskin lamps make his chin look like it is carved from granite. He has begun to believe that he can read her mind. It's one of her strategies, to let him think he can.

"Fighting didn't solve anything, did it?" she shouts, going along.

Though what she's actually thinking is, tongue's spice, row of teeth, even breath, the way the words *you're mine* embroider the heart with delicate, worn threads. When Anshe mentions it she begins to think, it shames her to admit, that all of them being in the same room may have been exactly what she'd secretly wanted—the three of them together so that she wouldn't have to leave part of her life in one place while she went away to live the other part. It's utterly selfish, she knows, to want a thing like that. The musicians cease at last and argue among themselves near the kitchen.

"I'm grateful no one was hurt, worse," Anshe says, showing her the place on the heel of his hand that has almost scarred over after a month. A chunk of skin had been gouged out—teeth or fingernail marks or a scrape against exposed brick. She thinks of the man in America's swollen jaw. He couldn't shave. In her mind she places her hands gently on his two-day growth of beard. The fight had made being together for them feel slightly dangerous. They walked down the back stairs to avoid someone standing guard at the elevator. He pulled his car around behind his apartment to the alleyway, where Yara got in.

Each day over her own soul's objections she tries to let the way she feels about the man in America tarnish in some diminishing, occluding way. She imagines the future unraveling between them into skeins of regret for what they would have to abandon. She tries to make the certain pressure of his focus, the demands of his whole attention, and her own elation inside it, into the close smells of frying fish in the market. She places a woman who would like to be her rival in bed with him, the eager hump of her ass lifted toward the ceiling. What if the accidental re-ignition of an old desire? She resorts to the potential eventualities of disease, the depredations of old age. What if a paralyzing accident? She can't impute, or won't, impotence.

Even the rug dealers in Istanbul speak of the symbols of harmonious longevity. *Bereket*, a fertile union, as evidenced in figs and pomegranates, poppies, heads of grain. *Bukagi*, which means fetter, the sign of permanent union. *El, Parmak, Tarak* (hand, finger comb), all these warring against the influence of the evil eye, the degradation of the holy union, as does *Congel* (hook), they are assured over apple tea. *Hayat Agaci*—the tree of life, means going on and on—the dealers move their hands in circles. They tell you that the rug they want you to buy was woven as a wedding gift. They say its value is precisely what you'll pay.

Yara and Anshe have been traveling together for over a month now, in and around Istanbul, city of new beginnings forced on one people by another. Travel is a world of comfortable shoes and phraseology. It involves the fair and unfair exchange of currency, gestures of strangeness, hospitality. It is meant to trigger, at the end of the road, a longing for home. On their way out of the restaurant, after they have finished drinking the lion's milk, a young man wearing a bright red vest shakes lemon scented water into their hands to splash onto their faces. She is certain it is a ritual meant to carry them together into the eternal future, like throwing rice at a bride and groom.

"Can you say you think that you'd like to try to love me?" Anshe asks quietly behind her on their way down the curved iron stairs. There are so many parts to his question.

Yara clings to the railing in order not to slip, and keeps going.

"I *am* trying," she says, which has never been enough, and still isn't she can see in the grim shudder of the night that spreads before them.

"I know you're trying," he says it patiently. "But do you *want* to try?"

Breakfast at the Metro

Rachel Hadas

Breakfast with a friend from out of town.
The diner window washed before our eyes.
As suds slide down the pane,
what was a grey January morning
yields briefly to an artificial blizzard
until the whiteness, squeegeed out of sight,
leaves the plate glass window near our booth
so squeaky clean that everything
(cup, syrup, my friend's face, the street outside)
looks closer than before.
So when a dark wing brushes across the sky
I flinch. At that same moment
a neighboring madman, happening to pass
the diner, cups his hands around his eyes
to shield his face from the glare
and peers in through the plate glass
and sees me and remembers in a flash
(he may be mad; his memory's in great shape)
our history, if you could call it that,
and what is more
(now in a trice he's at the diner door,
none too welcome to the maitre d')
immediately recognizes my companion;
is at our table in a blink; turns out
to have been a student of the startled breakfaster
thirty years ago in Bennington.

I could go on to braid these strands, but no.
What interests me is how the threads draw tighter,
crowding memories, people, and events
into one ever-shrinking space—the phrase
small world refers not to space but time.
How crowded is it, though? The socked-in throng
is an illusion born of artful doubling,
each person playing several parts at once.
Even in this incident we note
multiple roles: the madman as alumnus,
student as well as sculptor of a monumental piece
he invites us to visit on Upper Broadway;
my breakfast guest his teacher once upon a time
and many other things I scarcely know;
and me, translator, poet, breakfaster,
wife, mother, teacher, yada, yada, yada,
the usual human multiplicities,
but this morning mostly younger sister:
far from young but newly worried sister
of a woman who many miles away
is suddenly (I learned this late last night)
swept and shadowed by a blade, no, scythe,
no, dark wing brushing swiftly its
announcement in the January sky
seen with wincing clarity this morning
through a pane shining clean, still barely dry,
a few belated soapsuds
soundlessly and slowly slipping down.

Louis Zukofsky on Guillaume Apollinaire

(Translations of Apollinaire by Sasha Watson)

A few words on Louis Zukofsky's The Writing of Guillaume Apollinaire. *A major American poet discovers a major French poet and, out of that reading/meeting, comes not only a precise and informative analysis-appreciation of the poetics of Apollinaire but, inexorably intertwined in this work, a description of Zukofsky's own understanding of poetry. In this manner, the "other" becomes the mirror image of the reader.*

Two sections of this manuscript, Il y a *and* &Cie, *initially appeared in the* Westminster Review *(winter 1933 and spring 1934). In 2000, Wesleyan University Press will publish this manuscript as part of a seven volume edition of Louis Zukofsky's works.*

—Serge Gavronsky

The Stroller

"Le flâneur des deux rives" who visited "le plus rarement possible dans les grandes bibliothèques" and liked "mieux (se) promener sur les quais, cette délicieuse bibliothèque publique" listened receptively and wrote down the words of a singularly mindful reader of his acquaintance:

"A New York, j'ai fait de longues séances à la Bibliothèque Carnegie, immense bâtiment en marbre blanc qui, d'après les dires de certains habitués, serait tous les jours lavé au savon noir. Les livres sont apportés par un ascenseur. Chaque lecteur a un numéro et quand son livre arrive, une lampe électrique s'allume, éclairant un numéro correspondant à celui que tient le lecteur. Bruit de gare continuel. Le livre met environ trois minutes à arriver et tout retard est signalé par une sonnerie. La salle de travail est immense, et, au plafond, trois caissons, destinés à recevoir des fresques, contiennent, en attendant, des nuages en grisaille. Tout le monde est admis dans la bibliothèque. Avant la guerre tous les livres allemands étaient achetés. Par contre, les achats de livres français étaient restreints. On n'y achetait guère que les auteurs français célèbres. Quand M. Henri de Régnier fut élu à l'Académie française, on fit venir tous ses ouvrages, car la bibliothèque n'en possedait pas un seul. On y trouve un livre de Rachilde: *le Meneur de Louves*, dans la traduction russe, avec la traduction en caractères latins suivis de trois points d'interrogation. Cependant, la bibliothèque est abonnée au *Mercure* depuis une dizaine d'années. Comme il n'y a aucun contrôle, on vole 444 volumes par mois, en moyenne. Les livres qui se volent le plus sont les romans populaires, aussi les communique-t-on copiés à la machine. Dans les succursales des quartiers ouvriers il n'y a guère que des copies polygraphiées. Toutefois, la succursale de la quatorzième rue (quartier juif) contient une riche collection d'ouvrages en yiddisch. Outre la grande salle de travail dont j'ai parlé il y a une salle spéciale pour la musique, une salle pour les littératures sémitiques, une salle pour la technologie, une salle pour les patentes des Etats-Unis, une salle pour les aveugles, où j'ai vu une jeune fille lire du bout des doigts *Marie-Claire*, de Marguerite Audoux; une salle pour les journaux, une salle pour les machines à écrire à la disposition du public. A l'étage supérieur enfin se trouve une collection de tableaux."[1]

Years after the War, following the shadow of the flaneur's seeming divagations, his three books, *Il y a*, *L'Hérésiarque & Cie*, and *Calligrammes* disappeared from the "Bibliothèque Carnegie" for several months, and after that passage were again available for public use.

New York, March 14, 1932.

from *Il y a*

The stroller, living through the times he did, must have often appeared an isolated phenomenon to himself. He might have often said—Guillaume, what have you, what is there?—as he did say

Un jour
Un jour je m'attendais moi-même
Je me disais Guillaume il est temps que tu viennes
Pour que je sache enfin celui-là que je suis
Moi qui connais les autres[2]

As a phenomenon, that is not as a wonder but as a human entity, he thus isolated his time, literature as well as habit.[3]

There are, by way of self-, as well as, objective isolation, the three calligrammes:

1- Mon coeur pareil à une flamme renversée

2- Les Rois Qui Meurent Tour A Tour
   Renaissent au coeur des poètes

3- Dans ce miroir je suis enclos
   vivant et vrai comme on imagine
   les anges et non comme sont
   les reflets de Guillaume Apollinaire[4]

There are also the posthumous lines of *Chapeau-Tombeau:*

On a niché
Dans son tombeau
L'oiseau perché
Sur ton chapeau

Il a vécu
En Amérique
Ce petit cul
       Or
Nithologique
       Or
J'en ai assez
Je vais pisser[5]

As a pen-stroke, *Le Phoque* (possibly a self-portrait) is as reliable:

J'ai les yeux d'un vrai veau marin
Et de Madame Ygrec l'allure
On me voit dans tous nos meetings
Je fais de la littérature
Je suis phoque de mon état
Et comme il faut qu'on se marie
Un beau jour j'épouserai Lota
Du matin au soir l'Otarie

Papa Maman
Pipe et tabac crachoir . . .[6]

In *La Femme Assise*[7] in which the writing and the sense are often, of com-
punction, dry, there are the words of this notation:

Dans le milieu de poètes et de peintres qu'ils fréquentaient, milieu où
l'on n'est pas toujours enclin à la bonté, mais où l'on est toujours sensi-
ble, une anecdote émouvante remuait alors les coeurs—[8]

Never exactly given over to the times of Madame de Staël, and if there
were less haste his bonté might have exceeded the use of the word *sensi-
ble*, preferred *l'intelligent*, the emotive-intelligent: intelligence, emotive
intelligence of the stroller's writing dispenses with the mileposts of auto-
biography.[9] The poet reserved them for *L'Ermite:*

Seigneur que t'ai-je fait Vois je suis unicorne
Pourtant malgré son bel effroi concupiscent
Comme un poupon chéri mon sexe est innocent
D'être anxieux seul et debout comme un borne[10]

Amusingly secretive to the point of emanating a superstition, like
Descartes who kept his birthday to himself so that no astrologer could
cast his nativity, the poet's father according to biographers, was either a
Polish general or a Roman cardinal (the reader has but a perfunctory
choice); and the poet, a great friend of painters, found all portraits of
himself strange to himself.[11]

Of these, to the poet, strange likenesses, there are by Picasso:[12]

the linear, somewhat cross-eyed turnip head and tuft of hair, the pipe
and brief mustache indicating a mouth—

a similar head with a plump, black-inked body attached, the black,
glancing white, of formal and busy full dress, a fat seemingly small sensitive hand dragging the ruffled or feathered or laced chevalier (he was
never of the Legion of Honor) hat, not so busy tho formal; the other
hand holding a paper away from itself—all in all, an embarrassed pomp
which seems to have inveigled humor and irony in action[13] seducing and
traducing the scatter-brained, from the poet's appearance, evidently not
there: remaining intact himself, if doubtful, the eyes squinting doubtful—

the unwieldy heresiarch, if he may be guessed, mysteriously weighed
down by the bishop's petticoats and mitre, fingers beringed, watch on the

wrist of the other hand, equivocally turnip-faced, still squinting and smoking his pipe above the chain of the cross, above the cushion under his feet, the crozier, held slanting, taller than his seated height, than the tall back of the armchair—

or meeker, the same, petticoats doffed, an overpowering Polish peasant, in uniform and smoking a pipe—

or the soldier, bandaged head, Apollonic profile and youthful beard (to the poet probably a portrait which never suggested his lines; Un grand manteau gris de crayon comme le ciel m'enveloppe jusqu'à l'oreille, Sans pitié chaste et l'oeil sévère.[14]

and the brigadier, linear, considerable body but lithe, Spanish-Semitic beard and nose. He is seated in an armchair, one hand on the left knee, and looks on and out.

The eau-forte of Marcoussis:

well-dressed business editor, smooth-shaven chin, eyes, lips, formed, geometrically outlined by planes, sectors and circles, intersected by the title pages of his books; his pipes and penholder, and from the fingers of a cleanly wooden sculptor's manikin, in calligraphy on a sheet of paper, Un jour je m'attendais moi-même.

On the word of the sweet and somewhat asthmatic voice[15] of the poet, he did not recognize these portraits. But consistently skeptical, he realized, writing of one of his dessinateurs: Les portraits les moins ressemblants lui coûtent le plus de peine. Il met parfois plus d'une année à les achever. Et lorsqu'ils paraissent bien éloignés de la réalité, voilà notre dessinateur content. La cruauté de cette méthode a donné quelques portraits surprenants qui, loin de la réalité, s'approchent singulièrement de la vérité.[16]

But the conditions of reality inscribed the plane of the poet's fact. (Vendémiaire) "Je vivais à l'époque où finissaient les rois."[17] He lived also in the time (du) commencement de la division du travail, en littérature. La nouvelle mode pour les écrivains, he wrote, c'est d'étre très peu les auteurs de leurs livres. Ainsi, M. F— écrit volontiers d'après un canevas que lui apporte son éditeur. Il ne reste à l'éminent critique qu'à amplifier. C'est en cela qu'il excelle.

Je connais un éditeur qui vient d'apporter un plan à l'illustre amplificateur. "Le jeune auteur du canevas, m-a-t-il dit, attend avec curiosité l'issue de cette collaboration. Il n'attendra pas longtemps. Il faut à M. F— deux jours pour écrire un livre, il en faut quinze pour qu'on l'imprime. Dans vingt jours, mon jeune homme lira cet ouvrage qu'il a conçu et n'a point écrit."[18]

Feat which was an impossibility to one who wrote:

La parole est soudaine et c'est un Dieu qui tremble
Avance et soutiens-moi je regrette les mains
De ceux qui les tendaient et m'adoraient ensemble
Quelle oasis de bras m'acceuillera demain

Connais-tu cette joie de voir des choses neuves[19]

If one does, writing cannot be a matter of setting down aesthetic principle by way of filling a sketch. Writing becomes the work of making art
of an intelligence, of a life, of using an era as an illustration of an emotion, of isolating the mutations and implicit historic metamorphoses of
an era to record them.

Such work does not innocently dispense with the writer by terming
him a catalytic agent or a medium—the criticism of "l'esprit scientifique"[20] in aesthetics, the metaphorical chemistry of the man of letters,
is a phase not too far staged from an "automatisme psychique" "la croy-
ance à la réalité supérieure de certaines formes d'associations négligées, à
la toute puissance du rêve, au jeu désintéressé de la pensée."[21] To make
an art of familiarity rather par les cinq sens et quelques autres:

Un jour je m'attendais moi-même
Je me disais Guillaume il est temps que tu viennes
Et d'un lyrique pas s'avançaient ceux que j'aime
Parmi lesquels je n'étais pas

Et le langage qu'ils inventaient en chemin
Je l'appris de leur bouche et je le parle encore
Le cortège passait et j'y cherchais mon corps
Tous ceux qui survenaient et n'étaient pas moi-même
Amenaient un à un les morceaux de moi-même
On me bâtit peu à peu comme on élève une tour
Les peuples s'entassaient et je parus moi-même
Qu'ont formé tous les corps et les choses humaines[22]

Intimacy has achieved distance and space with emotion. There is no
subject nor the pretense at an object. The writing is a period of vibra-
tion off the ring of intelligence which is an object. For the intimacy
revealed is not Apollinaire's, a reflection's, but that of an intelligence,

the fact and a life. The writing down of this intimacy has become the cast of forms of his time. For another time may be imagined when no such intimacy will or can be recorded, the cast of forms of that time so rigorous in its production as to pervade the writer involved in fostering it, become sharp tho unconscious as a tool.

His work, the lyric pace of his time or the tripping up of it and its modes of love or movement and their recoil a necessity, is, granted necessity, a kind of choice and a turning upon choice. Adventurer of invention, which takes cognizance of order but particularly of its vehemence, he left to that vide avenir l'histoire de Guillaume Apollinaire, realizing at once the future's illimitability as well as its indeterminate present; realized also, pitiless for himself, that there were many things which he did not dare, or was obliged not to say, and asked at the same time for the present's pitying disdain and the uncolored future's indulgence.[23] "Life without slippers or parallel, which is against and for unity and decidedly against the future; we know wisely that our brains become downy cushions that our anti-dogmatism is as exclusivist as the functionary and that we are not free and go crying liberty . . . severe necessity without discipline or morality . . . within the frame of European weaknesses . . ."[24] By the same necessity, Guillaume came close upon his followers:

demain est incolore
Il est informe aussi près de ce qui parfait
Présente tout ensemble et l'effort et l'effet[25]

Biography, its subsequence, comes in only as an axiomatic witness: Quant à son oeuvre, je considère qu'elle est à la fois remplie d'invention et du choix le plus intelligent. C'est un ami que je regrette profondément, il avait le charme incomparable de ne pas se compromettre pour être compromis.[26]

Any example taken at random may serve: the Soleil cou coupé of the christian era bid farewell to in the Parisian zone. The recoil of skepticism of Zone[27] strips turn by turn because it loves—Je suis malade d'ouïr les paroles bienheureuses. It is also perpetually active, which is the nature of love—ceasing to attract it would be merely enervated of its radiation (the medieval image is circuitous in these lines.) But it is there, too, to be emitted, to shift its quantum and form new energy, new substance. The transformation, the tiredness with being what it was, is natural, it will not be lost, but be a new substance—an entity—its related charges. Its friends suffer its impatience; if they do not tearfully linger to prove its honesty,[28] they grow impatient. They do not move instinctively as it does with the same unconscious conscience. The *te* of *Zone* is thus Guillaume Apollinaire; the identification of the *te* by surname and familiar name[30] might as well have been dispensed with, yet Guillaume is known only thru the name of his familiar, the familiar's emotions set down are Apollinaire's morphology. The poem is Apollinaire's image. Even sentimentality is objectified as in a Mozart fantasia. For there can be either intelligence or an erased slate following subjection to a code of subversive ritual. With intelligence, there is the handling of, and absorption by, a matter and a time for a creation which moves: intelligence as writing which to the concerned or the observant never becomes an attitude, the subjective grease in the cracks of brilliance.

"We don't recognize Apollinaire any longer, for we suspect him of being a bit too canny in the matter of art, of patching up romanticism with a telephone wire and of not knowing his dynamos. The stars are unhooked—it's very tiresome."[31] The difference is in the order of the voice: his critic "preserving modernity likewise, and killed every night" and Apollinaire, "C'est toujours près de toi cette image qui passe."[32] Guillaume showed the same impatience, saying[33] he had never read Rimbaud. Perhaps because in writing "Seuls des bateaux d'enfant tremblaient à l'horizon"[34] and the rest of *l'Emigrant de Landor Road*[35] he did not need to resort to Rimbaud's final decision in which thought no longer had its recoil and action was an enervation—not a passage to the cherished finality. Too skeptical to say that art was a stupidity, Guillaume found even the record of enervation not a stupidity.

Notes

1. *Le Flâneur des Deux Rives*, Paris, 1928, Librairie Gallimard, 75-77. First published, *Editions de la Sirène*, 1928. In New York, I put in long hours in the Carnegie Library, an immense building of white marble that, according to certain regulars, was washed with black soap each day. The books are brought in an elevator. Each reader has a number and when his book arrives an electric lamp switches on, lighting up a number corresponding to the reader's. Constant ruckus of a train station. The book takes about three minutes to arrive and a bell rings to signal every delay. The work-room is immense and each inlaid panel of the ceiling, meant to hold a fresco, meanwhile contains grayish clouds. Everyone is allowed entrance to the library. Before the war the library purchased all of its

German books. It was, however, limited in its buying of French books. The library purchased books by only the most famous French authors, and very few of those. When Mr. Henri de Régnier was elected to the Académie Française, all of his works had to be ordered because the library did not possess even one. One of Rachilde's books could be found: *le Meneur de Louves* in the Russian translation, with the translation in Roman characters followed by three question marks. However, the library has had a subscription to *Mercure* for a dozen years. As there is no stamping of tickets, an average of 444 volumes are stolen each month. The books that are stolen the most are popular novels, which is why one sees machine copied versions distributed. Yet, the 14th street branch (in the Jewish neighborhood) houses a rich collection of works in Yiddish. Beyond the large workroom that I spoke of there is a special room for music; a room for Semitic literature; a room for technology; a room for United States patents; a room for the blind where I saw a young girl reading *Marie-Claire* by Marguerite Audoux, with her fingertips; a room for newspapers; a room for typewriters for the public to use. Finally, there is a collection of paintings upstairs.

2. "*Cortège-Alcools*," *Mercure de France*, 1913.

One day
One day I was waiting for myself
I said to myself Guillaume it is time that you came
That I might finally know what I am
I who know others

3. cf. Paul Dermée or *Le Flâneur des Deux Rives in L'Esprit Nouveau* 26, October 1924.

4. "*Calligrammes*," *Mercure de France*, 1918.

–My heart like an overturned flame

–The kings who die each in turn
are reborn in the heart of poets

–In this mirror I am held
Living and real like angels might be
And relfections are not
Guillaume Apollinaire

5. Philippe Soupault, ed., "*Reflets de L'Incendie*," *Les Cahiers du Sud*, 1927.

A nest was made
in his grave
the bird sat

On your hat

He lived
in America
This little ass
ornithological
But
Enough of this
I've got to piss
6. *Reflets de l'Incendie.*
I truly have a sea-calf's eyes
And Madame Y's allure
I attend our every meeting
I work in literature
I am the seal of my state
And since a man must wed
Some fine day I'll marry Lota
The Sea-lion from morn' to night
Daddy Mommy
Pipe and tobacco spittoon . . .
7. *Nouvelle Revue Française*, 1920.
8. Ibid., page 189. "In the milieu of poets and painters that they frequented, a milieu whose members are not always inclined towards benevolence, but are always sensitive to it, a moving anecdote touched every heart. . ."
9. For what has been done, though, in the way of biography see the complementary bibliographies of 1. Hector Talvert, *La Fiche Bibliographique Française*, 1931; 2. Hector Talvert et Joseph Place, *Bibliographie des Auteurs Modernes Langues Françaises*, 1929; 3. M. Elie Richard in *Les Images de Paris*, and subsequently in *L'Esprit Nouveau*, October 1924.
10. *Alcools.*
Lord what have I done for thee Look I am a unicorn
Like a beloved child my sex is innocent
In spite of its fine terror concupiscent
Of standing like a post upright anxious and alone
11. cf. André Rouveyre. *Souvenirs de Mon Commerce*, G. Cres et Cie 1921: "Je le savais monégasque, et il pretendait qu'il était né Romain. En tout cas il fut baptisé à Rome, le 29 Sept. 1880 à la Sacrosanta Patriarcalis

Basilica Santa Maria Maioris." Billy's date of Apollinaire's birth is Aug. 26, 1880, in Rome.

12. See: André Billy, "Apollinaire Vivant," *Editions de la Sirène*, 1923; the frontispiece to *Contemporains Pittoresques*, 1929, *L'Esprit Nouveau*, October 1924.

13. "naturally, irony when put down in writing is insufferable, –but naturally you are well aware that humor is not irony." Jacques Vaché, *Littérature* 6.

14. *Gravé sur Bois* by R. Jaudon, see *Calligrammes*. a great coat pencilgray like the sky envelops me up to my chin, pitiless chaste and severe of eye.

15. Alberto Savinio, *L'Esprit Nouveau*, October 1924.

16. *Anecdotiques*. Librairie Stock 1926, a collection of *La Vie Anecdotique*, articles which appeared in the *Mercure de France* from April 1, 1911 to November 1918 (he died November 9). The first three articles of *La Vie Anecdotique* appeared under the signature of Montade. The portraits that look the least like me give him the most difficulty. Sometimes it takes him more than a year to finish them. And when they seem quite far from reality, only then is our illustrator content. The cruelty of this method produced several surprising portraits that, far from reality, come singularly closer to the truth.

17. *Alcools*.
I lived at the end of the age of kings.

18. *Anecdotiques*, page 9.
of the beginning of the division of labor in literature. The new style for writers is to be as little as possible the authors of their books. Thus Mr. F— is willing to write according to a framework that his editor gives to him. All that remains for the eminent critic is to amplify. This is where he excels.

I know an editor who recently brought an outline to the illustrious amplifier. "He told me that the young author of the framework is waiting curiously for the result of this collaboration. He won't wait long. It takes Mr. F—two days to write a book, it takes fifteen to print it. In twenty days my young man will read this work of which he conceived and of which he wrote not a word."

19. *Calligrammes, La Victoire*.
Speech a trembling God is sudden
Come hold me up I miss the hands
That both tended and adored me

What oasis of arms will welcome me tomorrow
Do you know this joy of seeing things new

20. André Breton, "La vanité de l'esprit scientifique," preface, *Manifeste du Surréalisme.*
21. André Breton, *Manifeste du Surréalisme.* psychic automatism ... the belief in the superior reality of certain neglected forms of association, in the all powerfulness of the dream, in the disinterested game of thought
22.
One day I was waiting for myself
I said to myself Guillaume it is time that you came
And my loved ones came forth with a lyrical step
And I was not among them

And the language they invented on their way
I learned from their mouths and I speak it still
I looked for my body in the passing retinue
All those who happened by and were not me
Brought bits of me one by one
They built me little by little as if I were a tower
Peoples gathered and I appeared
Who had formed all bodies and all human things
23. *Cortège Alcools; Merveille de la Guerre, La Jolie Rousse, Calligrammes.*
24. Tristan Tzara, *Manifeste par Monsieur Antipyrine.*
25. tomorrow is colorless
It is formless too next to that which perfect
Presents every thing together and the effort and the effect

26. Francis Picabia, *L'Esprit Nouveau,* October 1924. His work is simultaneously filled with the most intelligent invention and choice. He is one friend whom I miss deeply. He had the incomparable charm of never compromising himself in order to be compromised.
27. *Alcools.*
I am sick with the sounds of joyful speech.
28. André Salmon, *Nouvelle Revue Française,* Nov. 1920.
29. "L'arbitraire si, du long charmant, nul si peu que lui n'est enclin à se libérer," André Breton, *Les Pas Perdus.*
30. René Dalize.
31. Jacques Vaché, *Littérature 6.* Also Breton's edition of Vaché's lettres de Guerre (1919).

32. *Zone. Alcools.*
This passing image is never very far
33. André Billy, *Apollinaire Vivant.*
34. Only children's boats trembled on the horizon.
35. *Alcools.*

Big Game Hunting in the City

Joyce Mansour

Translated from the French by Sasha Watson

Your hands are in the motor
My thighs on the dashboard
The brake between my legs
Your flesh against my skin
There's a bird on the ventilator
A man beneath the wheels
Your hands in the motor
Playing with a nail
There's a scream in the motor
A policeman and his book
A road in the rear-view mirror
Wind between my legs
A headless giant drives the car
My hands on the steering wheel
My candid pleading sex

*

You scowl and my heart unravels
I talk about my nose
My hair falls
You laugh
You open your mouth
Light and empty like a new mother
I leap into your arms
A string of jokes comes unexpected

My bed dives into the night
My clothing falls
You laugh

*

The rhythm of money
In our pockets and in our hearts
The radiophonic love of night-time crowds
Cradled by money broken by money
Protected by money
Putrefied by poverty hairy with money
Chirping desperation
The chilly imbecility of vaginal laughter
Gazing at itself in the glacial fire of bouncing lights
Electric electric electric
The crushing superiority of money on our bodies
Trembling caught in glue
In spite of the looming web of old age
In spite of the boilers of shame
Where woolly-maned fools roast
In spite of silver-cheeked death
Who frets and paints her face in the mirror
Naked under a cloak of night

*

It's not my fault
If my skin is molded
To my thighs
I didn't want to unhook the gaping smile of your desire
When I pulled back my skirt
Strangled by joy you seized my opening
It's not my fault
If the alarm went off
And your hand caught in the act
Was torn off judged turned upside down
And hanged by the neck like a creamy doll
It's not my fault
I wanted to pardon you

*

The bird must fill his beak with earth
Before taking flight
The dirt that sticks to pigs' feet
Must follow women to the shade of their beds
That flesh might renounce touch
I must clasp your knees
In spite of the blood flowing from your stomach
Such a scream
In spite of evil genies their horns and their tails
I must kiss your feet before running 'round the world
Sinners must sin their way to bestiality
To forget it all to start all over again
To learn to wait

*

The road winds its way through grey dust
Seeds die in fields
Lightning strikes rods
An Indian older than storm's hot wind
Scorching
Bent beneath the weight of his father and his past
Tied to his burden with a belt of flesh
Stumbles lone shadow travelling between the folds of long-jawed earth
A bad kind of omen
To come from the moon
The Indian lets his father slide from his back
Like sand that slides like water on a dune
The pleasure car whips the road with its tail
And darkly serpentine passes the scarlet crest
On bodies standing and out-stretched tired of being Indians
Curled up in loneliness like eggs in a nest
Two bodies on a deserted road

*

Since I've known you
Soul of my soul

Every hydra that I swallow turns into a spirit
The sad longings of sealed women who stand before love
Weigh on my legs like batrachian nests
And the swamp buttercup opens before you
Such is an unclean mouth lit up by mockery
You make my path beautiful
Soul of my boundless love
Such a leaf on a grave
A tear in the soup
I await you stretched taut in the night I nearly break
Wishing for your arrival before knowing myself
A bubble of sobs ready to hatch
Shrivels between the unhooked hinges of my jaw

Contributors

★★★ **L.S. Asekoff**, coordinator of the M.F.A. Poetry Program and faculty associate of the Wolfe Institute for the Humanities, is currently the Donald I. Fine Professor of Creative Writing at Brooklyn College. His two books of poetry are *Dreams of a Work* (1994) and *North Star* (1997), both published by Orchises Press. ★★★ **Judith Baumel**'s most recent collection of poetry, *Now*, was published by the University of Miami Press (1996). She is also the author of *The Weight of Numbers* (Wesleyan University Press, 1988). ★★★ **John Berger**'s most recent novel is *King, a Street Story* (Pantheon, 1999). ★★★ **Susan Bergman** is the author of *Anonymity* (Farrar, Straus & Giroux, 1994) and the editor of *Martyrs: Contemporary Writers on Modern Lives of Faith* (Harper, 1996). ★★★ **Jake Berthot**'s paintings have been displayed in dozens of galleries and exhibitions. He has received a Guggenheim Fellowship, a grant from the National Endowment for the Arts, and currently teaches at the School of Visual Arts in New York and at the University of Pennsylvania. ★★★ **Julie Carr** lives in Brooklyn and teaches creative writing and dance to many different populations. Her poems have appeared or are forthcoming in *New England Review, Poet Lore, Pequod,* and *Salamander.* ★★★ Born in Mexico City in 1952, **Pura López Colomé** long maintained a regular literary column for the newspaper *Unomásuno*. She is the author of several important books, including *El Sueño del Cazador, Un Cristol de Otro, Aurora,* and *Intemperie*. She has translated into Spanish works by Samuel Beckett, Virginia Woolf, Gertrude Stein, and Seamus Heaney. ★★★ **William Corbett** is editing James Schuyler's letters for publication by Black Sparrow Press. ★★★ **Greg Delanty**'s most recent book of poetry is *The Hellbox* (Oxford University Press, 1998). He has also published versions of Aristophanes' "The Suits" and Euripides' "Oreste" for the Penn Greek Drama Series. ★★★ **Jean de Sponde** (1557-1595) was a poet of the French Renaissance. ★★★ **Leslie Epstein** has published eight books of fiction, most recently *Ice Fire Water*, from which "Hip Hop" is excerpted. He is the director of the Creative Writing Program at Boston University. ★★★ **Ingrid Fichtner** is a translator and author whose work has appeared in various literary magazines in Germany, Switzerland and Austria. She lives in Switzerland. ★★★ **P.N. Furbank**'s books include the two volume biography, *E.M. Forster: A Life* (Harcourt Brace, 1977-8), *Diderot: A Critical Biography* (Knopf, 1992), and *Unholy*

Pleasure: The Idea of Class (Oxford University Press, 1985). ★★★ **Forrest Gander** is the editor of *Mouth to Mouth, Poems by 12 Contemporary Mexican Women*, and the author of several books, of which *Science & Steepleflower* (New Directions, 1998) is most recent. He teaches at Harvard University as the Briggs-Copeland Fellow in Poetry. ★★★ **Barbara Guest** received the Robert Frost Medal this year from the Poetry Society of America. Her recent publications include *Rocks on a Platter* (Wesleyan, 1999) and *If So, Tell Me* (Reality St. Editions, 1999). ★★★ **Rachel Hadas** is the author of many books of poetry and essays, most recently, *Halfway Down the Hall: New and Selected Poems* (Wesleyan, 1998). ★★★ **Brian Henry's** first book, *Astronaut*, will be published in the Arc International Poets Series next year in the United Kingdom. His poems have appeared in the *Paris Review, American Poetry Review*, the *Yale Review*, and *New American Writing*. He edits *Verse*. ★★★ **Daniel Kane's** poems have appeared in the *Denver Quarterly, Hanging Loose*, and *Exquisite Corpse*. ★★★ **Claudia Keelan's** most recent book of poems is *The Secularist* (University of Georgia Press, 1997). ★★★ **John Kinsella's** most recent books are *Poems 1980* and *The Hunt* (both from Bloodaxe/Dufour, 1998). He is the editor of *Salt*, co-editor of *Stand*, and a fellow of Churchill College, Cambridge. ★★★ **Wayne Koestenbaum** is the author of three books of poetry, *The Milk of Inquiry* (1999), *Rhapsodies of a Repeat Offender* (1994), and *Ode to Anna Moffo and Other Poems* (1990), all from Perseus Press. He has also written several books of criticism, including the forthcoming *Cleavage* (Ballantine, 2000). ★★★ **James Lasdun's** most recent book of poems is *Woman Police Officer in Elevator* (W.W. Norton, 1997). He is a Guggenheim Fellow in Poetry. ★★★ **Rika Lesser** is a poet translator of Swedish and German literature. She has taught literary translation at Columbia University and Yale University, and is the author of three collections of poetry, *Etruscan Things* (Braziller, 1983), *All We Need of Hell* (North Texas, 1995), and *Growing Back: Poems 1972-1992* (University of South Carolina Press, 1997). ★★★ **Jan Heller Levi's** *Once I Gazed at You in Wonder* was the 1998 Walt Whitman Award winner of the Academy of American Poets and was published by Louisiana State University Press (1999). She is the editor of *A Muriel Rukeyser Reader* and is currently working on a biography of Rukeyser. ★★★ **Phillis Levin** is the author of *Temples and Fields* and *The Afterimage*. Her poems have appeared in the *Best American Poetry 1998, The New Yorker, The New Republic, Paris Review*, and *The Nation*. Her third collection, *Mercury*, is forthcoming from Penguin in the spring of 2001. She is currently editing an anthology of sonnets from the Renaissance to the present. ★★★ **Joyce Mansour** published her first book of poetry, *Cris*, in Paris in 1957, at the age of 25. She was associated with the Surrealist movement and collaborated with such artists as Pierre Alechinsky and Hans Bellmer. "Big Game Hunting in the City," from *Rapaçes*, was published in 1960. ★★★ **Charles Martin** is the author of the book of poems, *What the Darkness Proposes* (Johns Hopkins University Press, 1996), and has translated the poems of Catullus (also published by Johns Hopkins). ★★★ **Donna Masini's** book of poems, *That Kind of Danger* (Beacon Press, 1994), won the Barnard Women Poet's Prize. She has published a novel, *About Yvonne* (W.W. Norton, 1998), and is at work on her next collection of poems. She teaches poetry at Hunter College and Columbia University. ★★★ **Molly McGrann** is a contributing editor to the *Paris Review*. She lives in Oxford, England. ★★★ **Jane Mead**, author of *The Lord and the General Din of the World* (Sarabande, 1996), is the recipient of the the Whiting Writer's Award. She is Poet-in-Residence at Wake Forest University. ★★★ **W.S. Merwin's** recent books include the narrative, *The Folding Cliffs* (Knopf, 1998), the collection of poems, *The River Sound* (Knopf, 1999), and the collection of Asian translations, *East Window* (Copper Canyon, 1998). ★★★ **Bruce F. Murphy's** first collection of poems, *Sing, Sing, Sing* (New York University Press) won the Bobst Award. His poetry and essays have appeared in *Pequod*, *Critical Inquiry*, and *Poetry*. ★★★ **Paul Nemser** lives in Cambridge, Massachusetts. ★★★ **Howard Norman's** most recent novel is *The Museum Guard* (Farrar, Straus & Giroux, 1998). ★★★ **John Peck's** sixth book of poems is *M and Other Poems* (TriQuarterly Books/Northwestern University Press, 1996). ★★★ **Melissa Holbrook Pierson** is the author of *The Perfect Vehicle* (W.W. Norton, 1997). She is currently at work on a book about women and horses, also for W.W. Norton. ★★★ **Claudia Rankine** was born in Kingston, Jamaica. Her most recent book of poems is *The End of the Alphabet* (Grove Press, 1998). She teaches at Barnard College. ★★★ **Donald Revell** is the author of six collections of poetry, most recently *There are Three* (1998) and *Beautiful Shirt* (1994), as well as a translation of Apollinaire's *Alcools*, all from Wesleyan. ★★★ **Mark Rudman's** most recent books are *Provoked in Venice* (1998), *Millennium Hotel* (1996), and *Rider*, which won the 1994 Book Critics Circle Award for Poetry, all from Wesleyan. He teaches at New York University. ★★★ **James Schuyler's** *Collected Poems* is published by Farrar, Straus and Giroux. Copies of his novel,

What's For Dinner? (1978), can still be obtained from Black Sparrow Press. ★★★ **Vijay Seshadri** is the author of *Wild Kingdom* (Graywolf Press). He is on the editorial staff of the *New Yorker* and teaches at Sarah Lawrence College. ★★★ **Jane Shore** has just published her fourth book of poems, *Happy Family* (Picador USA, 1999). Her third, *Music Minus One*, was nominated for the National Book Critics Circle Award. Her second, *The Minute Hand*, will be reprinted by Carnegie Mellon Press this year. ★★★ **David R. Slavitt's** latest books include *PS3569.L3*, a collection of poems, and *Get Thee to a Nunnery: Two Shakespearean Divertimentos*. His recent translations include Aristophanes' "Celebrating Ladies" in the Penn Greek Drama Series, of which he is co-editor. ★★★ **Charlie Smith** is the author of four books of poems, most recently *Cheap Ticket to Heaven* (Henry Holt, 1996) and *Before and After* (W.W. Norton, 1995). ★★★ **Göran Sonnevi** has published fourteen individual books of poems and three collections. He has translated the poetry of Ezra Pound, Paul Celan, and Osip Mandelstam into Swedish. The first book-length collection of his poetry in English, *A Child is not a Knife: Selected Poems of Göran Sonnevi*, was published by Princeton University Press (1993). ★★★ **Terese Svoboda's** most recent book of poetry is *Mere Mortals* (University of Georgia Press, 1995). She has a second novel, *A Drink Called Paradise*, forthcoming this year from Counterpoint Press. Her poetry has appeared recently in the *Atlantic* and *New Republic*. ★★★ **E. Beth Thomas** has published poems in *Epoch*, *Prairie Schooner*, and the *Bellingham Review*. She lives in New Jersey, where she is an editor at the Ecco Press. ★★★ **Alan Warner** is the author of *Movern Callar*, which won the Somerset Maugham Award, and *These Demented Lands*, which won an Encore Award. He lives in Dublin. *The Sopranos* was published by Farrar, Straus & Giroux (1999). ★★★ **Katharine Washburn's** most recent translation is "The Madness of Heracles," the Penn Greek Drama Series. She is the co-editor of *An Anthology of Verse from Antiquity to Our Time* (W.W. Norton, 1998), and is completing a novel, *The Translator's Apology*. ★★★ **Sasha Watson** is a writer and translator living in New York City. ★★★ **Susan Wheeler's** first collection of poetry, *Bag 'o' Diamonds* (University of Georgia Press, 1993), received the Norma Farber First Book Award of the Poetry Society of America. Her second was *Smokes* (Four Way Books, 1998). She has appeared six times in *Best American Poetry*, as well as in the *Paris Review* and the *New Yorker*. ★★★ **Joshua Weiner's** poems and essays have appeared recently in *Threepenny Review*, *AGNI*, and *Verse*. In 1998, he received the PEN New England

Discovery Award. He teaches at Northwestern University. ★★★ **Louis Zukofsky** was a poet and critic. The pieces appearing in this issue are excerpted from *The Writings of Guillaume Apollinaire*, which will appear as part of the Wesleyan centennial edition of *The Collected Critical Writings of Louis Zukofsky*.

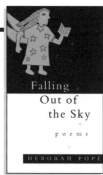

Announcing the *Witness* short-short fiction contest for emerging writers

$500 first prize and publication in *Witness* awarded to the winning story by a writer who has not yet published a book of fiction, poetry or creative nonfiction with a nationally distributed press. (Other entries will be considered for publication and payment at our regular rates.)

Complete Rules and Guidelines

1   All entries must be postmarked by December 31, 1999. Mail to *Witness* Emerging Writers Contest, 27055 Orchard Lake Road, Farmington Hills, Michigan 48334. Simultaneous submissions are allowed. Entries will be judged by the editors of *Witness*.

2   Entry fee is $15 per story, limit two stories per author ($30). Entry fee includes a one-year subscription to *Witness* (a $15 value). Make checks payable to *Witness*.

3   Previously published work or work accepted for publication is ineligible.

4   Maximum length is 1,500 words, typed, double-spaced. Author's name, address, phone number, title of story and "*Witness* Emerging Writers Contest" should be on page one of the entry.

5   No manuscripts will be returned. Please include a self-addressed, stamped postcard if you wish to have receipt of your entry acknowledged.

6   The winning story will be published in the next general issue of *Witness*.

HOPSCOTCH

Read
between
the lines.

A Cultural Review

New from Duke University Press

Editor: Ilan Stavans

Editor at Large: Antonio Benítez-Rojo

Forthcoming in the first volume of *Hopscotch*

Mario Vargas Llosa on haves and have-nots

Steven G. Kellman on John Sayles's latest film

Valdir Cruz on the rain forest's indigenous peoples

Ricardo Gutiérrez Mouat on José Donoso's legacy

Rosario Ferré on Puerto Rican identity

Lalo López Alcaraz on racist humor

Alberto Gerchunoff on Jews in Argentina

Roberto González Echevarría on Cuban *peloteros*

Joseba Gabilondo on Hollywood machos and spitfires

Alan West on Latino percussions

Antonio Benítez-Rojo on the New Atlantis

Roberto Schwarz on the pitfalls of the Brazilian Left

Judith Thorn on the labyrinthine Bibliothèque Haïtienne

Gregory Rabassa on (and in) translation

Ilan Stavans on Julio Iglesias

Plus, the editors on the broken sounds of Spanglish

Subscription Information

Individuals: $24

Institutions: $50

Add $12 for postage outside the US.

Send orders to Duke University Press, Journals Fulfillment,
Box 90660, Durham, NC 27708-0660.

To order *Hopscotch* using a credit card, call toll-free, within
the US and Canada, 888-DUP-JRNL (888-387-5765).

919.687.3602, Fax: 919.688.3524

E-mail: dukepress@duke.edu

Check out the *Hopscotch* Web site: www.hopscotch.org

MICHIGAN QUARTERLY REVIEW

RECENT AND FORTHCOMING

Spring 1999: Walter Burkert on the Greek heritage and Western cultural studies • Wendy Doniger, "A Response to Walter Burkert" • Susan X Day, "*Walden Two* at Fifty" • James Richardson, "56 Aphorisms" • Karen M. Radell, "A Meeting with Graham Greene"

Summer 1999: Richard Rodriguez, "Violating the Boundaries: An Interview" • Janet Landman, "The Confessions of a War Maker [Robert McNamara] and a War Resister [Katherine Power]" • Valentin Rasputin, "In a Siberian Town," and an essay on Rasputin by Elisabeth Rich • David M. Sheridan, "Making Sense of Detroit," with writings about Detroit by Julie Ellison, Camilo José Vergara, and Al Young

Fall 1999: Rudolf Arnheim, "Composites of Media: The History of an Idea" • Lawrence Kasdan, "The Craft of Screenwriting: A Commentary and Demonstration" • George Toles, "Obvious Mysteries in *Fargo*" • Jon-Christian Suggs, "*Blackjack*: The First Novel about a Black Boxer," by [Black author] Walter White, including a scene from the unpublished manuscript • William Baer, "An Interview with Stewart Stern [screenwriter for *Rebel Without a Cause*] • Joyce Carol Oates, A chapter from her novel-in-progress on Marilyn Monroe

Winter 2000: Helen Vendler on Whitman's poems about Lincoln, with one or more responses • David McGimpsey on Quebec poet Gaston Miron and the question of separatism • Alice Mattison, "Writing with Jane Kenyon: A Memoir" • Anne Herrmann, "The Aviatrix as American Dandy" [on Amelia Earhart]

Spring 2000: A special issue, "*SECRET SPACES OF CHILDHOOD,*" guest-edited by Elizabeth Goodenough

FALL 2000: A special issue, "*REIMAGINING PLACE*," guest-edited by Robert Grese and John R. Knott

Some copies still available: Fall 1998 special issue, *ARTHUR MILLER*, edited by Laurence Goldstein, ($7)

Send a check for a single copy ($5), one year subscription ($18) or a two-year subscription ($33) to *Michigan Quarterly Review*, 3032 Rackham Building, 915 E. Washington, Ann Arbor, MI 48109-1070

Bakhtin/"Bakhtin": Studies in the Archive and Beyond
Edited by Peter Hitchcock

Introduction: Bakhtin/"Bakhtin"
Peter Hitchcock

Bakhtin and Cassirer: The
Philosophical Origins of Bakhtin's
Carnival Messianism
Brian Poole

Bakhtin as Anarchist? Language, Law,
and Creative Impulses in the Work of
Mikhail Bakhtin and Rudolf Rocker
Robert F. Barsky

Bakhtin's Chronotope and the
Contemporary Short Story
Rachel Falconer

Bakhtin without Borders: Participatory
Action Research in the Social Sciences
Maroussia Hajdukowski-Ahmed

A Broken Thinker
Anthony Wall

Bakhtin Myths, or,
Why We All Need Alibis
Ken Hirschkop

The Bakhtin Centre and the State
of the Archive: An Interview with
David Shepherd
Peter Hitchcock

Vološinov, Ideology, and Language:
The Birth of Marxist Sociology from
the Spirit of *Lebensphilosophie*
Galin Tihanov

Questions and Answers: Bakhtin from
the Beginning, at the End of the Century
Vitalii Makhlin

Archive Material on Bakhtin's
Nevel Period
Nikolai Pan'kov

Afterword: A Two-Faced Hermes
Michael Holquist

Please send me ____ copies of *Bakhtin/"Bakhtin"* (*SAQ* 97:3/4) at U.S.\$12 each. In the U.S. please add \$3 for the first copy and \$1 for each additional copy to cover postage and handling. Outside the U.S. please add \$3 for each copy to cover postage and handling.

☐ I enclose my check, payable to Duke University Press.
☐ Please bill me. (No issues can be sent until payment is received.)

Please charge my   ☐ MasterCard   ☐ VISA   ☐ American Express

Account Number	Expiration Date
Signature	Daytime Phone
Name	
Address	
City/State/Zip	SQ9E0

Duke
University
Press

Box 90660
Durham, NC
27708-0660
Fax 919.688.3524
http://www.duke.edu/web/dupress/

To place your journal order by phone using
a credit card, call toll-free, within the U.S.
and Canada, 888.DUP.JRNL (888.387.5765).